TERRA NOVA

Pegasus Books, Ltd.
148 West 37th Street, 13th Floor
New York, NY 10018

First Pegasus Books cloth edition December 2022

Interior design by Maria Fernandez

Library of Congress Cataloging-in-Publication Data is available.

ISBN: 978-1-63936-242-4

10 9 8 7 6 5 4 3 2 1

Printed in the United States of America
Distributed by Simon & Schuster
www.pegasusbooks.com

TERRA NOVA

HENRIETTE LAZARIDIS

PEGASUS BOOKS

NEW YORK LONDON

For Nike

When I looked back, the coastline was all but imperceptible, and it was apparent that our footprints had been erased behind us, and so we splashed tracelessly on out to the tidal limit. It felt at that moment wholly true that a horizon might exert as potent a pull upon the mind as a mountain's summit.

—ROBERT MACFARLANE

1

88° 30'S

Soon they will have to send Tite and Lawrence back. There is no longer enough food for four of them. The men will protest, but it will be no secret that they will be crying behind their sun goggles, tears of relief freezing into grains of ice in the corners of their eyes. Watts catches himself. Their bodies are too desiccated for tears. There is no weeping in this place so stripped of human life. There is only cold. Cold like a presence they breathe and like a force to hold them down, hold them in place even as they inch over endless swales of white and gray, gray-white, blue-white. He wants to curse now, again, at this cruel palette. His lenses struggle to find nuance in this stark world, the camera eye narrowed to a pinprick and even that almost too much for his glass plates. There is only contrast here: white and black and darker black and brighter, impossibly brighter, white.

Cruelty reigns here. Is it not cruel to be forced to crawl like creatures of some frozen anthill or voles beneath the crust of this giant's pasture, eyes screwed tight against this sun? Is it not cruel to continue forward when they have lost most sense of their progress, when to spin like the compass's foolish needle and face in any direction, any!—he nearly sits up at the thought—and to set off would make no difference? Except to Heywoud. Heywoud who lies in his bag across the tent, who barely speaks all day lest human interaction distract him from his goal. It is a violence that they are

1

here at all. Four men, and four others waiting at Hut Camp and six more at the edge of a sea from which no ship will depart, no hailing voices ring, for two more months. All of them carried away from gas fires, hearths, fenders, beds by the desire of this man Heywoud to plant the flag in the center of this vast expanse of nothing.

Watts can feel the panic rising in him, his heart fluttering and a small guttural sound rustling in his throat. Anywhere else, he would shout and thrash. He would seize Heywoud by the collar and pin him until he gave a schoolyard's surrender. He cannot do that now. Not yet. They would know him to be mad, then, another casualty of the white cold, and they would leave him behind to die.

He fumbles in his clothing for his notebook, slipped inside the linen pouch he keeps around his neck. He pulls out the graphite stick but drops it, then scrabbles at the edges of his bag, fingertips already beginning to harden from mere proximity to the ice beneath, and retrieves the stick. Heywoud has not stirred. Watts rolls onto his stomach, the sour tang of the seal pelt thick in his lungs, and riffles the grubby pages. At the beginning of the little book is the list he began to keep when they made landfall. Curiosities sighted: penguin, seal, albatross, a band of vivid turquoise water at the base of a coastal berg. He was all eyes then, eager for the Pole's new vastness. With time he added to his list. Spit, piss, shit, cum, blood. Things that froze, one by one, elements of his body that this place had overpowered. It is as good a chronicle of their time here as any other. But this is no language for the Geographical Society. If they live, they will have to find other words with which to tell their tale.

Watts finds the first blank page. He does not know how long it has been since he has written. Heywoud keeps the calendar for them now. For Watts, it has been one long day, time marked only by the brief graying of the sky. His mind is in a state of agitation that he knows cannot be calmed, only diverted. He writes to Viola. Once he begins, he cannot stop until the verbs go and he is left with the language of a list, naming her body as if to conjure it beneath him. Neck, breast, legs, cunt. He moves against the bag but knows he mustn't come for it will mean peeling frozen wool from the only patch of skin that is still tender. He forces his mind to step back from her. Now she is across the room from him. Viola, brown eyes smiling and a laugh suppressed beneath the upper lip that pouts forever out. Her dark hair pinned up in the manner of an Ingres, her shoulder turned to him so that her jaw can cast a shadow, so that the hollow at the base of her neck can darken within her collarbone's frame. In his mind he squeezes the shutter bulb. *Viola, after the bath.*

Watts looks over at Heywoud. How can he stand it? Has the man no passions? Before the Pole, on Alpine climbs and in the Dolomites, Heywoud would laugh and jolly him up a rock face. Heywoud would reach a gallant hand down to Viola who would take it without need. He stood on summits and breathed deep the beauty of the view. He clapped arms around them both, Watts and Viola, and they three were the luckiest alive to be together. In all these months that they have journeyed, weeks they camp together in the low canvas tent, Watts has never caught Heywoud so much as sighing. He moves forward each day more like machine than man. Watts rolls onto his back and stares up at a sprinkling of pinholes through which the light pierces like swordpoints. Perhaps Heywoud goes out into the sun and fucks the cold. That is his lover: Antarctica, Terra Australis. And the rest of them have become nothing more than pimps and panderers to the great man's amorous folly.

Watts hears the clink of chain outside and then the dogs begin to snuffle and cry. Tite murmurs to the dogs and their whimpers become yelps. They think he has food for them, bits of potted seal and meat from the dogs' own comrades, dried in the sun and preserved with fat, a canine pemmican. Such cannibalism no longer offends. These are the exigencies of the Pole, demanding, in so many ways beyond just this, that those who venture there consume their own kind in order to succeed.

"Down," shouts Tite, and the dogs fall to silence, expectant and quivering, Watts knows, trusting and loyal. They don't know that Tite has marked Lulu, the oldest bitch, as the next to be slaughtered. If Heywoud sends Tite and Lawrence back to Hut Camp, perhaps the old dog's life will be spared. There is a future in which Tite lives out his days beside a hearth in Cornwall's tropic zone, wrapped in shawls and jumpers against even that temperate clime, the old dog at his feet.

"Edward," Watts says, for Heywoud has not moved at the sounds of the day's beginning. "Edward."

The man jolts upright, looking about him, quickly assessing. Still here, his gaze seems to say. Still not finished. Still in sunlight. Still cold and snow and ice. And still Watts. His eyes glance off Watts and he stares at nothing. His mouth opens and shuts as if practicing speech, or learning it. The men's lips go numb in the night despite the fur they pull up to their chins. There is always, but especially upon first waking, a limit on what they are capable of saying.

Without addressing Watts, Heywoud pushes his bag down around his waist and dons his outer parka. Over his head he lowers the long strap connecting his fur mittens. A band linking the ends of the strap rests across his chest. To lose a mitten here would be to lose a hand, a limb entire. With more smacking of his lips, Heywoud strikes a match and lights the Primus stove. Nearly instantly the tent fills with briny, dark-gray smoke. It is seal oil they are burning, made from fat boiled down at Shore Camp and carried from each depot to the next. This can is one of the last four they possess. They will need at least two to reach the Pole.

Watts sits up in his bag and watches the little pot on the stove where Heywoud has dumped a tin of hoosh, a thin gruel of oats and pemmican, a breakfast fishy and foul. There can be no nourishment in it but to keep them from maddening dreams of gristle, toffee, bone. He craves such things his teeth could wrestle with. He wants to chew.

Tite's ginger head pokes through the tent flap.

"Oi," he says. "I was just having my morning constitutional."

This is the way with Tite. Never afforded the leisure of a constitutional in his life as a farrier, up at dawn with the horses, he affects for Heywoud's and Watts' amusement the manners of the upper class.

"It's a fine morning, gents," he says.

But Watts can see the skin peeling off his pale cheeks above the copper beard. He has seen Tite limping and seen—once only and sufficient viewing, that—the right foot blistered and raw, the edge of black where the little toe is dying. There is a value to Tite's jollity, but they must send him back. If they do not, he will be the cause of all their deaths. They are as tied to one another as the dogs in their traces or the mittens strung around their necks.

"Where is Lawrence?" Heywoud asks, his voice cracked and hoarse.

"He's coming." Tite assumes a cheery smile.

Watts holds back the tent flap and winces at the shock of the sun. He makes a lattice with his fingers and peers through it, searching the white until he spots a dark figure approaching from the other tent. Heywoud still maintains the rank and discipline of his Navy life and keeps the men's tent at some remove from the one he shares with Watts. Unlike Heywoud, Watts is no officer, but he thinks he may still be a gentleman.

They take their bowls outside the tent and sit, two and two, on the sledges with their gloved hands cupping tin. For a brief instant the tin is hot and the steam rises up to moisten cheeks and beards and eyes. Watts dips his face so close that ice forms on his beard. There was no gray in it when they sailed from Cardiff.

The hoosh is quickly gone and the animals quickly fed with chunks of meat Tite throws for each dog separately so that they will not maim each other in the eating. Watts returns to the tent and emerges with his camera. He unfolds the tripod and stands the camera on the ice. The other three men glance up and look away. They do not like the camera. Lawrence complains about the weight of its glass plates—as much as seven stone—and even Heywoud has begun to worry that the record of their journey will never be seen if they cannot survive the hauling of it. Watts does not let the men see that he too has begun to find the burden heavy. He masks his grimace of effort as he heaves a box of plates and positions the camera on the hardpack surface. The men need no excuse from him to toss the plates into the snow like so many shards of ice.

He covers the camera with its thick, black drape and ducks beneath the cloth. He closes his eyes and breathes deeply in the darkness, a scent of wool so dry it smells like fire. The men's voices come to him as if along a corridor. The camera is what keeps him here, away from fires and corridors. But for his skill with it, would he not be the one to go, back to Shore Camp and then a homebound berth at sea? Heywoud will never let him leave, will never send him back, never forego the photographic proof that Watts creates for him. Nor will Watts volunteer to leave. It is his job to take the photographs that document the expedition. He serves his friend, now here his Captain, by capturing images of stunning beauty to bring back to London. For this he braves the dreadful ice. The faintest cloud of heat fills the air before his face, though to call it heat would be to name their exertions no more than a stroll.

He forces himself to reach into the cold outside the drape for the box of glass plate negatives, then once again inside the soothing blackness of this fabric room he selects a pane of glass and inserts it in the negative-holder and slides the wooden apparatus into place within the camera's box. They would mock him at the Slade for clinging to such cumbersome equipment in so inhospitable a place. But Watts began with a determination he has not yet shed: to document the southern lands as purely as he can. No film for him, but instead the immediacy of light etched in emulsion. When he shows his photographs in London—he impresses himself with this confidence in his own future—his viewers will see through the glass just as his camera has done. Viola will stand among the rest, staring in wonderment at his art, his vision, and she will look at him across the room. And there will be Antarctica, the thief of so much, yielding up in black and white some tithe of what it has stolen.

This photograph he frames for its documentary qualities. *January 1910, Captain Heywoud and two of his men at breakfast, one hundred miles from the Pole.* When the newspapers publish this one, they will place the word breakfast in quotation marks, reassuring wives and husbands at their morning meals that Antarctic exploration preserves all the rituals of English life, that even here in this extremity of land, Englishmen are civilized. In a photograph taken in September at Shore Camp, they had toasted blood pudding on long forks over a fire, Heywoud brandishing the package for the public: Harrods. Sent to Lyttelton in New Zealand with the returning depot ship, that glass plate has by now found its way into newsprint, the jovial scene so many months gone now gracing households across the Empire.

Watts squeezes the shutter bulb. The men's movements are so small—spoon to mouth, spoon to bowl—that they will never blur the image. The masses of their bodies and the sledges, and the smaller masses of the now-dozing dogs scattered around the men in a beautiful asymmetry, will be reproduced in sharp focus. At least there is that here, with the camera's eye closed so tight against the sun: the focus is pin-sharp. In London's gray, the shutter's little curtain moved with deliberation, as if it had all the time in the world. Here it draws forward and back with the alacrity of a train porter closing a carriage door. In the Antarctic summer, time is frozen. Nothing seems to move—not sun, not ice—though at Shore Camp they woke nightly to loud cracks and groans as the ice shuddered and swelled against the shifting of the sea.

"And now one more, boys," Watts says. "Give us a smile. Last leg and all that."

The last leg, they call it, as if there will be no return journey, no slog backwards against the slow unspooling of their southward path. They say this as a hope, to think only of the goal, the success, but it is at once an utterance of resignation.

Lawrence rises from the sledge and pulls Tite up beside him. The larger man sways a little as he stands and, throwing an arm around Lawrence's shoulders, conceals his unsteadiness with a swagger. Heywoud looks up and rests his bowl in his lap. In the camera's eye, Watts sees Heywoud's posture straighten. The man's expression is serious, almost stern. Unlike Lawrence and Tite, he cannot hold a smile long enough.

"Just a little longer," Watts says, and gives a quick squeeze to the shutter bulb. "All right."

He watches through the camera as the smiles drop from the men and Heywoud resumes eating his hoosh, and then he ducks beneath the drape once more to remove the glass plate. It joins nine others in its box and he knows the men are thinking of the weight of it. It is just light he has captured in Paget's solution of chemicals and egg whites, dried more than a year ago in London. It is just light and it has turned a burden for them all.

The men tend to the dogs and the sledges while Heywoud occupies himself with the sextant that is his constant companion. Watts begins to pack the camera but stops and gazes out in the direction he thinks they will take this day. With the Barrier and the Beardmore far behind him, he sees only a plain of gray-white ice, dimpled like the skin of a satsuma or the face of someone suffering from pox, and above it pale blue sky. Is it possible that this vast whiteness bears another expedition party like theirs hauling sledges and urging dogs onward? He sees no sign, hears no shout or howl. And yet the Norwegians cannot be too far, English and Norwegian paths from different coast camps converging surely now as both expeditions approach the Pole. Watts and Heywoud have been racing Olav Nilsen since before that September breakfast, even before their ship left port festooned with bunting and hailed by Navy bands. Who will be first man ever to the South Pole? This is the race they run. Watts knows that Heywoud scans the horizon daily, masking his search as a test of the sextant's readings. They all do it. He has seen Tite crouch down to shush the halted dogs and cock his head, listening for the sounds of other men's progress. Watts strains to hear now but there is only the hum of the wind.

2

15 January

Viola will have to run to catch the march. One hand rucks her skirt and the other grips the camera strap and she breaks into an awkward trot. The camera bumps her hip with every stride. She turns the corner onto Victoria Street and bulls through the stragglers. She makes no apologies, seeks no pardon. Even if she did, no one would hear her over their own shouts and slogans. Viola saves her breath, a thing she sees in puffs this January day, and pushes forward.

Where Victoria Street narrows she takes to the pavement and makes for the march's head. She glimpses the leaders—Emmeline Pankhurst, Christabel, Sylvia—their feathered hats like plumage. But today she will photograph the crowd, this legion of women who, when the Pankhursts summon, answer with voices, bodies, hearts. There is power in these multitudes, strength in the anonymity the crowd affords. What might a woman do here among so many others. Look at them! Delegates with sashes listing towns from all of England. Graduates in academic dress. *Votes for Women! Deeds Not Words!* Mothers, daughters, sisters, all linking arms and singing. Viola is none of these—not even daughter lest an orphan claim the name—but here she is, among them all, and their numbers are so great, their shouts so high and clear, success seems destined.

Months now she wades into these protest rivers like an angler in the current. It is no less a marvel than a sunlit Yorkshire beck, this stream of joyous women brushing past. She spreads her feet to brace against the jostles and lifts the camera to her eye. She turns the focus ring and takes a photograph. Women fill the frame. Hat brims overlap, signs clash. Lavender and green, the colors of the movement, on every brooch and sash. In black and white, these shades will be just paler grays. No matter. Color is no loss here when she has the women's figures for her work. She breathes on frozen knuckles and looks about for the next frame.

Ten paces off, a woman taller than the others sports a bandage on one eye, perhaps a casualty of last week's tussles with police. Viola calls to her, waves, and the woman glances. "Yes, you!" Viola shouts. The woman halts. Viola wants her sharp and still and with the blur of marchers all around her. She turns the shutter knob to slow, dials the aperture as small as it will go, and springs the shutter. "That's it," she says and the woman gives her a shy smile. "Thank you," Viola calls. "We must all fight as you have done."

She dashes to the front and looks out past the leaders towards the railings of Westminster Palace. Today's march seeks an audience with Asquith. Since the Prime Minister refuses all discussion of the cause, these women bring the cause to him. But the gate to Parliament is closed and by the time Viola reaches it the press of marchers is so thick she cannot even move to raise the camera. The women are shouting now and a constable's whistle shrills somewhere overhead. A surge forward buckles Viola's knees and she nearly tumbles. Constables break through to seize a woman who has climbed the iron fence. She hurls something over the crowd and it glints an instant in the sun. A key, ignored in favor of its lock now fastened around the woman's other wrist.

Viola pitches down into a storm of banners, boots, and constables' batons. Her cheek is scraped by buttons on a woman's sleeve. A shoe steps on her skirt. The Midg catches on something and the strap snaps and it is gone. On hands and knees she feels for the hard edges of the camera box. Let the box hold or her day's work will be glass shards. She saves her head with one raised arm and forces through with the other until her fingers close on the camera's corner. She brings it to her chest, pushes to stand. She gives the Midg a little shake as if to chide a prodigal and sighs relief at no sound of broken pieces. The plates are packed in velvet and thick oak, thank god for that.

The crowd squeezes close again and she scrabbles for purchase but it is too late; she is aloft among the bodies. "Stop!" people are shouting. "Move back!" She keeps her arms wrapped tight around the Midg. It is like tumbling down a snow face and the rope not yet paid out. From James she learned the safest way to fall. But now, pressed to the fence, chin tucked to save her neck, Viola has no safe route out but up. Toe to the fence, one hand at the rail and tugging with her climber's grip, she pulls free of the crowd and feels an awkward twist in her ankle. She seizes the railing with one hand to hoist herself up onto the granite lip. An ache pulses in her ankle, but her vantage is so good she must ignore it. She looks out over the hats and bared heads of the march that has become a protest and the force of it near takes her breath away. Today's march spreads further, wider, than any she has photographed before. When she gives her photographs to the newsmen at the *Telegraph* and the *Observer*, everyone will see the scope of the movement's power. Surely, everyone will see that they must not be turned aside.

She spots a new band of constables brandishing a saw. They are a dark blue streak in a field of greens and lavenders. They shove towards the woman who has chained herself and she clings to the fence like a Prometheus, the constables like pecking birds. What these women want—and Viola too—some think it is as dangerous as fire. So many are arrayed against them—Anti-Suffrage Leagues and Government and men with daft ideas about what womanhood must be. Must women be punished like Prometheus for claiming what they should already own? A hand seizes Viola's shoe and she grunts at a jab of pain and nearly tumbles from the ledge. She breathes in deep and braces tight, watches the crowd moving like unruly clouds below a cornice. She has one plate left and she must choose. What has she not yet captured? No, that is not the question. What has no one, no photographer, artist, or journalist yet captured? What image makes the most of her stolen freedom to stand here, at this moment, with a camera, on this ledge?

She waits until the instant the police lay hold of the chained woman. One constable pulls at her, a dark diagonal. Another works the saw; he is an anchoring mass in the frame's lower left. She brings the camera to her eye and holds her breath. The crouched policeman takes the woman by the waist. The instant she is seized and shouting, Viola springs the shutter, feels the curtain dash across the lens. It is the same glorious sensation every time: the plate settles in the box and all the light and shadow she has stolen from the air is caught between her hands.

She makes her way along the rail until she reaches open space and lowers herself gently to the street. She weights the foot and sees that she can walk with careful steps. Breathless, she looks back at the march still pressing at Parliament. Her photographs will show the country women must be independent. They will show James and Edward, too. Yes, you traveled to the world's last place, but see what a world grew while you were gone. Look at the power of these women. Is it not almost as great as the strength of you few exploring men? Or greater, driven not by desire or curiosity but by the need for freedom.

It is an hour's walk home to Margaretta Terrace, but even with her ankle sore she cannot imagine taking the Underground and being stuck inside a tube after such excitement. She walks slowly west instead, ignoring the cold that nips her ears, bearing the camera at her hip like a creel lined with silver shining fish, each one a piece of light tugged from a brilliant stream. There is a tale somewhere of fish who leap from creels or rivers to grant a stranger's wish. If such magic sprang now from the camera at her side, what would she ask for? Her single and constant wish comes to mind quick as a superstition: may James and Edward return safe. She rests the ankle, waiting for a line of cabs and omnibuses to cross and, in the moment she is still, her other, deeper, wish arrives, like something she cannot outpace. May her photographs astonish. May she capture light like a live thing to flash silver and white and black inside her darkroom and then leap out into the world. Viola shakes her head to shed the idea, the hubris of it, the folly, but the thought clings to her like the cold. She is not sure the photographs she took today will generate that sort of living awe. What can she do to match what James does with his camera at the Pole? What can she find in this world to surpass his reflections of a new one?

In Chelsea, she turns onto Margaretta Terrace, a small street that forms a loop one block before the Thames. Three years she has lived here with Edward, his choice of this address a marriage gift to her. With their home here, she could stay near her artist friends from the Slade School—though Isabella, whom she missed the most, was off in Soho, and Edward never knew Viola traveled further to see James in Camden, never knew that she had taken up again the line to James that she had once let go. Now, she takes the two steps up from the pavement and lets herself into the house where she finds Mary already in the hall.

"Ma'am!" Mary says. "The sight of you!"

"It's nothing, Mary." She touches her cheek where a welt makes a raised line.

"And your hat."

"Yes. That one's gone, I'm afraid."

Viola sets the Midg on the hall table and checks her image in the mirror.

"You'll catch your death of cold," the girl says, and then a hand flies to her mouth. Such statements are not uttered now in Margaretta Terrace. "I'm sorry, ma'am."

"I have apparently survived," Viola says. "And that hat was useless anyway. But I do seem to have hurt my ankle."

The sounds of Viola's return have summoned Samuel Miner from the rear parlor that is Edward's study. In the shadow of the stairs, he bends over some object he is always fussing with and always secreting away before she sees it. A strand of hair, a locket, a medal from the Boer War he would rather not pin to his chest? She does not know.

"Samuel."

"Ma'am."

The face no longer shocks as it once did. She knows to look him in the eyes. The nose ends in a puckered stub, like a twisted bit of clay, the skin discolored to a shade of darkest oxblood. Miner is a man mutilated by weather. One day and one long night in a Mont Blanc crevasse after his rope to Edward failed have robbed him of a nose, a thumb, and several fingertips. His left boot holds a block of molded leather where half his foot should be. What if James and Edward return like this, with pieces of their bodies lost to cold, with feet misshapen, toes and fingers gone? Even this fear, Viola knows, is a luxury—to think that they will be only diminished.

"You've been out taking photographs?" he says.

"Yes," she says. "With the Midg." When she uses her larger camera, Miner attends, her truculent familiar, the rude spirit of her art. At Edward's request, he has fashioned a cart from wood and leather, with wheels along the bottom and a handle with which he steers it like a sledge down city pavements. It contains everything she needs—her lenses, tripod, flares, her glass-plate negatives and cloth drape. To Edward she made the promise that Miner would escort her. She did not tell Edward she could choose the Midg, which she can work without his help.

"I assume there was another march," he says.

"There was."

"Sure, she was in it again, with all the suffragettes," Mary says. "Look at the state of her."

"I *am* a suffragette, Mary." She hands the girl her coat and winces at a new pain in the ankle.

"You're hurt," Miner says.

"It's fine, Samuel."

"She twisted her ankle."

"I'm fine, both of you. It's not the first time I've rolled an ankle and it won't be the last."

"You should have it looked at, ma'am," he says. "I'll send for Mr. Hickham."

Viola sighs loudly, but she does not stop him. Bertie will come and drink some tea and wrap the ankle in a bandage. It will be good to see him.

"You shouldn't be going," Miner says. "These things are dangerous."

"Hardly dangerous at all compared to what Edward endures."

"Dangerous for London, then. And I see you've hurt your face as well."

This last remark unsettles her, said with no seeming connection to his own state.

"I'm fine," she says. "Both of you. Stop it."

Mary's freckles vanish in the flush of her cheeks.

"And Mary will give me an ointment, won't you?"

"Yes, ma'am," the girl says, with a little bob.

Viola takes the Midg and limps towards the back stairs that lead down to the darkroom.

"What would Mr. Edward say if he knew you were joining with these marchers?" Miner says.

She looks at him.

"Mr. Edward is not here." She imagines for an instant that Miner will send a telegram to meet Edward in New Zealand. *Sir, your wife has disobeyed you. Stop. Come home soon and make her stop. Stop.* "I can do what I choose," she says.

"If he were here," Miner says, "would you be going?"

"Mr. Miner, it is not your place to comment on my actions."

"Mr. Edward charged me with your safety, ma'am."

"But he needn't have, as I am perfectly capable of keeping myself safe."

"I'm sorry, ma'am," Miner says. "I was simply concerned for your well-being."

Viola cannot always read his face—even when he bares it as he does inside the house, shedding the special mask he wears outdoors—and now she wonders if, with so much time away from Edward, he cares more for her than for her husband's edicts.

"It's all right, Samuel. I spoke too harshly," she says. "And thank you for sending for Bertie. But now you must both leave me alone. I need to work."

Theirs is a strange balance of need and independence. Three years in Margaretta Terrace, Miner has been with her more than Edward has. Miner, her husband's man, his climbing scout turned family retainer—though there is no family in the house save the false one they make with Mary. Yet they observe certain rules. Despite his injuries, Miner serves. And despite Viola's desire for self-reliance, she accepts his help. They play these roles as if Edward were watching—as if to drop the pretense would melt the very ice that Edward walks on.

She finds that she must lean on the handrail to take some weight off her ankle as she descends to the ground floor. Edward agreed to have a darkroom fashioned here, carved from a larger workroom. The darkroom abuts the kitchen, but with two doors closing the space off from the tiled corridor, Viola hears no sounds of Mary's cooking. In a grander house, there would be both maid and cook, but Edward saves this luxury for later when his adventures have brought him fame and fortune. Viola's is a lean home, with only Mary and Miner to attend her. She closes the two doors behind her and flicks the toggle for the ruby safety light. She puts on her leather apron and drags out from beneath the workbench the tubs of chemicals: developer to bring the silver crystals together where the light has found them, fixer to halt the process when the blacks and whites are clear, and stopper to stabilize the image once and for all. It is a tricky task to do this without standing fully on the injured foot, but she will not confine herself to bed or to an armchair with her foot raised on a cushion.

She fills the timing tank with developer and slides the first negative from its waxed-paper envelope. In the ruby light, she makes out the green of the exposed plate, a dusty green like the spring silt of an Alpine river. She moistens the plate from a bottle of distilled water and stands it on its edge inside the tank. She does the same with ten more plates, then shuts the tank with its metal cover. She rocks the tank gently, bathing the plates in the developer until her clock ticks off its time. She rinses once more, glimpsing the images in their reversed blacks and whites, and sets them one by one into a basin filled with fixer. Once the fixer binds the silver halides to the glass, she rinses off the last of the emulsion and dries them with her chamois cloth.

When she has set each plate in the enlarger and printed a photograph from each one, she will dispatch a set of prints by evening post to the

Observer. What began as the newspaper's favor for the wife of a man soon to be famous has now become sincere demand. No one else has photographs like hers, in compositions that arrest the eye and taken with the intimacy of someone allowed into the movement's heart. She signs her prints Colfax, not Heywoud, a large V and X bracketing her name. *ViolacolfaX.* She likes the look of it. Edward liked it too, until they married and he expected this to change. But there is no harm in her publishing these photographs under her own name now while he is gone. She will give up Colfax once again, when Edward comes a second time into her life.

When, she tells herself. Not *if* but *when*. And in a few months, she hopes to have them both. James the slight and wiry figure beside Edward's stocky one. James dark-haired and Edward light, both of them with dark eyes smiling. Their ship will come to Cardiff's port and someone will take Viola up the gangplank and bring her to a cabin where Edward will rise slowly to embrace her. In her thoughts he always rises slowly, as though he has only just left the Pole and not spent weeks on board to rest and heal. They bring James to her in Edward's cabin and she holds him just too close and just too long and hopes that Edward does not see.

Mary is at the door.

"Ma'am, I have the ointment."

Viola checks that her photographic paper is within its wax-sealed box and that she has left no undeveloped plate out on the workbench. She tugs off the heavy gloves and opens the two doors into the corridor.

"If you must," she says to Mary, who bears a tray with a little ceramic pot and a wooden spreader.

"I must."

Mary dips the spreader into the pot and presents it like a warning to comply.

"How's that ankle?"

Here below stairs where it is just the two of them, Viola allows this more familiar attitude. A mere five years her junior, Mary might have been schoolmate or sister in different circumstances.

"Bertie will fix it."

"That he will. But he can't fix your fancy to go out romping with those marchers. Chin up," Mary says, before Viola can chide her for the comment. Viola tilts her cheek to the girl's ministrations.

"It is no fancy, Mary. And when we win, you also stand to benefit."

Mary makes a dismissive sound. They both know the movement leaves the working women out for now, that no one—man or woman—without property can vote.

"You'll be glad Mr. Hickham's coming."

"I always am." Bertie who shared the medical office with her father, who came to find her at the Slade with news of the railway crash. Bertie and Alice who took her in when she was newly orphaned.

The ointment is cool to the skin and smells of something dusky, floral.

"Just a bit more, ma'am. You don't want this to scar."

Here is another in the list of statements they should not make in Margaretta Terrace. How can Viola prize smooth skin when Miner bears his disfigurement and when James and Edward may return the same?

"You'd have a job explaining that scar to Mr. Edward, wouldn't you?"

"I've no intention of keeping any of this secret, Mary. I will tell Edward I am still fighting for the cause. I was already marching when I met him." She does not say that when Edward asked her to stop marching, she agreed. She wanted to please her new husband. But by the time he sailed from London, the movement had sparked hotter and she could not stay away from that new blaze.

"Well, I agree with Samuel," Mary says. "Mr. Edward won't be happy."

"Let's not have this again." Viola looks her in the eye, and Mary sticks the spreader into the little pot as if in comment. "When Edward returns," Viola goes on, "we will have more interesting things to talk about than whether I photographed a march."

Mary gives her a look of mock prudery.

Back in the darkroom, Viola cinches her gloves tight around her wrists and resists the urge to touch her cheek where the ointment has roused a sting. She knows of one photographer who wiped a tear away at the image of his dead child and lost the sight in that eye thanks to the halides. Mary and Miner are both right. If Edward were here now he would chide her. For all of it. For going to the marches, for taking the photographs, for using the name Colfax. He would insist that she stay safe at home and that she return to painting—a noble art, an art for women—not this new thing photography that uses chemicals and gadgets. Let men do it. Let women—let my wife—maintain a household, raise our child.

She wanted a child, too, before Edward departed. Or at least she wanted what he wanted. There was such sweetness to be joined to him, first on a climbing rope and he sending her up ahead to marvel at her prowess, and then in love and savoring the ease of his embrace. He made a dashing figure in his woolens and his cap that first climb at Great Gable. But it was his voice that drew her to him, so commanding and so sure. Edward and James were to attempt Napes Needle, a feat James thought a good beginning to this new bond between his friends. Theirs was a modern companionship—old lovers with passion spent, and romance taking form in a new pairing. That day in the Lakes, Viola was to stay at ridge's base while the men climbed up the spire. But before they reached the Needle, mist rolled in and Edward declared they must head down. Know the cost and know the value, he said then. This is not the risk to take. From pub windows in Wasdale they watched black clouds claim the sky and lightning scratch the crags along the ridge they would have climbed.

From that day, she and Edward climbed together, away from each other but always in sight, and he was always there for her return. When she lost the child Edward wanted so much, she discovered a relief to be free a little longer from that other kind of tether. She could not fathom a rope that bound its climber with so tight a knot. There would be no rescue there but by shrinking small enough to slip away. Now, with Edward gone, she has had respite from that tie and from the thought of it. It is like breathing deeply after gasping in thin air.

She takes up one of the glass plates, now developed and stark in the black and white of the negative. She slides it into the enlarger and reaches for the paper where she will print the image. When Edward returns—her heart jolts a little at the hopeful certainty of *when*—she must convince him she will not give up this life of her own choosing. James understands the pull of it. Like her, he knows the joy of catching light and shadow, the thrill of summoning it forth in darkness like a kind of god. But Edward grasps at hard shapes of rock and ice. What can she offer in her currency that he will value? Is there some quality of light she can yield up to him to seal the bargain?

3

88° 30'S

Heywoud motions to him from the tent. Watts finishes packing up the camera and the glass plates and joins Heywoud who is sitting on his bag, folded onto itself to fashion a low stool. Watts does the same with his own bag. If they could spare the matches he would light a pipe.

"I've made new calculations," Heywoud says. "We have twenty tins of hoosh, six of seal meat, ten boxes of biscuit, seven of lard, and eleven of potted beef. Each man hauling over one hundred miles, with the assistance of dogs, assuming progress of three miles each hour"—Watts knows this is far faster than they can advance but says nothing—"consumes 4,000 kilocalories each day."

"How many do we have left?"

"Not enough."

Watts waits.

"The dogs must be calculated too," Heywoud goes on. "But if we eat them, we gain several more days' kilocalories each."

Watts makes a disapproving noise.

"We gain, James, in the eating and in saving what it takes to keep them alive."

"I'm not going to eat the dogs, Edward."

"Would you rather die? No, I ask you," Heywoud continues when Watts begins a challenge. "Would you rather die without having eaten dog or would you rather live? Because it may come down to that."

Watts does not answer.

"If we keep the dogs alive," Heywoud says, "we have only enough for 1,000 kilocalories each man each day. If I send Lawrence and Tite back with one dog, we can kill and eat the other three over time. That gives us more food for the last leg. I don't know how much is in a dog." Heywoud's voice trails off.

"You're trying to do the mathematics for a life."

Heywoud snaps his gaze to Watts.

"Exactly. If I do not do that, we are lost."

Watts must concede the logic. The dogs are worth more to them as fuel than as workers. Four men to travel the more than one hundred estimated miles from their current position, and to return more than one hundred again, and then from there to continue to the depot at Hut Camp: the effort will starve them and the starvation will freeze them to death. But Tite and Lawrence will be robbed the heroism of the Pole. If Heywoud sends them back, they may at least survive, but their names will never be remembered.

"What of the camera?" Watts says.

"Of course, we will keep the camera. Don't be an idiot."

"The weight of it means work. Have you done the maths for that?"

Heywoud rises and looks down at him with a wry smile.

"The camera is worth its weight in hoosh, James. I'm not sure I could say that for you."

"And the photographs. I want them safe," Watts says. "I want them to reach London."

Watts wants Viola to see them, to hold the gelatin prints in her hands and peer at the men's faces.

"I do too," Heywoud says, and looks at him. "If nothing else," he adds, "mementoes for my widow."

Watts affects a chuckle and forces himself to meet Heywoud's gaze. The man's face is deeply creased, brown as a brogue, and the lips are cracked and scabbed. The blond beard is thick with gray. Patches of skin below his eyes have begun to blacken, deadened by persistent ice where he does not sweep it from the hollows. Watts supposes his own face presents a similar chronicle of exposure and hardship. His earlobes burn now when his body warms from work. He suspects he will lose them. Watts waits for a sign from Heywoud, a sign of anger or disgust or even sadness, but the man speaks of his widow and gives away nothing. Then Heywoud's face cracks into a smile.

"I've not come this far in this fucking cold to have nothing to show for it, have I now?"

Heywoud stoops and passes out of the tent.

Watts looks at the space that Heywoud has vacated, vaguely aware of the sound of men and dogs outside, the hardpack creaking beneath booted steps. He wonders at the sharpness in Heywoud's voice, that touch of the cynic new for a man of such honest ambition. He fears he knows the reason for it, though there are ample causes here for the stripping away of kindness. It is a marvel they have come this far without greater savageries.

When Heywoud thinks of London, what does he imagine? What does he think Watts conjures of his own future there? Watts sees them now returning, greeted first by crowds in Christchurch and its harbor Lyttelton, outpost of Empire granted pre-eminence in this one thing: the welcoming of those mad enough to embark for Antarctica. Mawson, Shackleton, Scott: the great men who have come South before them and whose living ghosts Heywoud chases and now overtakes as he pushes towards greater latitude, towards the very Pole itself. Their welcome, his and Heywoud's, will be far greater, offering to the crowd a common dream, the shared fantasy of the Union Jack in virgin ice. Watts sees himself descending from the ship in Cardiff, Heywoud at his side, and between them Viola, the great man's wife. Will the crowds watching them discern what he fears Heywoud knows? Will it pulse off Watts like a heat even then, the heat that warms him when he wakes in the sun-blazing night, and off Viola too, or will it dissipate once and for all in London's sooty air?

"Watts! Get out here!"

Heywoud's voice rouses him and he stumbles in the tent to take up something, anything, in his hand as a cover for his idleness. He steps out of the tent, pulling his sun goggles over his eyes.

"Come on, man. We've work to do."

"Right you are, sir!" Watts attempts a smile at his own joke, his mockery of the very obedience Tite and Lawrence live by. Heywoud turns his back and continues with his work of carrying boxes to one of the two sledges. Tite is freeing Lulu from a knot in the traces, made from her immobility within a tangle of restive dogs.

The wind has been building. It is what Watts has come to think of as a rope wind, a thick cord of surging air formed of several breezes come suddenly together, twisted like a braid. From some unseen tether to the South, always to the South, it bucks and snakes, snapping and whipping as if to scatter them away. The rope wind is gathering now. They will be lucky to have their belongings secured before it begins to lash.

Watts joins Tite who now is fixing leather straps around the bundles on his sledge.

"How are you, Angus?" he says.

"Peachy." Tite does not look up from his work.

"How is the foot?"

Now Tite glances up at him. He cinches up the strap as if it were a saddle girth and he back in a Cornwall barn.

"Foot's fine," he says. "It'll hold."

"You've been limping."

"Aye. And he's lost half his face." Tite tips his chin towards Lawrence. "That's not stopping either of us."

Tite fixes him with the strange stare of a man in sun goggles, black circles for eyes.

"Haven't come this far to turn back now, have I, sir?" he says.

"I suppose not, Angus. Nor have I."

But there it is again, a whisper telling him he could change direction, march North, let this rising wind push him homeward to the shore. Keep Tite, he would say. Send me in his place.

"What's he saying, sir? The Captain."

"We're close. Handful of days now," Watts says and marvels at the easy slide of the lie.

No more than twenty yards of hardpack stretches from the two men to where Heywoud bustles back and forth between the tent and the sledge. The Polar wind and cold expand distance, so that a man could starve to death or lose a toe to frost with food or fire mere steps from where he lies. In this space of ice no larger than a London drawing room Heywoud is alone, as isolated from companions as are they from the men who await them at the shore.

They do this packing and unpacking of the sledges at every stop, like travelers on the Grand Tour unloading trunks and cases at a succession of approved hotels. It has become a quiet joke shared by all but Heywoud, though their cheeks rise now in grimaces not smiles and they curse the theater of these furnished camps. They desire only to sleep in deep snow trenches warmed by dogs and pelts and wool and with their eyes closed against the glow of Antarctic dusk. Now Heywoud loosens the guy lines for the tent pitched as last night's shelter and Watts wonders why he squanders the very time and kilocalories he deems so precious.

It is nearly certain Heywoud has been watching Watts and Tite as he works. That he has not shouted at them and at Lawrence to join him is testament to his awareness. They might speak mutiny, but the weight of the sledges will counter their flyaway words. And so he trudges from the tent and stacks another heavy crate onto the pile.

Watts steps around Tite's sledge and walks into a landscape altered by the thrashing of the air. The hardpack blurs, the line between snow and sky erased by the scouring of the rope wind. Solid ground turns to a cloud of crystals rising and falling, throwing up plumes and wraiths. The dogs have disappeared and everything—sledges, boxes, blocks of ice they sat on for their pemmican moments ago—is lost to the white cloud. A ground cloud, they call it, and they fear the storm it presages and the confusion it creates.

Watts sees a corner of the tent caught in the wind and flapping towards a tear. He calls to Heywoud. The man does not hear him so he shouts the words again, this time downwind. Heywoud looks up from the strap he is affixing to the sledge rail as if to spot a bird on the wing, and, disappointed, turns back to his task.

"The tent," Watts bellows.

Heywoud sees him finally and Watts waves to the tent whose edges he can hear thrumming against the snow. Heywoud has removed the boxes and crates they place around the tent's perimeter to block the wind and the fabric is vibrating in the rush of air.

"Come." Watts steps into the tent without waiting to see if Heywoud has followed. But he has, and both men take a single deep breath in the hush of the enclosed space. A gust pries a windward corner of the tent from its mooring, and the men pounce at the canvas that bucks with a sound like gunfire.

The storm is nearly upon them. Watts and Heywoud both know the storms of Snowdon and the Peaks. They know the *orages* of Mont Blanc where black clouds surge like ocean waves, tumbling and grinding down upon the summits. At Shore Camp, too, the storms were familiar, terrestrial. Here in the interior of this blasted land, storms come with the force of an idea, in a clear sky, on a dry day. The wind tumbles the snow until the men are all blind and lost in white and blue, while the indolent sun ignores their struggles.

The tent again secure, they work together to dismantle it properly, beginning with the stays and snow anchors. Watts notices in Heywoud a tightened expression, a stiff carriage of the neck. In this Antarctic summer, the man warmed during his solitary work before the wind arrived, and he has been caught without his balaclava. Watts fetches the wool hat from Heywoud's bag of coverings and pushes it over his head when he throws off his hood. Heywoud stands still, like a child, while Watts nudges the wool into the man's coat as best he can with his broad gauntlets, and pulls the hood around Heywoud's face. They must move quickly now. They finish loading the sledges, evenly dividing their supplies between the two, and they marshal the dogs to their traces. In the ground cloud, Watts loses sight of the dogs until one creature frantic at the coming run leaps up at Tite's legs. He sees Tite crouch down briefly. He is saying something to the dog.

They step into their skis and set off into the wind. The harness tugs against Watts' chest and presses shoulders down as if to drive him through the snow's hard crust. He steps and kicks a heel back and glides forward with the other ski, one glide and then another and this is how it will go this day as on all others. He steps and kicks and draws the sledge forward one more yard. They are one hundred miles from the Pole and he is contemplating yards. He looks across at the other sledge where Lawrence takes the harness. Already that sledge leads and Watts knows again the panic of being left behind. He is no different from that antic dog desperate for its master's notice. But in this ground cloud, they must not lose one another. There have been days when the cloud has teased and tempted men away like some atmospheric Circe and at haul's end they have been two groups not one, the errant sledge some crucial compass points off course. Then to travel east or west is an indignity, the extra miles heaved onto day-weary men like as many blows.

Ahead of them is more of the same they left behind. White swales, shadows of the palest turquoise, sun. Watts skis towards an image of Viola, her right eyebrow arching upward as she smiles. She had risen while he slept and in the thin light of the Camden morning she had pulled his shirt and trousers on against the chill. Stay there, she told him when he reached for the sheet to cover himself, waking to cold. Turn sideways, she said, and then her eyebrow again. She took his photograph, naked to the groin. She photographed herself then, holding the bulb on its long cord, both hands in pockets, shoulders hunched and hair tucked in a cap. I could pass for a man and what would this picture prove? You're not fooling anyone, he said, and pulled her down onto the bed. But they were proof, those images. They were art and they were proof of something. Later that morning, before she gathered up her things to return to Margaretta Terrace, they had staged it properly. Viola dressed head to toe in Watts' clothes, kohl pencil on her face to make the shadow of a beard, shoulders curved in to conceal the swell of breasts.

When they stop again, the second sledge is so far behind that it appears like a mote upon the hardpack. Heywoud stands beside him, looking back at the mote turning to coal, turning to shadows, turning to men, and he says nothing, offers no explanation for the gap he has allowed. Heywoud and Watts are mountaineers enough to know such separation is unsafe. A crevasse encountered by one team on its own would almost certainly mean death. And yet, as he stands by Heywoud, joining him in silent watching of the other, weaker team, Watts knows that this is what awaits them all—not death, if he can help it, but the onward journey of one single sledge.

4

15 January

When Bertie Hickham comes to the house that evening, Viola has finally given in to the injured joint and sits on the parlor divan with a book, a new novel by Mr. Forster. She rests the ankle on a small ottoman but when she hears Bertie's voice in answer to Mary's at the door, she goes to spring to her feet.

"Halt right there, young lady. Just where do you think you're going?"

"To see you," she says.

He bends over her and she kisses him on the cheek. He keeps his face close-shaven over a thin curve of beard, a counter to the white curls that peek from his hat.

"Mary, some tea for Bertie, please," she says.

"Thank you, Mary," he says, and brings a smile to Mary's face. "What have you done, my dear?" He takes a seat beside Viola and scans her face.

"Twisted it during a march. That's all."

He touches her cheek lightly where Mary has daubed the ointment, looks at his fingertips and seems to approve the quality of the medication.

"Been in a scuffle, is what I'd say."

He stoops to open his medical bag.

"Where was this particular march?" he says.

"Victoria Street."

"In front of Parliament, then?" He gestures for her to lift the foot. He undoes the laces.

"There were thousands of women, Bertie. It was a big one."

"Yes," he says, distracted now as he gently pulls off her shoe and moves the ankle this way and that. Viola grimaces and tries not to let him hear her grunt in pain. "I can see your ankle hurts you," he says. "You're not fooling me, you know. Have you ever fooled me, Viola Colfax?"

"Heywoud."

"Yes, and have you ever fooled me since you were a little girl?"

"I suppose not."

"You have not."

He pats the ankle and sets the foot down on the ottoman.

"It's a sprain, but not a very bad one. But you probably knew that."

"They insisted that I send for you."

"And I am grateful for it. Samuel," he calls out. "Mary. I thank you for your concern."

He pulls a rolled bandage from his bag.

"You'll rest the foot for a few days," he says. "And you'll keep it bound like this."

He begins to unroll the bandage around the ankle. The delicacy in his movements reminds her of her father's hands, the way he would affix a sticking plaster to a cut or place a compress on her forehead. She was nearly nineteen when her parents died, but Bertie cared for her the way her father had, and his wife, Alice, as her mother had, in those first years.

"Do I smell a cigar, Bertie?" she says. "Alice will not approve."

"I didn't hear you promise," he says.

"But there is so much I want to do, Bertie. I need to photograph those marches, to get the photos in the papers."

"You have an injury, my girl, and you must rest the foot for a few days. Promise me?"

He waits until she sighs acceptance.

"I promise I will try."

He ties the bandage off and takes up her shoe and pulls the laces loose.

"You won't be able to fasten your shoelaces. That will keep you from those marches."

"Perhaps I shall ride a bicycle."

"Like a true suffragette."

"Bertie, I am quite serious. Since Government won't listen to petitions or delegations, we must march. Women must have the right to speak for themselves. And I don't intend to be silent about it. You know more than anyone that I was raised to speak my mind."

"Indeed," he says.

Bertie at her father's side as he showed her Gray's *Anatomy* and da Vinci's sketches. Conversations at the table over Sunday lunch about why were so few women admitted to medical schools or to the Slade, and why did so few women have work hanging on the walls of London's galleries. Her father showing her the Slade's acceptance letter, smiling. *Why not you?*

Mary comes in with the tea and Bertie takes up the cup Viola pours for him.

"But I worry about you," he says, "out among those crowds and with the constables. I don't want to hear from Samuel one day that you've been struck with a baton like some of the other marchers. And no arrests! Do you hear me?"

"I can't promise you I won't be hurt. And I can't predict what the police will do and whom they will choose to arrest."

He lets out a long sigh.

"You never change, do you?"

"Should I?" She smiles at him.

"Not really. Not someone as marvelous as you, my girl. You realize I worry."

"I know."

"About what your parents would think."

"I know," she says more seriously. "I'd like to think they would be proud." She tamps down her sense of loss, but Bertie seems to tend it like a fire banked with coal. After a while, he clears his throat.

"I have been paying some heed to the calendar," he says. "I calculate your Edward will be quite near the Pole at this very moment."

"Yes. That is my hope."

"It is important, my dear Viola, that when he returns you accept him for whatever has occurred."

"Why?" For a moment she wonders does he somehow have news. "What do you mean?"

"I want to be certain you are prepared for any outcome."

"Of course, Bertie. All I want is for him to be home safe and sound." She does not tell him about James, about how she longs for James and Edward both. "People say I pushed him to go."

"Who says such a thing?"

"I hear things from my artist set." She shakes her head. "The idea that I drove him to the bottom of the world. I only care about the Pole because Edward cares. If he could be happy climbing Alps the rest of his life, I would be happy for that too."

"And that will be a lovely future for you both. He'll return safely." He punctuates his words with pats on her knee. "He'll return victorious. He will do his climbing on the Continent. And you will settle down to start your family."

She sits up on the divan.

"I'm not so sure."

"Nonsense. You'll be just fine. You needn't worry about the miscarriage, dear girl. It is entirely safe for you to try again and I am confident that you will have a child. Alice will be so pleased."

She winces at his words. She takes his hand in hers.

"Bertie. I am not certain that I wish to be a mother. Even if I can be."

"Why not?"

She squirms in the cushions and it is suddenly as if she is a little girl caught in the surgery pouring out chemicals to make a potion.

"The tie is too great, Bertie. A mother and a child. It's—" She lets out a long breath. "It's this connection to your *self* and it never goes away, mustn't ever go away." She shakes her head. "Perhaps I am a very selfish person, Bertie, and you will not like me anymore."

He looks at her. He does not accuse, but simply studies as if to learn her.

"I am not sure I can give up a fundamental kind of independence. The ability to be simply *alone*."

"Now, that sounds like you've taken this suffrage movement a bit too far."

"The entire point of the movement is that women should have their own voice. Which means that if I wish to be alone in that way, if I don't wish to give up that kind of independence, then I can choose not to."

"Well." He presses his lips together in displeasure. "You shall see what Edward has to say about that."

She begins another protest but decides against it. He more than most knows all the means available to her on her own. Bertie claps his palms on his knees and makes to stand.

"Your injury must be fatiguing, dear girl. I will leave you to rest and we can speak of this another time." He picks up his medical bag and stoops to kiss her on the forehead. "You must keep the bandage on for a few days until the swelling stops. I know you'll be in that darkroom of yours. Have Samuel find you a tall stool to sit on so you can rest that foot. Do you promise?"

"I promise."

She remains in the parlor for a while longer, stirring her tea without drinking it. The thought she fights away comes back to her in Bertie's words. *When he returns.* But for Viola it is always *they.* When they return, both of them, Edward and James together and she faced with the choice between them that she never wants to make. It seemed so simple when it first began, James introducing her to his climbing partner, she turning back to James a year after the wedding, telling herself she could be with them both. To love two men at once—there was exhilaration in the balance of it, as if she walked a tightrope from one man's arms into the other's. But when they return—if they both return—she does not know what she will do. She fights in front of Parliament for the right to be her own fate's captain, and yet her love for these two men pins her to her place.

5

88° 45'S

Heywoud skis to Watts' right, taking his turn out of the harness now. The dogs ignore him. Once set to run, they look only ahead. He has given Lulu to the other sledge, along with Travis, a male whose power should offset the weakness of the ailing bitch. To his own sledge Heywoud has tethered Kip and Dagger, the last two of the Russian dogs. When Watts sees them through his camera lens, they stare back with changeling faces, their blue-white eyes like chips of glacier.

Inside his parka, Watts is sweating and already he feels the grip of ice on his chest and small of his back. He turns his head to let the wind take his hood and hopes to find some respite with this invitation to the air. An odd place where a man fights cold with cold.

They travel on the hardpack for two more hours, though Watts does not know the time, nor can he judge from any passing of the sun. The storm has passed and the footing is good and the dogs delight in the easy haul. Heywoud shouts a halt and Lawrence's sledge, ahead by several yards now, slows and stops. Heywoud frees his boots from their strap bindings and stoops over his own sledge to extract the sextant from its bundle. He holds it out before him but struggles to work the pieces with his mitts. Watts takes Heywoud's hand and nudges off the mitten. It dangles from its strap and Heywoud looks at Watts mutely before sliding the other hand free. With leather gloves he works the sextant to learn how far they've come.

Watts feels a shiver starting and swings his arms to shake free of it.

"88° 50'," Heywoud says. "That's five miles gone. Good."

When Lawrence and Tite join them, Heywoud repeats the words for their benefit.

"Good."

"See?" Lawrence says, more to Watts than to Heywoud, and Watts sees the other two men notice this.

But speed has a cost and when they hunch their shoulders around the Primus where Tite is melting snow for their tea and the dogs' water, their stomachs protest at the rations. Two pieces of biscuit each man and those so dry it squanders all their spit and water just to swallow. Seeing something in their eyes, Heywoud opens the tin again and gives two more. Double rations. They eat the biscuits with a mingled gluttony and fear.

They go again. Boxes lashed to sledge rails, dogs in traces, men in harnesses on skis. Now it is Heywoud and Tite who pull. Watts skis across the hardpack, into a whiteness so vast he cannot tell ice from sky. He thinks of the Broomway at home, the steely sand that spreads for miles off Southend's coast, and how a man can lose all bearings when the tide is out for miles and neither house, nor rock, nor ship mark his direction. He turns to look behind, and finds relief in two black lines—sledges, dogs, and men—drawn like a painter's signature at the base of this blank canvas. Ahead there are no lines of other men's dark progress. But if they merge upon the Pole, should the Norwegians not be coming into view? Who is lost, Watts wonders, they or their rival Nilsen?

Watts halts. Where wind has abated and ground cloud sighed to rest, motes of ice dance in the air. They hang more than fall, a crystal rain from a sky of no clouds. Diamond dust it has been named by men from other Polar parties, and Watts lets it settle on his shoulders, turns his face up to the sun, closed eyelids orange despite the goggles, to let the diamonds dust his cheeks. The particles are too fine or his skin too numb to feel them. There is no time to retrieve the camera. Heywoud glides past without stopping.

Now Watts sees the other sledge has gone ahead though on a course that veers eastwards. Watts shouts and waves at Lawrence, attempts a cabman's whistle but his lips are too numb for the job. He searches on his body for anything to clang or smack for noise but it is all wool and fur and cotton. He speeds a few strides and, heavy-thighed, pulls up, panting. He watches through the veil of diamond dust as the sledge draws an invisible line towards the wrong place.

For a moment, he wonders if this is some conscious act by either man, a suicide by wandering. But no, they move too slowly for an act of such pure purpose. Watts shouts and waves again. His hands are on the straps of his ski bindings and he fumbles with the buckles. Tite and Lawrence hear nothing within their hoods of fur and over the sounds of their own breathing and leather creaking and the excited rustle of the dogs.

And then it stops. The sledge pitches forward and is gone, both dogs and one man disappeared into the white. Watts screams and, free of skis now, starts to run, his legs like iron lifting boots of lead. His hood falls back and icy cold grips the clammy skin around his neck. The lone figure—it is Tite—crouches at the edge of a crevasse from which only the stern end of the sledge protrudes. The dogs yelp and Tite shouts down at Lawrence. Watts seizes the wood frame of the sledge and leans with Tite against the enormous weight. Nothing moves and it is as if they are posing for a photograph, still for the camera. *Men in Peril. The Pole Claims Another.* Watts grunts and heaves again and something yields upwards.

"Again!"

Tite plants his good leg in the ice and slowly straightens the knee so that his side of the sledge rises slightly. But the sledge begins to twist, its top-heavy lashings driving Watts' side down.

"No," he shouts. "Hold it."

"Lawrence," Tite hollers down. "Can you climb at all?"

There is no answer save the dogs squealing. Now Heywoud has arrived and takes hold of Watts' side of the sledge where it has dug into the ice, and all three men pull hard. The ice creaks beneath their boots and they inch the sledge out, its bow visible but still no Lawrence. Their boots churn the ice to dust and they lose purchase. The sledge descends again, and Lawrence's cry reaches them. They heave once more and yank the sledge further than before. Lawrence's head appears. Heywoud takes his arm and then his shoulders. Tite and Watts hold the sledge from losing ground. Braced on the edge with Heywoud, Lawrence reaches into the maw for the dangling traces and hauls up one dog then the other, writhing creatures glazed in frozen piss. His skis clack like cricket bats as he twists to hurl the dogs onto the ice, then hangs at the edge, mittens slipping.

"Don't stop," Heywoud says. "Come on, man." He pulls and shoves at Lawrence until his entire body is out of the crevasse and he lies on the ice like a drowning man on shore. The dogs lick his face and tumble over him, but their motion rocks the balance of the sledge.

"Someone free them," Tite says.

Heywoud fumbles at the harnesses then sheds hood and mittens to work the buckles loose. Freed, the dogs lick at their soiled fur. Heywoud kicks at Travis who blocks his access to the sledge and then, space cleared, takes hold of the rail.

"On three!" he bellows. "One! Two! Three!" And the four men yell as they strain muscles, bones, and lungs, taking the sledge rail hand over hand until momentum sends the sledge entirely free and it glides back from the lip, retreating as if in horror at its folly.

The men collapse onto the ice and lie there sending steam-engine puffs of breath into the air. The dogs go from one man to the other, excited still by all the irregular motion. They have already forgotten the moments they spent hanging by chest and haunches, their paws touching nothing, legs flailing.

Watts and Tite are first to stand and brush the snow from their parkas. Tite goes to check the sledge. His limp is worse. Lawrence sits up but he does not rise from the hardpack.

"I'm a bit banged up," he says and smiles. Tite comes back from the sledge. They glance at him but it is Lawrence they must hear from.

"Twisted the knee when the thing started going in. Skis caught."

"Can you move it?"

Lawrence tries this, winces.

"It's just a little stiff."

"Walk it off," Tite says.

"What happened?" says Watts.

"You were off course," Heywoud says. He has not stopped looking at Lawrence.

"We were going to veer back," Lawrence says.

"The dogs were pulling left," Tite says, and they all know it was Lulu on the right whose weaker tugging skewed the sledge's path. "But we knew. We weren't lost or anything." Tite attempts a laugh.

"And the next thing I know," Lawrence says, "I'm falling into a hole. Ground gave way." There is no ground here, only ice packed miles thick. But there are snow bridges hiding rents in the surface. They have lost two dogs and crates of unlashed cargo to crevasses on their journey, and yet they go on blindly because the hardpack gives them no choice. Watts has learned to read the surface for shade and light, but none of them, not even Heywoud, can see where ice hides a void beneath it.

"We weren't even going that fast," Tite says.

Lawrence slides one foot beneath him and pushes up slowly. He holds his injured leg out like a Cossack. When he is upright he attempts to stand on both feet, winces again. Watts sees he holds the left foot off the surface of the ice. Matching injuries, man and dog, the weakest of the dogs, strongest of the men. The men would all trade ailments if they could. Let them lose the weakest man instead and spend less of the currency they use to buy survival.

Tite makes to take Lawrence by the arm.

"Leave me, Angus," Lawrence says.

Heywoud crosses to the sledge and tosses traces onto it from the ice. He tugs it by the man-harness so that its bow points truly south. Tite clucks at the dogs.

"Come on, pups," he says. "Back to work."

The dogs tremble with wagging as Tite slips the traces over their heads and haunches. He and Lawrence go to set off, but Lawrence's injury is obvious now. He sinks down onto his good leg with each stride and nearly drags the other ski along its edge. Watts fights the urge to shiver. He breathes deeply, the air like steel into his lungs.

"He can't ski," Heywoud mutters and then calls out to the laboring sledge. "Lawrence! Lawrence, stop!"

"Make him ride for now," Watts says.

"Then Tite would be hauling even more. No." He shakes his head. "Come back, Lawrence."

Lawrence stills for a moment and the dogs jump and dart at this sudden halt. Tite flaps the traces to settle their attention. Lawrence frog-steps his skis like compass needles to point back the way he came. Already his shoulders sag with defeat. Watts and Heywoud watch him tug the sledge towards them with the one ski ungovernable by the injured leg.

"Your nonsense about the four of us at the Pole," Heywoud says to Watts.

He retrieves the sextant from the sledge and pulls his goggles down around his neck to take a reading. The labors of Lawrence and Tite do not matter to him anymore.

"As if it matters who we reach it with." He turns the knob of the microm-eter. "We've barely moved since our last stop before all this," he says. "One and three-quarter miles."

Watts knows Heywoud is right. This is too slow, even without Law-rence's injury.

No one speaks a word when Lawrence reaches them. He hands his harness to Tite and crouches to undo his skis. Once the dogs have been released and fed, the two men join the others at the stove and hold out hands for bowls of hoosh. They eat with faces low over the steaming gruel. Lawrence makes little humming sounds, of relief or pain, Watts cannot tell. Heywoud does not wait for them to finish their meal.

"From here on," Heywoud says, "only Watts and I will continue."

There is a noise from Tite but Lawrence doesn't flinch.

"You two will take one of the sledges back to Shore Camp and wait for us there."

There is barely a change in the rhythm of their eating.

"Lawrence, you heard me?"

"I heard you."

That is the entirety of Heywoud's announcement but other messages whisper: the last leg will remain beyond their knowledge, and they may well leave Shore Camp after a long and fruitless wait. Heywoud waits for some other sign and receives none.

"You can hardly question my decision," he says.

"I'm not."

"You'll be better off returning," Heywoud says.

"What about dogs?" Tite asks.

"You'll take Travis and one of the other dogs with you."

"And provisions?" This is Lawrence.

"We'll divide it all up. Watts and I will need more as we will have longer to go and more to haul."

None of them looks at Watts but it is understood that Heywoud is speaking of the camera.

"Which dog?" Tite's voice is hoarse. Heywoud doesn't hear him. "I said which dog?" The question now comes as a challenge.

"Lulu."

The single word falls like a coal in the frigid air and for several seconds no one moves or speaks. Lulu herself is puzzled by the mention of her name with no accompanying human command or activity and she lets out a single sharp bark like a puppy's plea.

"You won't survive without us, mates," says Lawrence. "You'll have pretty pictures of your death."

"That's enough from you," Heywoud snaps.

He takes only a second to contemplate the men now freed from his command and free to challenge him.

"Tite," he says, "take leads for Lulu and Travis, and two of the harnesses."

"Lulu can't pull a sledge, sir," Tite says. "None of the dogs can on their own. Especially Lulu."

The dog's tail thwacks three times on the ice.

"Take her as passenger then," Heywoud says. "But if I were you I would make her earn her keep."

Lawrence and Tite finish their hoosh, scoop up some snow from the hardpack and swab their bowls with it. They hold them out to Heywoud, first Lawrence then Tite following his lead. Heywoud, flustered, pushes the bowls back.

"Keep them."

Lawrence's lips curl with a cynic's smile.

"Thanks."

Though the air is calm, all four sleep fitfully that night. Heywoud murmurs in his sleep, or possibly wakes and calculates: dogs, miles, and calories. Watts leaves the tent and stands by the dogs they keep hooded against the sun the animals cannot otherwise ignore. Strange figures these, like executioners at rest, hangmen lolling before the next day's grim assignment. He listens. Nothing but the snore of dogs.

Watts hears steps creaking on the ice and turns to see Lawrence, limping towards him in his heavy boots and wool puttees.

"Do you agree with him, Watts?"

"Does that matter?"

"But do you?" Lawrence takes him by the shoulders.

Watts exhales deeply. He tries to turn his back to the hooded dogs but Lawrence holds tighter.

"He's giving us Lulu."

Both men understand what this means: a lame man and a lame dog and injured Lawrence piloting this triple-anchored sledge on an impossible course. It matters not at all they have a second dog. Not even a rope wind at his back could bring a man home safe with such companions.

"You heard him say it. One hundred miles. That's nothing. It's six days' hauling."

"Not if the wind picks up," Watts says.

"Eight days then."

"And what would you do, Will? He's right. There's no sense in starving all of us so we can touch the flag before we die. I want to make it home."

"And I don't? I have a wife and two boys. I intend to be a hero to them."

Watts has no counter to this, with no one waiting for him but an aging mother and a sister with a household of her own. And a lover lost in marriage to the very man from whom he steals her back with every thought and dream and deed. He steps closer to Lawrence and in the quiet he wishes to tell him heroism does not require survival. Watts wishes to return. Better to return without a hero's glory than not return at all.

And yet in this moment as he stands close enough to Lawrence to feel the other man's breath, he does not speak the words he suspects Lawrence would like to hear. Though Watts' greatest strength lies in his eyes and not his legs or back, he does not offer himself up as the pilot of the returning sledge, to share this Charon's ferry with two doomed souls. He does not yield his place on the southward journey, and his silence consigns Lawrence to one of two lesser fates: banal survival or ignoble death.

"Give us a chance," says Lawrence. "My knee feels better already, and maybe we'll gain on his calculations. Let us *try*."

Lawrence utters the last word with the vehemence of a man who knows the seductive power of this gentleman's belief—that there is honor in actions undertaken out of risk. Like all the other men in the expedition party, Lawrence is no amateur, paid for his service, so many pounds sterling each day—though it might as well be payment by the mile, the box hauled, the step taken, the degree of Fahrenheit measured in the thermometer's mercury bead. Watts wonders which payment makes the men richer: for their suffering or for their achievement.

Lawrence has seen the hesitation in Watts' face.

"Come on, man. Tell him. Just one more day and if we're not fast enough, then he can send us back."

A dog whimpers in its sleep and raises its hooded head to the sky.

"I'm sorry, Will," Watts says, and heads back to his tent.

6

20 January

Viola pauses at the open door to Isabella's flat. The large room is packed with sculptors, painters, art collectors from her Slade set. She tests her ankle again and wades in among them, pecking one friend on the cheek, patting another on the arm or shoulder. She is trying to reach Isabella, whom she has spotted on the far side of the room, near a table laden with platters. Izzy has invited them all to gather in honor of the Daylight Comet, so bright that it is visible to the naked eye even in the daylight from which it takes its name. London waits for Halley's, timed to come in spring, but this upstart star has arrived in winter to skip ahead of its more famous rival. Who best to celebrate a flaming star, Isabella's invitation read, but a pack of artists burning up their lives.

The sofa and table are pushed to the edges of the room next to the bed Isabella has turned into a sort of divan for the occasion. Three women lounge upon it, feline and unblinking. Isabella frees herself from the knot of people around her.

"My darling Vi!"

"My darling Iz!"

"Come see," Isabella says, and seeing her make a grimace, scans her up and down. "What's happened?"

"Ankle twist. During the last march. I can't go as fast as you."

Isabella takes her by the arm in mock stately fashion to the back of the room. On the table a shallow flower vase doubles as a punch bowl. Small fruits of yellowish green float in the pale-yellow liquid. Isabella goes to scoop them into a glass for Viola, but they bob away from the ladle. She plucks out two of the strange things with her fingers and pops them into Viola's drink.

"They're meant to be like a comet," Isabella says. "Aren't they marvelous?"

"Where did you get them?" Viola asks. The fruit tickles her lips. The punch is made with gin and it has turned the fruit sour.

"Morton brought them and sliced them up. They come from India," Isabella says.

Isabella tips her glass up and parts her lips for the fruit. She brings a hand to her mouth while she chews and her eyes share a joke.

"Now you must eat," she says. "Come. I'll find you a place where you don't have to stand."

But someone calls Isabella away. Viola watches her friend pass through the guests, her lithe form swaying and a single long necklace swinging like a pendulum, a cigarette holder in her hand. She drifts to the table where the food is mostly gone and finds a finger sandwich cut into the shape of a comet and its tail, like a veil extending from a tiny head. Cucumber and caviar. From a corner, two young men pretend they are not watching her. One wears a full beard. It is Bomberg, and beside him Gertler with his smirking eyes. They began at the Slade after Viola and Izzy had finished, and then Charles Aitken at Whitechapel Gallery took them up and gave them a name to make them famous. The Whitechapel Boys. Viola wants their fame. She wants the space they claim on the Gallery's white walls.

Isabella is at her side again.

"Have another, darling. God, it's better than fish paste."

Beads of caviar hang on her lip and she tucks them into her mouth with a knuckle, chewing.

"Did Morton bring this too?"

"I bought it! Landscapes, darling. There's money in them."

She waves to the wall where Viola now sees several new paintings in a thick gouache. Landscapes and boats.

"See? I've got a man who loves these things."

"Who?" Viola casts her gaze about the room.

"He wouldn't come," Isabella says. "You wouldn't like him anyway."

"What about your other work?" Viola says. She remembers lying on the floor in this same flat, her head on James' chest, while Isabella showed them paintings of subtle form and abstraction.

"Can't afford it. Doesn't pay for parties like this."

She brings the cigarette holder to her lips and draws in with sunken cheeks and tips her head back to expel the smoke. It is a pose she mocks so she can relish it.

A hand on Viola's arm. She turns and sees Morton. He kisses her cheeks in Continental style.

"So, we have you to thank for this?" Viola shakes the punch glass at him.

"Or blame," he says.

"Morton, it is lovely and exotic," Isabella says. But then she drops her voice. "How are you, Vi? I mean really." She and Morton move in close around her.

Viola takes a sip of the punch but likes it no more than she did before.

"All right, I suppose," she says. "I worry about them."

"Of course."

"I worry about what I will do." She makes a gesture with her head.

"Darling, Morton knows. I think everyone here knows."

"Well, then." Viola shouldn't be surprised but suddenly feels as if the whole room watches her. "I should never have let them go with that secret between them. I don't know what to do when they return. I don't know whether I can go on the way we were before. I don't know if I want to." She laughs wryly. "I don't know anything." She takes a long drink.

"You don't have to know anything now," Isabella says. "You still have plenty of time."

"Where are they supposed to be by now?" Morton says.

"They should be close to the Pole." She thinks of Bertie and his calendar. "Almost there," she says, and startles at her ready tears. Morton pulls a handkerchief from his pocket and dabs her cheeks. He is among the many, Viola knows, who think her already a widow to the man who dragged their friend James to likely death at the world's end. They do not see as she did James' eagerness to follow, his hope that in another person's exploration he might deepen his own. Edward did not drag James to Antarctica. James chased.

"And how are you, Viola?" Morton says.

"I do better when I'm busy."

"She's been working for the newspapers," Isabella says.

"I've seen the photographs." Morton swings a punch glass free from a passing tray. "Very admirable."

Viola winces.

"Is that so awful?" he says.

"I don't particularly want to be admirable. At least not *only* admirable. Have *you* seen the photos, Izzy?"

"I have. And a good job, too, to show Government what's what."

"Government doesn't seem much bothered by my photographs."

"That's Government's job, darling. Not to bother. Secretly, they must be seething," Isabella says. "They'll have bitten right through their cigars." Someone takes her elbow and she turns away for a moment. When she turns back, she brings with her the laugh at someone else's joke.

"It's not enough," Viola says. "Photographs and banners. And I don't know why the movement called this truce. Why would Mrs. Pankhurst agree to such a thing? For months! It's clear Asquith won't listen."

"Viola, darling." Isabella jostles her. "It's a party. For our lovely comet." Viola sets her punch glass down.

"Don't you wonder, though," she says, "what more we should be doing? Take the march I was at five days ago, where I did this." She dangles her foot. "A thousand women pushing at the gates of Westminster, and did anyone in Government care? Did anyone change his mind? Not that I know of."

"You could set someone's house on fire," Morton says. "Throw a bomb."

"It's been done," Isabella says.

"And clearly it was not enough, Izzy. We still don't have the vote. This truce is meant to show that suffragettes can be diplomatic. Isn't the whole point of the movement that women shouldn't have to be polite, especially when it comes to the right to speak their minds? Aren't we fighting for exactly this, the right to be rude, angry, demanding?"

"Must we be, Vi? That sounds so tiring."

Viola lets out a long breath.

"I'm sorry, Izzy. It's a lovely party. I'm simply frustrated that everything seems to be standing still. And I'm running out of time. Edward will be back soon. I want to *do something*."

"Ah," Isabella says.

"What?"

"Edward." She raises an eyebrow.

"Yes, fine. He is a part of this. They both are. They go into new territory every day. What can I find in London that no one has seen before? And I don't have forever, Izzy."

"Must you stop when he comes back?"

"It depends. You know how Edward feels."

Soon after Viola married she came to Isabella, perplexed at the change in Edward. Everything he loved about her was now source of threat or danger to the child she would have and the mother she would be. Her art, her independence, even the climbing he had taught her, all now worried him when they had brought delight.

"I did tell you, darling. A man is bound to think he can control his wife. If you wanted independence, you were going to have to take it, whether Edward liked it or not. Look at me. No one to tell me what to do. Not even mater and pater down in Wiltshire."

"And you've got none of their money either, Izzy."

"That's what the landscapes are for!"

"Well, I have seized my independence," Viola says.

"Well done, you." Izzy takes a swig of punch.

"That's why I can't keep filling my darkroom with photographs of women singing and marching. I need to find something more powerful I can do to help the cause. Something more extreme."

"If it's extreme you want," Isabella says, "you must talk to Lucy." She points to a tall woman in a yellow dress with garnet beading. "Lucy Bellowes. She's part of the Artist Suffrage League."

"And what is that? Paintings and posters?"

"So much more, Vi. Lucy Bellowes is one of the true warriors. And Margaret Lyons. Look."

"What am I looking at?"

"Don't you see it?"

Across the room, Bellowes places a hand on the shoulder of a woman matching her height. The woman's burgundy dress hangs loose on her frame, and her eyes are deep-set over high cheekbones. She has a gaunt appearance that is striking for its air of deprivation in a room of such excess.

"She's a hunger striker, isn't she?" Viola says.

"Just released from Holloway after ten days of not eating."

"Good God."

"As if it weren't enough to protest and be arrested. They have to starve themselves as well to have the cause taken seriously."

Though the newspapers report on the hunger strikers of Holloway, Viola has never seen a woman freshly freed from prison. Those who emerge from Holloway after refusing food in protest are too weak to join the marches that she photographs. Now here is Margaret Lyons, ten days refusing both food and water. When she neared death, the wardens would have forced a tube into her throat and pushed down it a mash of meat and starches. Beneath her too-large clothes, Lyons must bear the bruises of that struggle.

"It's a miracle she and Lucy came tonight. Constables everywhere ready to snatch her up," Isabella says.

Viola knows how the police proceed. Women on hunger strike near death are force-fed and released in order to recuperate. When they are well enough, the constables arrest them once again so that not even starvation can stand in the way of a Holloway sentence.

"Margaret Lyons will give you something powerful to photograph. These hunger strikers are at the very edge, Vi. It's only the forced feeding that saves them. Otherwise, they are prepared to die for the cause."

Viola knows she is staring at the two women across the room but she cannot look away. For an instant, Lucy Bellowes catches her eye and seems to squint at her. Isabella takes her arm.

"Come to the ASL with me. I'll introduce you at the next meeting."

"You've joined?"

"What's an artist to do, if she wants to win the vote?" Isabella makes a flourish with the cigarette holder.

"For one thing, you could march," Viola says.

"And be arrested and then have to choose whether to give in or starve? No thank you. Not for me. But these women are the real soldiers." A young man cuts in and says something to her. She tells him she'll be there in a moment. Isabella bends close to kiss her on the cheek. "Darling, I've an announcement to make," she says. "But I mean it about the ASL. I think it could be what you're looking for."

Isabella drifts away and suddenly Viola stands alone among the guests, her ankle faintly throbbing. She watches Margaret Lyons give Bellowes her glass. Bellowes takes a sip and passes it back. Viola guesses they are lovers. She can see this in the ease of their gestures, the way their bodies tilt into hip and knee and shoulder.

Morton is by her side again.

"Quite a creature, isn't she?" he says.

"Lucy Bellowes?"

"Our dear Isabella. Did she needle you about her suffrage league?"

"Only a little." Viola laughs. "I'm intrigued."

"I blame it on her landscape man," he says. "She's compensating."

She turns to share her laugh with Morton but sees a sadness settled over him.

"How are you, Morton?" Morton who knew Muybridge and whose paintings capture the forms of fast machines. Famous once when his work did what Muybridge did with photographs, he has not had a show in years. He drains his glass and shudders at the tartness of the drink.

"Same as you, my dear. I'm waiting for my ship to come in." He sets his glass down on a Moroccan table. "I think of them often, you know," he says. "I think of James, at any rate. Never met your Edward. Here we are drinking and eating and they are in so harsh a place." He shakes his head in wonderment. "I don't know how he manages. Veritable heroes, they are."

She need not remind Morton the men's fate is still unknown. Dead or alive. Successful or failed. Each of these possibilities might be true. It astonishes Viola to think that all these hang in the balance until a telegram arrives. Fresh tears threaten at the thought that at this very moment—as at so many other moments when she has had the thought—they might both be dead. She wants to tell Morton how she tries instead to imagine James and Edward on their ship, scanning the sky for constellations that belong only to Viola's hemisphere, to the northern half of the globe that holds their home.

"Viola, dear." Morton is saying something to her but a cabman's whistle pierces the conversation. Isabella steps onto a chair and lifts her glass.

"To the roof!" she announces. She remains standing on the chair like a woman watching mice scurry around her as her guests press towards the flat's front door.

Morton joins the others in filing up the narrow stairs that lead to a small parapet among the chimneys, some builder's fancy for the distant view of Primrose Hill. Viola arrives last, taking the steps one at a time to spare the ankle. She holds the railing and gazes up at the night sky. The comet they are there to celebrate. It is like a firework, but unmoving. She cannot quite believe she is witnessing a comet, its long tail extending in a graceful arc, from right to left, its glow rising up above it. She understands that it is moving. She understands that it is hurtling across the heavens, that it has come from across the earth, from Southern Hemisphere to hers, a duplicitous thing that straddles the sky's equator. Here it is, a fixed shape, as all the newspapers said it would be: a halo and an arc, unmoving in the heavens. Just this, exactly this, James and Edward must have seen mere days ago. Perhaps they held a railing as she does now, their feet planted on a deck rising and falling in rough seas while this thing of heat and speed hung still above them.

"A toast!" somebody shouts. "To Mr. Halley!"

"Mr. Halley!" cheer the guests.

"Daylight!" Isabella shouts. Someone pulls her skirt and she laughs. "It's the bloody Daylight one, you fools!"

But no one listens. They cheer for Halley's and point to Halley's all the rest of the evening and it does not bother them at all that they are not looking at what they think they see.

7

88° 52'S

They rise in light no different from the light they bedded down in. Heywoud ignites the stove, Watts trudges off to retrieve the camera and tripod, and the other men prepare their sledge. They confer with Heywoud, and Watts sees Tite take a box from his sledge and place it on the other. Heywoud commandeers his allotment for the Pole.

Not for the first time Watts marvels at the thin leash that stays the men from turning on their Captain. At any moment, they could change course against his order. They could drive away both sledges while he and Heywoud sleep, going Poleward alone for fame and glory. That Lawrence and Tite have not done so is a testament to their sense of class and rank. But more than that, Heywoud has become, in their minds, the very South he marches towards. Even if their bodies had not betrayed them, to go South without him would be as if to go without a flag.

Watts sets up the camera to take a photograph of this last four-man camp. Watts captures an image of tents and sledges and crates ranged low before the distant peaks of the Transantarctic Mountains, the ridges of the Beardmore Glacier that they wove through weeks ago. Watts calls to Heywoud to come pose. He wields the idea of the captured image like a drug. And indeed it is like laudanum or whisky for Heywoud who, even now as Watts turns back to look at him, stands straighter for posterity, fixes on his face an expression of endurance. Watts quickly performs the sequence of movements that are his own narcotic: open tripod, throw drape, insert glass plate, squeeze bulb, and most powerful of all: frame shot. He wonders if he would be mad by now—or madder—if he did not several times each day place four edges around this limitless expanse, if he did not enclose the whiteness in the camera's box. He wonders if madness has struck the others. He watches them convene, the two slow men attempting heartiness when both are ailing and the third attempting sharpness when already Watts sees something of despair.

He frames the photograph. Tite standing on the left and Heywoud on the right, Lawrence between them on the sledge, a horizontal between two poles. He doesn't like the way their bodies face the camera square on. There is no artistry to the pose, but he squeezes the shutter nonetheless. There is something else to capture here, not artistry but proof. The simple proof that four men were here, together, in this moment. Is proof art's opposite? There are times here he thinks art proves a greater truth than any accuracy of science.

At the sound of the shutter, Heywoud turns.

"Not like that, for Christ's sake," he says. He crouches beside Lawrence and tugs Tite down so that all three men are low, equal, squatting like rugby players serried to celebrate a triumph. Watts slides a new plate in.

"All right," he calls. "Hold."

The men stiffen while he squeezes the bulb. The shutter sounds again and Heywoud rises from his pose.

"Right," he says. "Keep going."

In Lawrence's face, Watts sees what none of his cameras can detect, an emotion that unfolds in time. In two or three seconds, dismay rising and then mastered, settling into resignation.

All four embrace. They clap mittened hands on padded backs. They feel an instant's heat on frozen cheeks.

"Good lads."

"Safe journey."

"Plant one for us."

This last from Tite, accompanied by a vigorous thrust of hips. Heywoud turns away in displeasure. Lawrence breathes not a word of complaint. He stands from the sledge, wraps the leather bindings around his boots, slings the harness over his head, and begins to ski.

"Will, let me," Tite says, but Lawrence shrugs him off. Watts sees that he has splinted to his knee a length of tent pole and it lends his skiing a look of demented pride.

The sledge starts off, with Travis pulling hard enough to skew the path. Watts watches until Tite lifts Lulu and places her on the sledge where she sits like a figurehead sailing back to harbor.

Heywoud and Watts travel swiftly, barely speaking to each other during infrequent stops. They are blessed with continuing calm air and a plateau of hardpack that rises steadily but at an angle so gradual they cannot perceive it. They eat hoosh, they piss and defecate, they feed the dogs Dagger and Kip without releasing them from the traces, they throw their own harnesses over their shoulders once more and go on. Heywoud looks always forward, his head tipped up to the flat line of the receding horizon. He turns neither left nor right. When his hood falls off, he leaves it draped on his back and continues. His balaclava crusts with frozen breath.

Heywoud signals the end to the day's march and together they erect the tent, one small low structure in a vast white plain. Watts straightens and looks around him, turning slowly where he stands. He tells himself he is not searching for the others, the Norwegians who chase them or whom they chase, but he cannot help but scan the ice for those dark figures. He and Heywoud are alone. He scans the snow at his skis. Would he sense the Pole were it beneath him? Would he spin or tip or would he feel the ground fall away in a great curve? Would it all crack beneath his feet? He imagines the plain of hardpack flooded all at once by a rising sea, the ice melting beneath him, slab rocking like a raft out of Gericault, the grip of meltwater like a vise on his limbs and heart. His eyes open in the turquoise water and he sees Heywoud dangling, a russet figure suspended in the blue. He sees the undersides of ice floes, the black, the endless black, of the Antarctic ocean.

He gasps for breath, spins, looking for purchase on the truth. Someone grips his arm. Heywoud.

"James! Stop it."

He stands on firm ice. He breathes air.

Heywoud holds his shoulders.

"Control yourself."

"I'm fine. Just a little dizzy," Watts says.

"Help me with this then."

He follows Heywoud to the sledge where he has been unpacking food and fuel. Watts bends to the work but still when his eyes blink shut against the sun he sees the blue-black water and Heywoud's body, a man drowning where he stands.

"Why do you keep lashing everything down like this?" he says.

"So that we don't lose it." Heywoud laughs.

"Can't you put it in its own tank? Every day we have to go through this." He tosses the straps down. "Just to get our food."

"Easy, Watts."

"Do you see me with the camera? I keep it in its own bundle. On top."

"You do that because I told you to."

"It was a good idea, Edward. Have another."

"Shut up, James. You've got the jumps."

"I've got the jumps. Because it's you and me now and there's no other living thing for miles, except a bloody bunch of Norwegians out there somewhere. And these two dogs. Whom you want me to eat when we run out of food. Because we will run out, won't we?"

"You should have gone back with Lawrence."

"What?"

"You should have gone back with Lawrence. I'd be better off with Tite."

Heywoud turns his back to him and Watts cannot hold the fury rising up in him like his imagined flood. Tite, the dogs, Heywoud's rules, this desert place.

"Turn around," he says, even as he flies at Heywoud.

He catches Heywoud at the shoulder, half-twisted towards him, and they fall together to the ice. Heywoud gives a guttural cry and beats at Watts with mittened fists about his head. Some article of Watts' clothing rides up and ice touches him, like a toasting iron to the skin. He is distracted by the shock of it, and in that pause Heywoud lands a blow to his ear from which the hood has fallen away. Watts pummels Heywoud where he can—shoulders, neck, chest. Heywoud tugs down on an edge of collar. He grabs that hand, twisting free of it and turning Heywoud, pushing him over, face towards the snow.

"Watts!"

He finds the other arm, brings both together behind Heywoud's back. He presses him down. He has won.

Heywoud's voice is muffled.

"Are you quite finished?"

Watts gives one last shove and releases him, coming slowly to his feet. Heywoud sits up, patting snow from his clothes, adjusting his hood.

When Heywoud makes for the tent, Watts follows him, all too ready to resume his fight. He is still breathing hard and there is a target of fresh pain on the back of his right hip where, he is sure, a disk of snow the size of a sixpence rests against his skin, caught beneath the waist of his trousers. He has fought Heywoud and won, but this stab of cold torments him. He must remove his parka now, remove his gloves, hike up his jumper, to find the thing. It is like some imp, some malevolent spirit, stuck to him, part of him. He feels that sixpence of ice and nothing else, no other pain or comfort. Only that small circumference of cold beneath which he feels the cells of his skin dying one by one.

"Keep your clothes on, man," Heywoud says.

"I need to get this out."

Heywoud comes towards him.

"Leave me alone, Edward."

Watts snatches his jumper over his head and lashes his belt buckle open. He folds down his trousers waist and twists to find the spot on his hip. It is there. He plucks it from him, a coin of snow flattened to ice. He holds it up like a Catholic with a wafer. The light glows through it, the palest blue.

"Fucking bastard ice," he says. And then he crunches it between his teeth. His mouth is too cold for it to melt.

"Are you happy now?"

"I wasn't going to go to the Pole with that thing in my trousers, was I?"

Watts assembles himself, not before noticing that the skin on his hip has turned white. He pushes through the canvas flaps and looks south. He cannot occupy the tent with Heywoud, each of them breathing in the very air the other has breathed out. His own inhalations now come long and heavy and he realizes as his chest swells and falls that he has been nearly undone by a biscuit's worth of ice. He stares at the horizon to steady himself. They spend their waking hours tipping from side to side, he and Heywoud, tilting the line of that horizon one way and the other. They are level only when they stop to rest or sleep. And yet they never rest, never sleep. How can they keep their balance when to wake, to be in the world, is to be askew?

Watts takes a deep breath that knifes his lungs and he ducks into the tent. Heywoud is standing, holding something in his hand.

"What is this? What is this, Watts?"

It is his notebook and Watts lunges for it, but Heywoud tosses it aside. In his other hand he grips the linen pouch, its string snapped, and a sheet of card, an image on it, sepia tones and the low gloss of gelatin.

"That's mine, Edward." He regrets the words.

"Yours?" Heywoud's face folds in on itself. This is what crying looks like without tears. "Is this from before, James?"

A moment passes before he can speak. His head floods with words of chastisement. He should never have kept the photograph, never have brought it.

"Or is it from now?"

"What do you mean now? Look where we are."

"Before or now, James?"

"Does it matter?"

"What are you telling me?"

Heywoud moves about the tent. In a drawing room, he would stalk the windows, the mantel. He would perhaps find false composure in the lighting of a pipe. He spins to face Watts again.

"I don't know which of us is the bigger fool. You, for keeping this photograph of Viola." He speaks the name with extra clarity and Watts can see he is determined to keep his voice from cracking. "Or is it me, James? Am I the fool?" Here his voice trembles and that arid crumble begins again in his weather-cracked face. The blackened skin beneath his eye takes on the look of greasepaint.

"You're not a fool, Edward."

Heywoud looks up.

"Tell me how you see it, then. Frame the image for me. *Edward Heywoud. Polar Cuckold.* That's a fine title, isn't it? But wait. Why only Polar Cuckold. London Cuckold too."

Cuckold. The word sounds like a man choking, like a man whose throat is sere from days of skiing in this icy desert.

"When did it begin, James? Tell me that."

"You know that we had been together."

"Then when did it resume?" He draws the word out like a moan.

"I don't know. With all our climbing, our excursions. And we worked together."

"What does that mean? You worked together."

"She came to the studio. I went to hers. We worked on things. She wanted me to show her about the camera."

"But this was before me."

"Yes. At the Slade. But it kept on. She became a good photographer."

"I don't give a damn."

They stare at each other for a moment. Watts wants to remove his hood but dares not stir.

"You bastard," Heywoud says. "You introduced me to her. I thought she learned to climb for me. Why in heaven's name did you introduce me to her?"

"Because she asked me to."

Heywoud makes a sound like a surprised sob. Watts remembers Viola from the time when they were finished with each other. She was his friend then, passion spent or in abeyance, and took his elbow, pointed across a room. That man there, she said, your handsome climbing chum, you'd like me to meet him, and they had both laughed at the contrivance.

"You've been managing this entire thing then, haven't you, James? Your lover expresses interest in another man and you introduce her to him. Then she marries him and you go back to fucking her." Heywoud utters the word like a pain he suffers. "You disgust me. Both of you. It's disgusting."

"We were finished," Watts says.

"What?"

"When I introduced you. Viola and I were only friends. We were finished."

"Get out."

Heywoud scrambles to his feet and comes towards him.

"Get out. Get out or I swear I will kill you. God, what did she think of sending the two of us off together. Did she not think I would find out the truth? That you would let something slip?" Heywoud's attention drifts from Watts and his words turn inward. "I had my suspicions. I should have heeded them. It didn't occur to me to wonder who my wife had been fucking. Or some new man she might be fucking while I am in this godforsaken place."

Watts moves to sit down.

"I said get out."

"Edward, let me rest."

"You gave up rest when you took that photograph."

"You can't be serious. I need to eat, Edward."

"So do the dogs. You can join them."

Because he feels the weight of his thievery, Watts requires no shove or tussle to send him from the tent. But he exits backwards, his eyes on Heywoud whose face betrays a growing fear—Watts can find no better word for it—with each of Watts' retreating steps. Heywoud is afraid of his own fury. This is no place for human emotions, and Heywoud knows the danger of the exposed heart.

Watts nuzzles the dogs, for something to do as much as for warmth. They yelp and whimper. They think he brings them food. He sits on the ice, instantly feeling the greater chill rise through him, and the dogs climb on his outstretched legs. They push muzzles up the slope of chest towards beard and mouth. The dogs' tongues rasp Watts' nose and eyes and he lets them topple him, stretched full onto his back. This is a game now and the dogs play it with an edge of panic. They growl and snarl and bite each other's cheeks, bared teeth inches from Watts' face. He bats at them, tries to grab scruffs.

"Hey, pups," he says, attempting lightness. "Dagger. Kip. Hey, pups."

He rolls out from beneath them and the dogs become a twisting knot. They are lost in their fight, a true battle now. Watts could stop them. He could grab Kip's tail and pull him away as he once saw a Shoreditch grocer do to a street mongrel. But he does not. He watches and he listens as the dogs snarl on the snow. And then a howl from somewhere far away. He is certain of it. To Kip's and Dagger's growling comes an answering howl from somewhere to the east.

"Shush," he says, and strains to listen.

He pulls his goggles down for better vision but can make out nothing. Now the dogs have heard it too, for they stop and cock their heads. It comes again, a single short howl from the east. The dogs run to him, tails wagging and tongues lolling, all viciousness and strife forgotten in a new unease. He hugs them to him.

"Good boys."

"And I thought you were all hungry." It is Heywoud. He stands by the tent and looks east, the telescope in his hand. Watts does not answer for there is enough message in the distant sound and in Heywoud's emergence from the tent. Heywoud has heard it too. Nilsen's dogs are somewhere to the east.

"I'll light the stove," he says, and when Watts still does not move, he adds, "I'm not asking twice."

When he has lit the Primus, they sit with bowls of hoosh. Watts ventures a question.

"Did you see anything?"

"It's impossible to tell. There's a bloody Fata Morgana if you look east."

They are haunted by these mirages, tricks of atmosphere and light Watts sometimes captures in his lens. Iceberg towers appear where none exist, bays of open water where there is only ice and more ice. He and Heywoud travel always with the possibility that what they see ahead of them will vanish.

"We both heard the howl," Heywoud says. "Nilsen is close. I have no time to waste on you and your betrayal." Heywoud looks at him. "If we were anywhere but here, I would kill you."

"I know."

8

21 January

Samuel has found Viola a high stool for the darkroom and has even fashioned a clever system of wheels that she can lock in place at the press of a small lever with her shoe. Today, after a late night at Isabella's party and more of the sour punch to drink than she is entirely pleased with now, she is grateful for the seat. Rolling the stool around the darkroom's small space, she pours out her chemicals into the three trays for prints and sets the enlarger in place on the workbench. She wants to work again on that photograph of the tall woman with the bandage on her eye. When she took the photograph, the sun was low in the sky and slightly behind the woman. Now the exposure requires adjustment. If she renders the crowd in proper light, the tall woman becomes too dark and undifferentiated. If she wants the woman herself to be properly highlighted and shadowed, the crowd around her will be overexposed, a gathering of pale ghosts the woman walks among.

On hooks to the side of the workbench hang her manipulating tools on long wire handles. Small bits of thick card in various shapes, a feather, a scrap of black fabric—all of these she can use to cover a portion of the silver gelatin paper and keep the enlarger's light from shining on it. There is a utility knife for carving stencils out of sheets of the same thick card, and a set of stencils she has already made. She scans the tools now and selects a dodger in the shape of a small rectangle. She slides the glass plate negative into the enlarger and starts the timer. She flicks the switch for the enlarger bulb while dodging the projected image for four seconds by the clock, and then she pulls the dodger away for two more seconds. Four seconds with and three without. She makes a mental note and slips the exposed paper into the first bath to wait and see if her exposure is correct.

The image swims up at her as she jostles the paper in the liquid with her tongs. Gray darkens to black until she pulls the paper out. Once she has fixed and rinsed it, she holds it up to see. But already she sees that it is not quite right. The crowd is far too dark behind the woman with the bandage. She must try again with slightly different times. She repeats the process, but as she looks down at the image on the enlarger base, her thoughts drift to the party and to the women from the Artist Suffrage League that Izzy pointed out across the room.

"Sod it," she says, to see she has left the bulb on too long and knows the entire print will be likely solid black. She does not bother to take it through the sequence of baths but tosses the print into the bin. She begins again, and this time pays attention to the timer: three seconds with the dodger and two without. Now the crowd is correct, but the woman's form is still too dark. She must try once more, changing the ratio of lighting between the woman and the crowd. Three seconds with the dodger hovering over the woman's form, and one second with the woman exposed to the light. There it is. The exposure in the print is even, clear, and balanced.

But now there is a new challenge. Viola has been holding the dodger too still during that single second of light from the lamp. The outlines are too clear and too defined. She must do it again and this time move the dodger ever so slightly in that tiny period of time so that the edges between light and shadow will be too blurry to perceive. She tries this three more times until she has a satisfying image. She adds this one to the line where the others hang to dry.

She brings the best print towards her, touching the bottom edge of the damp paper, and looks at the woman's face. There is still more Viola can do with this print to make the bandage more clearly, starkly, visible. She would like the white of the bandage to be truly white, in great contrast to the black of the woman's shoes and of a bit of lamppost visible behind the crowd. She lets out a groan. For this she must cut a stencil so tiny as to make a miniaturist proud. And yet, if this is the effect she wants, she has no choice. She lets the print swing free from the line, joining the five others who all look back at her with the same gaze of confident defiance. In each print, the bandage over the woman's right eye is almost lost among the other details. And is this bandage not the most important thing, the very reason she singled the woman out?

But even when she does send the image to the *Observer*, and even if it appears on the front page of the paper, it will show readers no more than a familiar sight. A woman protesting a government that will not yield. A woman—foolish or brave, it hardly matters—who has got herself in trouble over nothing. Because nothing will come from repetitions of the same. Marches grow in size but they are still no more than marches. Women fall under constables' batons and more women step up to be struck again.

She cannot stop thinking about the hunger strikers. How much more stark, how much more striking, than even the clearest, most distinctly rendered bandage over an eye would be an image of a woman emaciated by her self-imposed starvation and then injured as she was forced to eat. What would that look like, Viola wonders. What would the *Observer*'s readers think to see that with their eggs and toast? How would she frame the image, pose the sitter? Would she place the woman against a background, like the tall woman at the march? Perhaps a closer frame is better, to emphasize the marks left on the body from the feeding tube and from the straps the warders use to hold the strikers down.

She flips through her negatives from the march and selects another three that she will work on. But as she works, she is already forming in her mind the letter she will send to Izzy later on, asking her to secure an invitation to the ASL. Izzy was right. She will find something at the ASL and with those women. She will find something more extreme.

9

89° 07'S

They begin the next march side by side in the traces and Watts wants to laugh, to share with Heywoud the joke of their forced union. Strange marriage, this, the husband and the lover. They need only Viola astride the sledge to complete the picture. The woman driving both men in a race neither can win. A harsher race than any Poleward competition.

Clouds gather and the sky turns lead. The air awakens and it is not a rope wind they ski into but another storm. The wind is restless, tumbling like the dogs. It shoves and pushes from an ever-changing source, sometimes hiking them up and forward, a tailwind so strong it frog-marches them across the snow, sometimes nearly stopping them entirely. In those moments, the traces go slack as the sledge slides up behind them, churlish. Watts feels the cold slide a bully's fingers into every buttonhole, every pocket and vent of his garments. He can do nothing but endure it.

The storm offers at least no chance of conversation. He and Heywoud stoop over their boots, leaning with each stride into a current of blown snow. Watts wonders what passes through Heywoud's mind. He has no doubt of the man's desire to cause him harm, and yet he feels no fear. Not until they reach the Pole. Would Heywoud kill him then or spare him until sure of his own safe return? And how would he achieve the deed? Watts would have fair warning, for the gun is buried deep inside the sledge.

Watts chuckles at the thought. He stops for an instant, laughter weakening him. Heywoud turns, sees him resume, goes on.

Watts thinks of Viola on the sledge—a photograph she would stage if she were there. She would create a sign for them to hold, some sort of written message within the photograph itself pronouncing triumph. She would dress herself in stage raiment, perhaps Boadicea, and the photograph would speak of something more than what it showed. Watts can imagine this but the true creativity itself escapes him. For so many hours he watched her conjure scenes of her own staging, though he could only capture what was already before him. And afterwards her hands on his waist, turning him to see first this print then that as they dripped from the drying line. Even after all of that, he could not command ideas as inventive as hers. Viola cares for more than light or shadow though she wrings from them ideas with no match in the known world. Watts could only look and envy. He can bid light and shadow do their best. He can do it even here where a gelatin print would shatter like an icing-sugar bottle on a stage. Was that not part of why he came, accepted Heywoud's invitation? To win a race with Viola for who can conjure up a newer world from what is given. Terra Nova. What new land can Watts find here where Viola has no map? It is another cruelty of this cruel place that the light he thought would make him best has only shown him he falls short.

But as Watts skis on, he knows he lies. For has he not begun, here in this frozen waste, to see things that are not present? The cold alters his sight and he attends to these new visions. Mountain ranges inverted, distant ships present before him on the ice, twin halos around the sun. Falsehoods and fantasies created for him by this sun and ice. He no longer needs his photograph of Viola and her smooth-skinned shoulder. He summons her without it, memories and waking dreams or nightmares all combined, all swimming up into the amber light of his closed eyes.

He skis blind for several paces. Why not? What difference does it make? This landscape bears no cairns or steeples to guide the mountaineer or rambler.

"Watts!"

He stumbles, opens eyes. He has skied into Heywoud's traces.

"What the hell are you doing?"

Watts holds up a hand to stay him, skis on.

The bully cold will not relent. When it is time to stop, Heywoud merely feeds the dogs with strips of pemmican and hands a piece to Watts and takes one for himself. They do not sit or heat water. They stand beside each other, loosen flies, urinate, bare hands sheltering their penises from the stab of cold that comes with each release. Their piss is brown as stout.

"I told you I could starve you," Heywoud says, when they crouch later by the Primus.

Heywoud utters the words as if he were offering to take a burden.

"I could ride you like a nag, Watts," he says, "and I could leave you to die five miles from Shore Camp."

"Nothing's stopping you."

"You won't defend yourself?"

"I don't have to."

Heywoud pauses his pumping of the stove. The flame goes out.

"God damn you, Watts." Heywoud seems on the point of crying. "God damn you. Both of you."

"She loves you, Edward."

Heywoud lashes out a mittened hand and smacks the side of Watts' head.

"Don't you dare. Don't speak for her. And don't tell me who she loves."

He resumes pumping and relights the stove. He turns the knob so that the flame burns high.

"Edward, stop it. That's too much."

"You're afraid we'll run out?" He turns the knob even higher and the stove hisses loud enough to make Dagger cock his head.

Watts seizes Heywoud's arm in both of his and pulls it from the stove. Slipping his mitten off, he twists the knob until the flame settles to a quiet blue.

"You need me, Edward, so you need fuel for me. Without me, who'll take your picture at the Pole?"

"I can do it."

"You can pull the shutter cord. But you don't know how to treat the plates."
Heywoud falls back on his haunches.

"I will make you, Edward. And you will make me. We have no choice now but to go on together."

Heywoud shakes his head.

"I can't trust you."

"What could I do here to betray you?"

"I don't know, James. But you and I are not on the same rope anymore," he says and Watts sees he is bereft. "I'll keep you alive. But only until we reach Shore Camp. After that, I don't give a damn what happens to you."

Watts has been tied to Heywoud so many times, across glaciers and up faces and crags. He and Viola and Miner too, all of them tethered to Heywoud without a thought to challenge the connection. What was it made them trust when they knew nothing more than what they saw before them? He simply told them to trust him, and they did. Because they loved him. And he loved them, cheering from the base of Attermire Scar when Watts reached the top first, or tugging a flask of hock out of his bag to toast a good day out in the Dales.

Watts watches Heywoud melt the ice for the day's tea—the leaves rationed out from a sparse supply—and knows this is why Heywoud nearly wept and why even now tears freeze at the man's goggle edges. He can endure betrayal, but he cannot withstand a loss of love.

They stow their supplies in the sledge and prepare to take up the traces. Kip does not move.

"What's wrong with him?" says Heywoud.

"Come on, boy," Watts says, and then to Heywoud, "I don't know."

Watts crouches by the dog, who whimpers and wags his tail in swift vibration. He takes hold of the collar but Kip pulls against him, listing to one side, rolling over to expose his belly. A sign of play now turned defense. The dog cannot be lifted or led on.

"Come on, Kip." Watts speaks under his breath.

Heywoud joins him low beside the dog. He holds Kip's paws, one after the other, squeezes, waits. He begins the test again, now tugging out the leg until, on the third, the right hind, the tug yields a yelp.

"Damn it," Heywoud says.

"What?"

"Shoulder. Strained or pulled or torn."

For a moment, they don't speak and they are allied once again over the tending of the dog. They sit back on their heels while the snow billows around them, the storm diminished, breathless. Kip, sensing that this business of theirs is completed, licks his genitals.

"I'll do it," Heywoud says and Watts swears he hears a catch in the man's voice. Later, if they ask about this day, Watts will be able to tell them of his leader's tenderness for this mute beast.

Heywoud rises and stomps to the tent.

"Let me take a photograph, Edward."

"Are you quite mad?"

"No, now," he says. "Before."

Watts follows slowly, thinking there will be time while Heywoud unpacks the gun buried in their cargo to use the camera for one more portrait. *Kip: Heroic to the End.* But Heywoud loosens one strap only and turns with the gun clasped in both hands.

"You have it," Watts says foolishly.

"Yes." It is a question. "One must be ready."

For what, Watts wants to ask. He wants to ask when the weapon made its way to ready access, what prey or target it emerged to strike. The target might be Watts himself, the traitor. Now it is Kip, poor Kip, snatched from a Petersburg dacha and brought so far away, for nothing.

A shot cracks the cold and the same instant Watts becomes aware of the sharp new smell of powder. He spins and Heywoud stoops over Kip while Dagger lies nearby, flattened on the snow, tail wagging, ears back.

"Take him away," Heywoud shouts.

Watts thinks he must mean Kip's corpse and stumbles closer.

"Dagger! Take Dagger away. For God's sake."

Watts cajoles the creature into untrod snow and makes a pantomime of play. He knows what Heywoud is busy at and keeps his back turned and Dagger occupied. He hears the grunt and gasp of Heywoud vomiting. It is a horror what they do now, both of them. Complicit, both of them, in turning acts of horror into matters of survival.

"We'll dry it," Heywoud says.

Heywoud lies the gun flat on the sledge's top, wrapped in its oilcloth but ready to hand. It is a threat. Were it not for Kip's pained yelp, Watts would have thought the kill itself had been contrivance. They move on, with Dagger running alone and panting at the extra work. Their ugly business done, the men resume their silence.

But soon enough it becomes clear that a new energy propels them. Propels Heywoud. For he kicks his skis out in long glides so that they clack against the hardpack. His ski poles fly out from him and lash ahead. He is a schoolmaster caning a miscreant boy. Watts struggles to keep up and even Dagger cannot stretch his traces away from Heywoud's urgency. Watts' breath comes fast and shallow. He lacks even the time to take a deeper swallow of the cold. He begins to sweat. Somewhere upon his person a strap or string sheathed full in ice swings and taps the frozen rest of him. Each glide forward on his skis rocks this icicle in an arc Watts can only hear, its rhythm three notes in a waltz. Watts slows for a second, but is nearly knocked off his skis from the pull of Heywoud's movement. So, he goes on, the icicle tapping into his thoughts. He thinks of his linen pouch, its string snapped and trailing from Heywoud's hand.

He imagines the thing dangles down his back, a vicious spike of ice formed around something so innocuous as a hood-lace or a bit of balaclava frayed and dangling. One twist would snap it, ice and fabric both, and he would wield it like a dagger. Could you kill a man with a spike of ice? Could he kill Edward? No. The Pole has not robbed him of so much. But he could arm himself against the man. It is a mad idea. Himself bristling with ski poles and a bit of ice and Heywoud turning on him with the gun. And then both of them dead, one instantly, the other days away.

Watts looks across at Heywoud, two strides ahead and leaning, driving, thrashing onward. The man is racing, hurrying, to the Pole. If their movement did not make a din of breath and skis and ice, they would listen for another howl from the east. Have the Norwegians overtaken? Is this why Heywoud flies ahead? Did he hear a howl in answer to his gunshot?

"Move!" Heywoud shouts and nearly jumps ahead to yank Watts forward.

Watts goes faster. His legs burn with fatigue and blisters rise on his feet where this new speed forces new movement. This is madness.

"I can't," he says, but not so loud that Heywoud hears. "I can't."

It is not protest but discovery. Watts breathes the words almost with wonder. He stops, digs his skis in, crouches low, and pulls. Heywoud glides two steps before the sledge swings out and rolls and its weight yanks him back.

"The hell, Watts!"

Heywoud leans into the harness, seizes it with both hands, ski poles flailing, and pulls at Watts. They face each other across six feet of ice and Dagger darts back and forth between them. Watts digs in deeper, skis splaying, knees bending in on each other. Heywoud remains upright, tipping back as if too proud to crouch.

"We're stopping," Watts says. "Stopping now."

"You don't decide." His upright posture costs him strength and he begins to list towards Watts.

"I'm not moving," Watts says.

The harness loosens slightly and Watts uses the slack to sit down on the snow, skis to one side, knees together like a woman on a horse. He is surprised at the ease of his own action. He does not mind the greater cold beneath him, feels instead the fever of fatigue leave his muscles, his breath lengthening into sighs. How good it is to sit, an act so simple it seems necessary, obvious.

Heywoud sways where he stands. His face is as slack as the harness drooping between them.

"Sit, Edward. It's much better."

"No."

"Then go without me. I'm resting."

"We need more miles."

"I don't want any more today. No thank you." Watts attempts a laugh.

"Nilsen will catch us."

Watts turns to look behind him, but the plain is etched only in light and shadow.

"Nobody there," he says.

"If we slow up now, they'll beat us."

Watts removes his mittens and works the leather strap of his ski binding to free it from its crust of rime. He sheds one ski, begins work on the other.

"I said they'll beat us," Heywoud says.

But he moves closer to Watts, as if with curiosity for these new movements. By the time Watts has removed both skis and slipped his hands back into mittens, stinging with new freeze, Heywoud has joined him on the snow. The straps of his ski poles are still wrapped around his mitts and, with hands in his lap, Heywoud has the air of a child defiantly inept. Now Watts sees Heywoud's face deformed by cold. His eyes are fringed with frost, nose hung with icicles of snot, his lips cracked and swollen. Leaning closer, Watts sees that he is shivering.

At once Watts registers this worst of news and understands that the day's rush has cost him less than Heywoud. He suffers mere fatigue. Heywoud is cold.

Watts takes Heywoud by the arms and drags him, skis attached, to the sledge and sets him gently down. Untying straps and lashes, he produces stove, pot, pemmican, tea. He pumps the Primus, lights it, places a pot above the flame, fills the pot with pemmican, stirs. He hands Heywoud a bowl and spoon, fits the spoon into his hand.

"Edward," he says, "we must stop for the day."

"No."

"Yes. We must stop for the day. You are cold."

Heywoud takes a spoonful, gruel freezing in his beard.

"We must stop," he says, as if the notion is his own.

Watts builds the tent and settles him within. He wraps his own bag around Heywoud, and brings Dagger inside, the dog's tail lashing in excitement at this rare privilege. Watts calms the dog, presses him beside Heywoud, tucks the heated pot of pemmican inside the man's parka, and waits. He watches for a sign of the hypothermic's desire to undress, braces himself for the first move to pull a toggle, twist a button. The man who sheds his clothing at the Pole is on his way to frozen death. Naked or not, bundled and wrapped against his will or tossing clothing like a crazed Salome, the man is gone. Watts takes an inventory: long johns, breeches, trousers, puttees, liner, jumper, waistcoat, smock, parka, balaclava. Let him list them again and again, until the danger that he and Heywoud shed them is safely passed.

After some time, Heywoud sits up as if from sleep.

"I'm better now," he says. "Just a touch of chill."

"You were in danger."

"I'm better now."

"I gave you extra rations."

"You should not have."

"That's rubbish. You'd have died. And remember? I'm the one who is supposed to starve."

There is a pause, then Heywoud clears his throat.

"I'll make new calculations," he says, announcing it in such a way that Watts fears the cold addles him still and that he thinks he speaks to multitudes.

10

22 January

The Daylight Comet is still in the sky when Viola pulls her muffler close against the chill of the day and heads west on the King's Road. There, where she can see an expanse of sky over Carlyle Square, she makes out the comet with its upward arcing tail. In the Square a handful of people aim Brownies at the sky to capture it. Viola considers the composition but does not regret leaving her own Brownie behind. The image is already too familiar, and London full of postcards and snapshots of the dying star. And she is already at Brittany Studios at number 259, a tall building with a grocer on the ground floor. In her bag she carries Izzy's reply to her letter, sent by afternoon post. *You are in luck. Come! They will be at the ASL today. They are the suffrage vanguard, darling, I promise.*

Edward is not here this time to tell her no. Their first June together as husband and wife when nearly half a million women gathered in Hyde Park, she was brimming with eagerness to join them. Isn't it marvelous, Edward? So many coming together to have our voices heard. Viola, this is not your fight, he told her. We are together now, and together in our views. I can vote for you. You can trust me to do what is best for us both. I would never support anything that would cause you true harm. He said this as a kindness so she did not insist, and when reports came of windows smashed that day at Downing Street, she let herself agree with Edward to ally with him over the marchers. But there were other stories, too, from that day and from later days—of women singing together, voices raised in unison to ask for that simplest of rights: to represent themselves—and they raised in her a shame she had so quickly given in. Edward is not here now, and he will not say she is no suffragette. James would let her march, she thinks. Or would he assume her already free in ways that in truth she can only pose and posture at?

Beside the entrance to the grocer at number 259 a door leads up the stairs to the first floor. Viola pulls the bell and above her a door opens and a woman's greeting rises over a murmur of other voices.

"Up here," she calls and disappears.

Viola takes the stairs, one at a time still for the ankle. She arrives at the landing and nudges the door open onto the large space of a studio with tall windows across the back. Groups of women stand or sit around large tables ranged about the room, working on fabrics of various colors and shapes. The space looks like a drawing room for gentlewomen, quiet and domestic. It looks nothing like the extreme edge of the movement that Isabella promised her.

Viola is on the point of closing the door quietly behind her to escape this too-soft place before the ladies there have noticed her. But she is too late. Isabella rises from one of the tables.

"You're here!"

"It's so domestic," Viola whispers to her.

"Don't be fooled."

From there, Isabella takes Viola around the studio and introduces her to several of the women, each one of whom sets down her needle and thread to offer a warm embrace. The women smooth their fabrics out to show her the designs. Some picture the castellated entrance to Holloway Prison, some turn the prison's tree-like arrow into a heraldic emblem, others show no images at all but only slogans, letters cut from silk as if for a jockey's jersey.

"I know enough about the artists, Izzy. I want to meet this vanguard you told me about before. Where are they?"

"They'll be here soon. Have patience."

"It's that I don't see how those bits of cloth are going to achieve anything. Show me the bomb throwers, Izzy. The arsonists. Where are they?"

"Slow down and don't be rude." Izzy speaks in a near whisper. "There is other work to be done, too."

Viola lets Isabella continue their studio tour. She is glancing at a large piece of card sketched with the design for a placard when conversation stops around the room. She turns to see that Lucy Bellowes and Margaret Lyons have entered the studio.

"You see?" Isabella says. "As promised."

Bellowes holds Lyons at the elbow and guides her to a low armchair by the windows. Lyons sits with some effort and turns her face to the winter sun as Bellowes leaves to fetch her something. Lyons is noticeably more frail than at Isabella's party. Viola wonders if the woman will not eat now that she is not forced. Is there a habit of deprivation even once a woman is released?

She watches Lyons as Bellowes returns with a shawl she drapes over her companion's shoulders. Lyons smiles up at Bellowes and her gaunt face hints at loveliness.

"Do you think she would have gone on not eating, Izzy?" Viola says. "If they hadn't forced her?"

"Do you mean would she have allowed herself to die?"

"I suppose so."

"Then yes. I think she would have."

"For the cause." Viola shudders at the thought.

She looks across at Lyons again. Viola knows what it is for the body's bones to reveal themselves in the face, the hips. She has seen Edward and James made lean from weeks climbing in preparation for the Pole. Margaret Lyons is different. This is a thinness Lyons does not simply endure but seeks for its power. Viola remembers evenings in her father's surgery and the Anatomy book he brought for her to see. She would trace a finger along the lineaments of muscle, organ, bone.

Isabella leans into her.

"So you see, Vi, it's much more than sewing and painting here."

"No," she says. "I see."

Something clatters at the room's far end and Viola turns to see Bellowes crouching at Margaret Lyons' feet to collect pieces of china from the floor. Lyons rests a hand on Bellowes' head and two young women rush to help with cloth to mop the spill from Lyon's skirt.

"Bloody Holloway," Isabella says. "Destroys them. Starving, feeding, starving, feeding, on and on. It's enough to kill a woman. You're sure you really want to talk to them?"

"Yes." Viola cannot conceal the excitement in her voice. She thinks of Edward and James, how these women too are willing to die for the goal they seek. And is the women's goal not nobler, one that could shake England to its core rather than add another jewel to its empire?

"Brace yourself," Isabella says. "Bellowes can bite."

She takes Viola by the hand and crosses to Lyons' chair by the windows and makes her introduction. Viola sees the badge of Holloway Prison pinned on Lyons' chest. A ribbon in suffrage colors from which hangs a medal stamped with the tree-like arrow pattern of the prison apron.

"Mrs. Bellowes," Viola says. "Miss Lyons, I have heard what you've endured for the cause."

Lyons' voice is hoarse and faint.

"Heywoud. Your husband is much in the papers." She places a hand on her throat and smiles an apology. "Are you a member?" She waves a hand out at the room.

"Not yet. I am Miss Purvis' guest."

"Your impression?"

Viola crouches so that she is level with Lyons' gaze. The woman's hand where it rests on the chair is bony and bruised.

"I very much admire what you do," she says. "I admire your sacrifice."

"Thank you," Bellowes answers for her. "But we must give Margaret some time to rest. As you can see, she is not in a position to socialize."

"My friend is a photographer," Isabella says. "She trained in painting at the Slade but now works with the camera."

"I have been photographing the marches," Viola says. "Documenting the movement for the *Observer*."

"Then we must thank you," Bellowes says.

Isabella makes her excuses and returns to the table at the far side of the room.

"As I'm sure you know," Viola says, "there are very few photographs of hunger strikers in the papers."

"Cameras are not allowed inside Holloway Prison, Mrs. Heywoud."

"I understand that. I believe that what you do should be documented in a way that helps the movement."

"And what would that be?"

"Perhaps I could photograph the women after they are released."

"That has been done. Have you not seen the images of Miss Wharry and Miss Forrester in the papers?"

"I have." Olive Wharry in a chair made giant by her emaciated form, her clothes loose and her gaze looking off at nothing. "But those photographs show women sitting docile and weak. Completely drained and listless. Swimming in their skirts and jackets and hardly daring to look at the camera. Photographs like these are easy for the public. All those anti-suffrage men and women—"

"There are far too many of them," Bellowes says.

"Right, well any of them will be almost reassured by these photographs," Viola says. "There is so much more power in what you do. People need to see what the suffrage movement *really* means. Olive Wharry hardly looks to pose any threat to anyone."

Viola sees a glint of interest in Bellowes' eyes. She goes on.

"Allow me to ask you," she says. "Who photographs the released women?"

"What do you mean?"

"Is the photographer a man?"

"The reporters are men. Sometimes the prison authorities take the photographs. And most of them are men as well."

"That's why they show the women in their overlarge clothes. They're keeping the most powerful weapon of the movement hidden."

"And what is that?"

"The bodies. The scars. The marks of the sacrifice they've made for the cause because the cause is that important. Their bodies are the most dangerous part. But the public never sees that danger now."

"Margaret's health is not good at the moment. As you can quite understand. I don't know that she has the strength to join in whatever you're proposing."

Lyons whispers something to her and Bellowes shakes her head.

There is in her figure the lassitude of the odalisque, though her pose is the result of illness and recovery. Viola thinks of the bruises beneath the clothes, the cuts and sores made by the feeding tube. What would it be like to photograph these women in the nude so that the wounds stood out in starkest contrast? She could achieve so much more with sores and bruises than with a white bandage across a woman's eye.

"Mrs. Bellowes," she says, and the idea takes shape with her words. "What if I photograph the strikers in classical poses? From fine art."

"I do not follow, Mrs. Heywoud."

"I could use the familiar poses of the classical tradition to show the most modern condition of women today. As hunger strikers fighting for their rights."

"What poses?" Lyons says.

"An odalisque. A Venus. A Sabine."

"Mrs. Heywoud," Bellowes says, "the figures in these sorts of paintings are hardly heroic. And they are of course all nude."

"Yes. Don't you see? That is the best way to make a powerful statement. I would use the very traditions of how women are seen as a way to overthrow them."

"Ah," Bellowes says. "This is quite unusual."

There is a long silence and Viola permits herself a glance out at the rest of the studio to see if their conversation is being followed. The women are busy at their tables. Isabella watches from a chair by the stove. Something seems to pass between Bellowes and Lyons, and Bellowes speaks.

"Perhaps you are right, Mrs. Heywoud. But you must realize you will see marks of torture. Many of our women have had wrists or ribs broken in the struggle to hold them down for feeding. Some have had their noses torn, even broken, by the tube. Margaret has been lucky that her face has not been harmed. She has kept all her teeth. If you are to do this, Mrs. Heywoud," Bellowes says, "you must be sure you yourself can tolerate what you will see."

Lyons takes Bellowes' hand.

"I am not easily shocked. My father was a doctor. And through my husband's travels I have seen the effects of frostbite and gangrene. I am so sorry for the pain you all have faced," Viola says. "But this is exactly why these photographs must be made. People must know this," she says. "People must see the truth of what is being done to women."

"The newspapers will never print them," Bellowes says. "Though I wish they would."

"These won't be for newspapers. We'll exhibit," Viola says. "In a gallery."

"People must understand the government's brutality. And the seriousness of our struggle."

"They will," she says. "We will break new ground."

"You are an explorer, then," Bellowes says. "Like your husband."

"Like him, indeed," Viola says and smiles.

But she knows she can be no such thing. Edward himself would not allow it. She cannot venture to the Poles, North or South, nor to the highest peaks, because she is a woman. Yes, she has climbed Snowdon and the Mettelhorn and Breithorn with James and Edward. She has traded her skirts for woolen jodhpurs and puttees to climb in bitter cold, and she has felt one earlobe blister with frostbite through a Cairngorm blizzard. But she cannot explore above a certain altitude, beyond a certain latitude, below a certain depth. There were always limits, spoken and unspoken, to what she was permitted, and after he married her, Edward set more. Now she maps a different journey for herself, a different expedition. A new world pushes into view, and it is not enough for her to simply document upheaval. Viola's photographs can fuel the force of the eruption.

"Why don't you come tomorrow, then," Bellowes says, "to Dalmeny Avenue in Holloway. Number 12. This is where many of us go to convalesce. Bring your camera."

Viola thanks the women and promises to meet them at the house in the morning. She crosses the large studio space to Isabella's table.

"Walk me out," she says.

When they are on the pavement on the King's Road, Viola grips Isabella's arm.

"I'm to go to their safe house tomorrow," she says. "With my camera. Thank you, Izzy. You have been my muse today."

"What did you tell them?"

"Nudes." Viola squeezes her arm. "Nudes, Izzy. And I will pose them as odalisques and Aphrodites."

"Like tableaux vivants? To recreate the paintings?"

"Recreate them, but in a different way. I want to make it obvious the subjects are hunger strikers."

"How?"

"I will show their injuries. The bruises and the scars. I plan to emphasize them. I'll make it so the viewer must confront the fact that these women's bodies are damaged."

"You'll never find women to pose. Who would want her pain on display like that?"

"Ah, but it won't be on display. Not like that. Not if I can pull the thing off the way I'm thinking, Izzy. Think of what an impact it will make. If I pose these women the way art has posed them for centuries. As visions to be stared at, right? But they don't show shame or pain. They stare back at you. They say *look!* Not *look at what happened to poor suffering me*, but *look at how I use my body in the fight against you. Who feels the shame now?*"

"I don't know, Vi. That's a lot of message to expect from a photograph."

"It is. But I can see it. I can see it working. I just need to make the hunger strikers get it right." She tugs Isabella close. "I do believe it will be wonderful."

"Be careful, Vi," Isabella says.

"I'm not the one being beaten and starved. I've done so little. Taking these photographs is hardly dangerous."

"Oh, but it is. There is something about these women, Vi, the strikers, that can draw you in."

"I'm on the other side of the camera, Izzy. I'll be fine."

Isabella returns to the studio and Viola begins the short walk to Margaretta Terrace. She remembers a trip to Ben Macdui with the men when she was friend to both—old friend and former lover to James, new friend to Edward. It was as if she hung between them, bound equally and they to each other. They hiked up the Lairig Ghru without a leader and, returning to the valley, nestled in the gorse to swig brandy from Edward's bottle. At the small hotel in Aviemore, already easy with the drink, they sat in the sun of the long June day. It's true she wants them to come back to her. But now—now she wants to have this news to tell them. How she turned Sirens and goddesses into suffragettes. How she turned suffragettes to heroines. Now she wants to stretch the winter days as if they were as long as June's.

11

89° 30'S

Watts' stomach twists in hunger and he discovers he has not fed himself. The hoosh has frozen, so he digs some biscuit from the box. He chews with molars only, gnawing at what seems too solid to digest. Dagger watches him and tilts his head as if for prey. How many days before the creature ignores its breed and training and he and Heywoud are no longer safe? Are dogs capable of such attack? Is Dagger? Watts wrests another bite from the slab of biscuit, but cannot generate the spit with which to swallow. He tosses the morsel towards the dog, who snaps it from the air and downs it whole.

"It's possible that we will die." Heywoud's words hang like a banner in the tent. "I don't expect to, James, but it is possible."

Watts eyes him, scanning for madness or revenge. But Heywoud's face is clear of enmity.

"Of course."

"We must arrange for it."

"I met with my solicitor before we sailed," Watts says.

"We must leave messages. We must make records."

Watts crossed to Lincoln's Inn on a summer day of high clouds. In the lawyer's office, everything sealed and stamped, his signature affixed to curling sheets of paper, the barely hidden giddiness of the clerk agog with explorers, a boy well-versed in newspaper accounts of Scott and Shackleton, as eager as a gambler in a cockfight.

"I've left her everything," Heywoud says. "Have you?"

"I have little to leave."

Watts thinks of the note he sent Viola—to the Slade, not home, he could not send to her home—the note that portioned out what mattered. Take the key here, unlock the case here, destroy what hurts you, keep only the smallest thing you can abide.

"Will she be all right, do you think?"

"Viola?" Watts laughs. "She'll be all right."

"You think she's better off a widow than a wife."

"No, Edward. She loves you."

Heywoud makes a sound.

"You can't expect me to believe that," he says.

"She loves us both."

They look across at each other, their faces neutral, slack.

"Then hers," says Heywoud, "will be a double loss."

"Yes."

"I should have liked a child," Heywoud says.

Watts takes in a breath and both men pretend that Heywoud has not noticed.

"You speak as though we have already died, Edward."

Heywoud looks at him, as if reminded they live still.

"I'd like a child," he says. "A daughter." Heywoud's face cracks open with a rare smile and Watts tries to hide surprise. "I shouldn't, should I?"

"Want a girl?"

"I should want a son, to carry on my legacy. But boys," he lets out a breath that clouds the air between them, "they are a burden."

Watts registers a sharpening in Heywoud's face, gone in an instant.

"If we do die," Watts says, "will someone find us?"

Heywoud shrugs.

"Who knows."

Watts breaks a silence.

"We'll never rot, will we?"

"Never," Heywoud says. "We'll freeze into the ice. If no one finds us, we'll be here forever."

Watts' vision flies up over where they sit, one speck on endless ice and snow, soon enough immersed in black of night, tent ripped to shreds across them. Two bodies, three with Dagger, in horrifying solitude.

"You and me and dear old Dagger," Heywoud goes on.

"Edward, stop."

"What's the matter?"

"Stop. I can't listen."

"It's no different from Mont Blanc or Monte Rosa."

"Yes, it is."

"We could have died there, too."

"Hardly."

"Yes, James. We could."

"We were in Europe, Edward."

Below them, there were little towns and restaurants and village squares where telescopes could track their progress. There were farms and chimneys and at expedition's start and end the scent of smoke and mown hay. Before Viola, they reveled in the company of men, Heywoud, Watts, and Miner to assist. Once Viola joined them, their outings held a special glory—to be two men with a woman in such friendship, such companionable love.

"What if we survive?"

"That's right, James. We may after all survive."

But Heywoud does not answer the question. They go forward so steadily into pain and cold and hunger that Watts has come to think these are their goal. They have prepared for death, but how do they prepare for life?

"In any case," Heywoud adds, "if we do die, it's far more beautiful to die here than in London."

Heywoud digs in a pocket of his smock and produces the expedition log in which he records their every halt and progress.

"You took no reading today," Watts says.

"You took no photograph."

Heywoud hunches over the log and begins to write.

"I suggest you do the same," he says, without looking up.

He is writing his farewell. Watts watches as Heywoud's hand draws the lead along in careful loops. There is no hesitation. He crosses out nothing. Heywoud has thought it out, has planned his valedictory before even arriving near the end. And why not? It makes no difference whether they write at 89° or 90°. They must write as if from journey's end.

"Do it now, James. While you still have your wits."

Watts frees his linen pouch from the pocket where he keeps it, untethered now, its lanyard snapped by Heywoud's angered pull. He turns to a fresh page and with the blunt nub of his graphite stick, he begins. *Dearest Viola.* They both write to Viola.

Watts has achieved little beyond this salutation, writing a false stoicism by which Viola will not be fooled, when Heywoud claps his log closed.

"I'll go out to take a reading," he says.

Watts nods and attempts again to compose his note. The longer he hesitates the more he fears an error he can correct only by crossing out, and that is no legacy for one's beloved, a penciled track of words gone wrong and doubled back. He sees Viola, months from now, reading through the strike lines to the ghosts beneath, trying to decide which words are truer. He forms full paragraphs in his mind, mutters them aloud, shakes his head, begins again. It is as if he performs a madman's play for an audience of the imagination. He places lead to paper, takes a deep breath that ends with a snatch of coughing, writes. *I cannot find words enough in this barren place with which to make you understand how much—*

"James. James, come outside."

"I'm not finished."

"Put it away. Come out."

Heywoud's voice is thin and reedy.

Watts stuffs pencil and notebook away and pulls on hood and goggles, slips hands into mitts.

"What?" he says with irritation, as he stoops out of the tent.

The sextant dangles by Heywoud's side.

"Are you hurt?"

Heywoud grimaces as if he answers yes.

"Come with me," he says.

Watts notices now that Heywoud's puttees are caked with snow as if he has been wading deeply.

"Where did you go?" Watts says. All around them, the ice is hard. The wind has scoured away the drifted snow to blue-gray hardpack.

"Over here." Heywoud waves towards the east. "Come."

Watts mutters a curse. The strange look in Heywoud's eyes would make him think this summons a ruse to lure him to a killing spot. But no, they have spoken calmly. They have sat together writing home, like boys at school. They have conjured together the single woman they love and Heywoud has not seized him by the throat.

"Slow down," Watts calls.

Heywoud has gone ahead some thirty yards and faces east. Watts rushes closer, leg muscles instantly afire.

"What is it?"

At Heywoud's feet, a form, two boots, fur trimmings snow-caked, green tent canvas shredded, flapping. Ten paces on, another form. No fabric. Nearest Watts and Heywoud a man's chest pokes up from snow. Wooden toggles, three, and a single strap of mitten-tether, the face concealed. Visible only the nose and half the frame of snow goggles, oiled leather.

"Good Christ," says Watts.

The words start Heywoud into motion. He kneels beside the man and paws at the snow, revealing arms, the head, the hind leg of a dog. Watts sees now that the snow has been disturbed already.

"How did you find him?"

"Goggles," Heywoud says. "I tried to pick them up. Thought they'd been dropped. I thought they'd dropped them as they passed."

Watts does not understand why the thought makes Heywoud cling to his arm.

"They're here," Heywoud says. "They haven't beaten us."

Watts shakes free. He sees the tiny rectangle upon the sleeve: the horizontal cross of Norway's flag, blue stripes, white edging upon a field of red, the colors pale. Beneath, a Norse word: *Sydpolekspedisjonen.*

"They haven't beaten us," Watts says. "The dog we heard."

"Must have been this one. Looks like their last."

They stare at each other, goggles and masks covering wide eyes and mouths.

"Edward."

"We have only to survive now, James."

Laughter bursts from Heywoud like a sob.

"We have only to survive," he says, "and we will win the Pole."

Watts laughs because it sounds like nothing, only to survive. It is a simple fact of sliding one ski before the other until the sextant proves their place. A simple fact of eating just enough and not too much, of keeping warm against this evil cold, of pushing on through wind and storms to a spot that looks no different from where they stand but that means everything.

"But Edward, wait," Watts says. "Edward. How do we know?"

"They're here, James." Heywoud laughs again. "Tomorrow we will already be past them."

"What if they were coming back?"

Watts feels a traitor even as he says the words.

"They weren't. James, they were not."

"How can you be sure?" he says.

Heywoud stills for an instant and it is long enough for Watts to see the two of them in a slow defeated turn for home, for North. But then he crouches by the frozen body and begins to scrabble through the rime.

"They'll have their flag with them," he says. "I'll find it."

"Edward, stop!"

"It should be here. I know it's here."

This is madness. Watts catches Heywoud by the shoulders and pulls him from his ghoulish errand.

"Stop."

Heywoud's breath comes heavily.

"Are you all right, man?"

"Of course I am," Heywoud says, and makes to pull away once more.

"Who am I?"

Heywoud scoffs.

"James Watts. Photographer to my expedition to the South Pole and my wife's lover."

Watts lets him go. It all belongs to Heywoud. The wife. The Pole.

Heywoud rises, takes a few strides to the South.

"Edward!"

"I'm looking for their tracks."

Watts walks beside Heywoud as he scans the snow for marks. They find nothing. The surface here is fine for sledging, poor for tracking rivals.

"You see, James? No tracks. No onward tracks. They were still on their way South. Not North. South."

"Or the snow buried their tracks," Watts says. "We should go further on to see."

Heywoud turns to face him.

"Why are you so set to tell me we have failed, James?"

"What do you mean?"

A wind has begun to hum across the plain. The fur trim of Heywoud's hood ripples in it like wheat.

"Do you want me to lose, Watts?"

"Of course I don't."

"If I lose, you lose as well."

"I know that." Watts' name will be everywhere if they return victorious. James Watts, photographer to the first expedition to reach the South Pole.

"But what?"

"If they've beaten us—"

"Then what, Watts?"

Heywoud goads him, as if to express defeat were to embody it.

"Then we can go home."

The words fall like a burden dropped into the snow. This is what he wants. Watts is as certain of it as he is that Heywoud can never turn around.

He and Heywoud do not move, cannot move. They stand there with their goggle-darkened eyes like eerie statues.

"You don't want to be second," Heywoud says finally.

No, Watts does not want to be second. He was wrong to think it second-best success, for there are only two alternatives here: to be first or to fail. There is no second Pole, no false summit or lesser peak to conquer. If the Norwegian flag flies from a length of sledge rail driven into hardpack thirty miles from where he and Heywoud stand, if it flies there now, they are transformed to losers. They need not even witness the planted standard. The thought alone that the flag is there alters them, diminishes them, undoes them.

"Even if you are right, Watts, there is honor in continuing. We have an obligation. To our country. To ourselves. Do you want us to give up?"

"We are low on supplies, Heywoud. If we go on without knowing for certain they were still on the way there, we risk thirty miles each way for nothing. At least we should not go on until we've found the flag."

"We will never find the flag in all this ice. There is nothing to prove they were returning when they died," Heywoud says, approaching as he speaks. "And yet you would still turn back?" Heywoud stands inches from Watts now, his breath casting ghosts onto his goggles. "You're trying to keep me from succeeding."

"I am not, Edward. Stop this nonsense."

"Perhaps I should go on without you."

"Don't be foolish."

"You can fail. I can't. I am the explorer who must succeed. But you can go back to Shore Camp and sail home to Viola uncontested. Think of that, James. The husband dispatched willingly. The hero's widow available. That's what you want. That's what she wants."

"She doesn't want you dead, Edward. Don't say that."

"She wants me the hero. Dead or alive, it doesn't matter."

"That's not true. She loves you."

"Spare me the sentiment. She's like a woman of Sparta, is our Viola. Come back either with your shield or on it dead." He laughs. "Though that could be difficult to manage. The coming back dead."

"What matters to her most is that we survive."

"If you think that, Watts, you have no notion of the scope of her ambition."

Heywoud turns towards the tent.

"We've used up too much energy. We'll rest now. We'll dig up the sledge tomorrow for their food. We'll find the flag."

Watts stands alone to look across that last half-degree of latitude. Somewhere there if his eyes could pick it out is a single dark shape, he is sure. Somewhere ahead of him is proof of his and Heywoud's defeat. He does not desire to go towards it.

They bring Dagger inside the tent again and the dog wags eagerly and lies down once no food is offered. Heywoud lights the Primus, melts snow for water, produces the canister of tea, and pours scant leaves into the battered tin pot. The tea is heat and no taste, just a weak scent of bergamot. Watts breathes in the steam and sees New Zealand gardens, a house in Christchurch where a pretty girl strolled with him at a party in their honor. They were feted then, gazed at with awe. Look at the men who may be going to their deaths. See the men who would freeze for glory. And with their pinched vowels and twangy southern speech, they said, gentlemen, how brave you are, gentlemen, goodspeed until we meet again. *Until*, they said, while thinking *if.* Heywoud thrusts a biscuit at him, then a bowl of hoosh. The porridge fills just half the bowl and the biscuit is a shard from box's bottom.

They slide into their sleeping bags, Dagger between them for his heat.

"Before we begin tomorrow, you must take another photograph."

"Of corpses in the snow?"

"A memorial photo for their king."

Watts lies with eyes open to the undersea green of the tent. The day's edges now show a different quality of light, the slow descent into Antarctic winter. He pulls the bag up over mouth and nose, feels breath warm briefly on his cheeks. His toes are numb again, and the lobe of his left ear has become hard to the touch. His stomach churns. His eyelids tap together when he blinks.

He should be a different kind of man. A man who sees the virtue of such suffering. Who sets above all others an achievement that may conclude in silence. Heywoud imagines even dead he'll be a masterpiece of courage, a frozen corpse turned self-museum. Exhibit 1: Antarctic Hero. See how the great man braved the elements, how he persisted until death. See how the ice preserves his broken body as evidence of fortitude. But this is no South Kensington, no Russell Square, where fine people will admire and gawk. If they die here or one day off or two, no one will ever find them.

Viola understands Heywoud's desire. Were she among them now, she would see journey's end itself, the death, as a performance. They share this, she and Heywoud, this improbable kinship of the man of action and the woman who takes action through her art. She left Watts once for Heywoud. But she has stayed with Heywoud even coming back to Watts. She loves them both, he said to Heywoud. Here they must always choose. Pick potted meat or pemmican, not both. Tea or tobacco. Rum or whiskey. Haste or food. In Hut Camp they left a gramophone, a magic lantern for Watts' slides, a game of chess, the pieces carved for Heywoud in stone brought from the Dolomites. In London, he left heavy damask curtains over tall windows, a transom open to the Camden light by Regent's Canal. A carpet threadbare by the bed but napped thick before a little stove where they could lie like figures in a Degas, Viola wrapped in bedclothes, shoulders lit like sunrise from the fire.

He was a fool to leave. What does he care of glory like that which Heywoud craves? To reach a summit is to feel the body's power and to find at greater altitude the possibility of altered and untested light. But to be first across an empty space? What does it matter? Or is it light he chases, sure that, by going further South, he can find in Antarctic sky some quality no one has ever seen? Viola again, chin resting on his hip. How could you not go? she said. The light! Eyes widening, chest lifting with her inhaled breath. Think, James. All that light! His hand in her hair, fingers in a snarl from a pin she had not noticed. "But I wouldn't have you," he said. "I'll wait," she said, "for both of you." He asked her then whom she loved best and she answered both. She pressed her lips against his navel and said it again. I love you both.

So, he had come with Heywoud for the light and for the promise of a gallery where he would hang his wonders from this antipodean world. So, he had come for Viola and for the way she had said it, for what she had seen, had conjured.

From Heywoud, a sound muffled by the quilting of his bag.

"Stop fidgeting," he says. "I can't sleep with you awake there."

"Sorry."

Watts did not know his body spoke his thoughts.

They lie silent, stiff as dead men.

"Watts, tomorrow we must make a cross for them."

"All right."

"I'll take a reading. Note it in the log."

"The public love a cross," Watts says.

"We'll build a cairn."

"With what?"

"Blocks of snow. We'll mound it," Heywoud says.

"Do you think they'd have done the same for us?"

"I don't know. Nilsen is a bastard." Heywoud's voice is languid from fatigue and numbness. "Cares only to get there first. He'd speed on by."

"And you wouldn't?" Watts pushes up on elbows to look at Heywoud.

"We're still here, aren't we?"

Watts falls back into his bag. Heywoud is lying. They did not halt their progress so that they could pay respects. They are exhausted to the point of kinship with the dead. These Norwegians and their dog, an expedition party like a mirror cast upon the ice to show them who they almost are, what will almost happen, what is about to happen to them. It is as if the landscape has a dream of vicious symmetry that he and Heywoud might realize in death. Two parties, both dead, one returning from the Pole, the other going. Or both on homeward march. If he and Heywoud turn for shore, let others have made this godforsaken place their own. They cannot all of them have been defeated by this monster land of snow and ice.

"Tomorrow," Heywoud says, "we'll make a cairn and then press on."

"What if there are others?"

"Where?"

"These two could have been sent back, like Tite and Lawrence. Nilsen could have gone on himself. He could have made the Pole."

"We saw no onward tracks, Watts."

"That still doesn't prove there was not a second sledge."

"I saw them."

Again Watts presses up.

"What do you mean you saw them?"

"The day we heard the dog howl. I looked. I saw them through the scope. Two men only. One sledge. Heading South."

"You said there was a mirage. You couldn't see."

"They were not very far ahead. And anyhow, we caught them."

After a silent moment, Heywoud speaks again and now his voice is hoarse.

"I know what Nilsen looks like."

"As do I."

Viola with the *Times* spread for him and Heywoud on the sitting room table in Chelsea. This is Nilsen, she told them both. This is who you're racing. A blond face like a Viking, pale eyes smiling from a frame of fur. Was she afraid? Watts asked. Of course not, she said, and she and Heywoud shared a smile and looked at him. Was he?

"The body," Heywoud says. "It's him."

"Why did you not say so? Could have spared us the breath."

"I didn't know you needed me to prove it."

They stood together looking down at the man's frozen face. Watts saw no Nilsen in him. How did Heywoud? Watts saw no identity in him at all.

"You're certain, Edward?"

Now Heywoud sits up fully. Dagger jumps awake and nuzzles him.

"Bloody hell, Watts." He shunts the dog away. "Yes. I'm certain." Heywoud rises from his bag.

"What are you doing?"

"Good morning. We're leaving."

"Edward, it's the middle of the night."

"There's no point," Heywoud says. "Neither of us can sleep. Get up and help me dig up the goddamned sledge."

Heywoud moves rapidly to fasten toggles on his coat, pull down goggles, pull up hood. Watts nudges the bag down, legs gripped instantly by cold. His toes stiffen in clammy socks turned ice. He draws on parka, goggles, mask.

12

23 January

Viola tells Mary to send Miner to her in the sitting room. She waits by the front window and looks out at the railings of her own and the neighbors' houses covered with woody stems and only ivy now in leaf. The day's raw air blows through the window sashes. She feels it like a paper's edge on skin, a thin line that teases and beckons. Miner knocks on the open door. He wears his customary covering, a muffler fitted with a set of stays that keep it tight over the bridge of his nose and hide his nostrils. It is fashioned with two rows of whale bones, thin like baleen, sewn into the wool as if into a corset.

"Samuel, please bring the camera case around for me. I've packed it already."

He turns to go but she calls him back.

"I won't need you today," she says and sees a question in his eyebrows. "You can call me a cab and load the case inside."

"If you're taking the large case, ma'am, I must come. Mr. Edward said you were not to carry heavy objects. For your health."

"I know what Mr. Edward said. But today I must go alone."

She sweeps past him into the hall to fetch her coat and gloves.

"Where are you going, then?" He has followed her. There is something almost plaintive in his voice.

"If you must know," she says, "Dalmeny Avenue. In Holloway."

She shrugs into her coat.

"Is that wise?" he says.

"Why? What do you know about it?"

"The place was in all the papers. After they threw that bomb at the prison."

Viola tries to picture Bellowes or Margaret Lyons in her weakened state hurling a bottle bomb over Dalmeny's garden wall to shatter the windows of several cells. The papers ran a photograph Viola was not there to take: a suffragette in prison uniform smiling out through broken glass and iron bars.

"It could happen again," Miner says. "You won't know what to do."

She almost takes the chance to ask him what he knows of bombs. She thinks sometimes he might have fought in Ireland with Parnell, though perhaps he is too young. His ruined face disguises age.

"If I don't come," he says, "who's going to help you on the other end?"

"I'll drag the case myself." She knows she cannot bring a man onto the premises. Number 12 Dalmeny Avenue is a safe house for suffragettes only. "Honestly, Samuel." She snatches up her gloves from the hall table. "Edward charged you with helping me but that doesn't mean that I am weak."

"I know that."

"I have held Edward on the climbing rope," she says.

"So I have heard."

"He is almost as tall as you."

"The next time I go climbing, ma'am, I'll be sure to ask you to belay me." She catches a wrinkle of humor in his eyes.

"Yes, you'd best," she says, and coughs to hide her own amusement.

He goes towards the back stairway and she hears his staggered tread on the steps, the slight knocking sound that accompanies him always from the block of wood inside his boot. He enters the hall from the front door of the house, his muffler pulled up so that its top edge rests at his lower lids.

"Ready and waiting," he says, with a nod to the pavement outside. He has pulled the camera case around from the darkroom and out through the alley in the back. "The cab too."

"Thank you, Samuel."

The cab travels north and east and soon Viola sees the green of Regent's Park and realizes they are coming into Camden Town. She glimpses the curve of a broad street and something jumps inside her, as if the cab has missed its destination. Gloucester Crescent where James' cottage waits for him. Waits for her too, at the bottom of the garden, with the scent of the canal and the steady northern light falling from skylights onto the bed. The cab comes to a stop in a scrum of motorcars and carriages and her thoughts rush up around her. The two of them working together on a set of photographs James took in Scotland. Edward ski training in Norway. The darkroom's ruby light and the growls of hunger they both laughed at but ignored until the prints came right. And then the twilight walk to the pub where heads turned to see Viola entering among the men. She watched James come back to her, hands full of pints and pies, and realized for months she had been taking only sips of air, as if to inhale deeply were to drown. James tasted of sour wheat when she kissed him.

So many times she traveled to James' cottage under pretense of fine art, inventing watercolor outings to London's parks and gardens. Her face burns to remember Edward thought these invented projects worthy, and that the ruse fooled him because he did not understand her lack of interest in this kind of art. But how could she have told him about James? What could she have said to make him understand she loved both him and James at once? He never asked to see the watercolors, never asked for proof of her endeavors. She wonders now did he think she kept a secret it would hurt to know.

With a jolt, the cab is free from the cluster of vehicles and gains speed over the canal bridge. Finally, Viola sees a church ahead on the left. St. Mungo's. Dalmeny Avenue, Lucy Bellowes told her, is just three crossings further down. Now the houses are lower, smaller, brick, and sure enough, just as the young woman told her at Brittany Studios, here are four policemen, lying in wait should any women be leaving Number 12 with time left on their sentences. She gives the cabman a shilling for helping with the case. He drags it out onto the pavement despite her urgings for care.

Until now, Viola has only seen the prison in newspaper photographs that show the gateway where suffragettes lose and regain their freedom. Now, the structure looms above her like a beetling crag. Beyond the tops of the outer wall, she can make out the battlements—there is no better word for them—of the entrance and the central feature, and the roofline of the buildings that form a star around the hub. The gray stone of the place seems to shroud all of Dalmeny, despite the day's crisp light.

"Oi," shouts one of the constables. "We'll be here all night. Tell your friends."

She ignores him and tugs the camera case up a flagged path through overgrown shrubs. She rings the bell and waits on the step with empty milk bottles. Viola cannot help but think how much of the stuff these women must need to bring them back to health. There should be vans here with deliveries of meat and bread. There should be boys on bicycles lined up along the curb with cheese and pastries. And yet, what good will full health do but send them back into the prison?

She sees a shadow in the frosted glass. A peephole slides open and Viola cannot help but let out a sharp laugh at sight of a single eyeball, large and blue, peering out at her. The peephole slides closed again and the door opens. A young woman tugs Viola in, but there is confusion with the camera case behind her and it bumps against her heels. Still, quickly enough, both she and the case are inside the cramped hall. The young woman with blue eyes gives her an earnest nod and slides three brass bolts across the door.

"There are constables outside," Viola says.

"We know. No one's going home today," she says and slips through a door into what appears to be a drawing room.

The air is close and stuffy, over-warm and redolent of boiling cloth, as if something is being laundered constantly, or people being bathed. Soft voices come from behind the drawing room door and then the young woman reappears ahead of Lucy Bellowes. Bellowes is dressed simply, in a pinafore over a collarless shirt. With her sleeves rolled up and her hair bundled loosely, she seems younger than at the studio, not much older than Viola herself.

"Mrs. Heywoud, I see you are determined."

"Did you not think I would come?"

"Perhaps I hoped you would not. You realize I must protect the women here. I feel myself responsible."

"I understand," Viola says. "I assure you, Mrs. Bellowes, that I will take every care."

Bellowes leads her into the drawing room where Margaret Lyons and three other women sit in low armchairs near a coal fire. Now Viola sees how the house is kept so hot—and why. The women hug themselves beneath jackets and shawls. Their cheeks when they turn to greet her are flushed with the heat, but still they do not move from the grate. They are all so thin that they are freezing. They were—they are—near death. Viola did not see this in Margaret Lyons in the studio, but she sees it clearly in these women now.

"Mrs. Heywoud, I am glad to see you." Margaret Lyons' voice is stronger than at the ASL and Viola hears its throaty timbre.

"I am glad to see you too, Miss Lyons, and looking already more recovered."

Bellowes waves at the other women.

"This is Eliza and this is Abigail." Abigail has dark circles under her eyes and a pinched mouse-like face. Eliza's face is rounder and she has blonde hair bound in a wiry cloud. Her skin is blue-pale as milk. "And this is Tess."

As the third woman turns towards Viola, her shawl slides from her head and reveals a mane of yellow hair. Bellowes has pointed Tess out separately, as if she, too, knows how striking is the effect of her coloring.

"For safety's sake," Bellowes says, "I cannot tell you their surnames. I'm afraid we can never be too sure of our guests. Do not be offended as it is simply our policy."

"I understand," Viola says again, though Bellowes' prudence rankles slightly.

"How long have you been with us, Abigail?" Bellowes asks.

"Two days, same as Eliza and Tess."

Lyons is free five days more than the others and those five days make her by comparison the bloom of health.

"These are to be your subjects, Mrs. Heywoud," Bellowes says. "I have explained your proposal and they have agreed."

"I will join as well," Lyons says. Bellowes gives her a quick glance and Viola sees the news has surprised her.

"It's too soon for you, Margaret," she says.

"Lucy, I have recovered longer than the others. You needn't worry. I am well enough," she says. "And it is for the cause. Isn't it, Mrs. Heywoud?"

"It is. Yes," she says. "But I must be certain that you really do all agree. You do all understand the nature of the project?"

"Pardon, ma'am," Eliza says, "but are we really to be naked?"

"Some of the poses will involve drapery. But, yes, you will be nude, just as the women of so many classical paintings are nude."

"But why?" Eliza looks to the others for support, but Tess stares at the fire and Abigail watches Viola with an avidity that looks like the hunger she perhaps still feels. Viola worries they will change their minds, but she must not appear to persuade.

"I don't mind, like," Eliza says, "if it's for the cause." Another glance, this time at Bellowes. "But I don't think I understand."

"It's revenge, isn't it?" Abigail says. Her sharp face snaps to Eliza and then back.

Bellowes lays a hand on her arm.

"Abigail, you must remain calm." She presses her gently into the seat she has begun to rise from. "We spoke of this. Keep your heart quiet, dear."

"It's to get back at the men," Abigail says in softer tones.

"I wouldn't say it's to get back at the painters or at men as a sex," Viola says. "It's to make a challenge. To ask a question that makes anyone looking at the photographs uncomfortable. If you look at an odalisque—"

"What's that?" Abigail says.

"It's Ingres," Eliza says, with perfect French pronunciation. "It's a nude painting of a servant woman."

The woman in the painting is most certainly a courtesan, but Viola will not correct Eliza.

"Or, perhaps, if you look at the Rokeby Venus. Do you know it?"

"The Velasquez in the National Gallery?" Eliza says, and Viola guesses there are drawing lessons in Eliza's past.

"Consider that painting. Anyone looking at it is looking at what a painter—a man—thinks is beautiful. How a woman looks in beauty. How a woman *looks*, full stop. Naked, vain, passive. Do you see?"

Abigail and Eliza murmur their assent but Tess remains hunched over the fire.

"But why must we women be idolized in this particular way? Why must this be our perfect form? I want to change that with these photographs. With your help, I will alter each famous image to make the nude figure powerful. The woman will be nude, yes, but defiant and questioning."

"I'm not sure how that works," Abigail says, "but I want to do it." She pushes from her chair.

"Abby." This time it is Eliza who slows her.

"You have all endured so much. No," Viola says. "Not endured. *Achieved.* You have shown so many powerful men that women can take the greatest risks. You have been so strong. I want to show that to the world."

Tess turns finally from the fire and Viola is struck by the likeness. With her long, fair hair, straight nose, and delicate eyes, Tess has the air of Botticelli's Venus. Beneath the girl's mannered form is a fury that strains the tendons in her long and slender neck. She is Venus defiant and she will be perfect for Viola's project.

"I don't see how taking photographs helps anyone," Tess says.

"Tess," Eliza says, "you said you'd join."

"Maybe I've changed my mind." She has not taken her eyes from Viola. "You haven't been to prison. Haven't gone on strike." The woman's voice is soft and reedy.

"You're right. I have been out there in the marches, but I haven't sacrificed what you have. My contribution is to document and show the world what women can do. But if you help me, Tess, my photos can do more than that."

"You have no idea what it's like. To go without food for five days, six days, seven. The feeding tube pushed up your nose, blood in your mouth and down your throat choking you even if the tube weren't making you choke already. Slammed against the special chair they hold you down in so your ribs crack and your back breaks."

"Tess, stop," Eliza says.

"And your heart leaping in your chest not just then but for hours and days after. How can you speak for us?" Tess' voice comes like a rasp. "What do you know about going without food for so long you can't stand up, about coming out of prison just in time before you die, because God forbid they kill you when all they want is to keep depriving you of your right? How can you ask to use our bodies when you haven't risked your own?"

Viola's heart pounds in her throat and she is sure her face is crimson. She will be asked to leave. This girl will destroy the project.

"I have no intention of *using* you," she says. "I want you to express exactly this. Your anger. Your frustration. Which I share."

Bellowes calls to the blue-eyed girl who met Viola at the door.

"Franny, take Tess for some rest," she says.

"I don't want to rest."

Franny holds Tess by the shoulders and stares at her until Tess will only look directly back, her eyes no longer darting with anger from one face to the next.

"Come now, Tess," Franny says. "I'll make you some nice chamomile. Come."

"She asks us to take our clothes off," Tess says to Franny, softly now. "But she keeps hers on."

Franny leads her from the room. She wraps her shawl around her as she goes, and the light of her gold hair is put out. Viola sees the tall figure of the goddess rising from the giant scallop shell, a zephyr in her hair and frills of water at her feet. Tess can stand in for that goddess, battle-scarred and battle-ready, where Botticelli's figure simply stands there to be seen. Viola clears her throat.

"Tess is right," she says. "I have not taken the risks you all take. I am an artist and so I have chosen to fight this fight with my camera. This is how I can help. I am angry, too, at Government, and at those who think women are too delicate for worldly things. But I do not mean to draw an equivalency. I know you have sacrificed much more than I ever could. I am sorry to have suggested otherwise."

"Do not apologize," Lyons says. "Never apologize for trying to do what you think is right."

"Yes, quite," Bellowes says. "Is that not what we march for?"

"I have offended Tess."

"She came closest to death of all our suffragettes in Holloway. She will take time to recover both in body and in mind."

"I would have liked to start with her today."

"Another time, perhaps. But we have lost some time already, Mrs. Heywoud, and these young women do not have the stamina for a long session with your camera. Best make haste."

Viola scans the faces in the room. Abigail and Eliza and Lyons are all expectant and smiling.

"Yes, of course," she says.

Bellowes leads the way down to the rear of the small house. Viola follows with the camera case, though the corridor is so narrow she fears that she will not pass. Eliza and Abigail follow behind until they reach a room containing only a bed and a washstand. The room is replicated twice more on the ground floor in spaces that once held parlor and library. Those furnishings have been moved upstairs and the bedrooms down. The women lack the strength for the first floor. Here, too, as in the drawing room, the fire in the grate is banked and blazing. The strangeness of the room makes Viola briefly hesitate. Stripped of most furniture, the place is neither home nor studio, the women neither friends nor models. They watch Viola, waiting for a signal.

"First I must set up the camera," she says and they are silent as she opens the case and unfolds the tripod, mounts the camera, slides the holder in with two glass negatives, attaches the velvet drape. She has never been watched with so much attention as she works to prepare, not even by James who watched her with a different sort of concentration. They used the camera between them as seduction. There will be no seduction with these photos now.

"Shall I begin with you, Eliza?" she says.

Eliza takes a small step forward.

"I'd like to do the odalisque," Viola says.

"I can do that." She seems to be steeling herself.

"We will make an altered version of the painting, as I explained. Ingres made the figure too long, too curved, for reality. Our figure—your figure, Eliza—will be sharp and straight and all too real."

"I am ready."

"Good. As we discussed, in the painting," Viola says, "the figure is nude. Would you mind, Eliza?"

"Undressing?"

"Yes."

She has never had to explain this to a model before. The Slade students who posed, like Isabella, knew what to do. The women hired from the pub or street simply did what they were told.

"I'll do it," Eliza says, but she holds back a moment, until Abigail murmurs something to her. "I said I'll do it," Eliza repeats to Abigail. "Franny," she says to the blue-eyed girl who has rejoined them in the little room, "please unbutton my dress."

As Franny works, Eliza's body sways with even these gentlest tugs and pulls. Dress, shift, camisole, stockings, all removed. There is no corset. A corset here would kill these bodies that already suffer. Viola wants to look away and senses that reserve among the other women, too. There is something wrong about what she intends to do, something unseemly. Though isn't it right to pose the nude as challenge rather than acceptance? Isn't it right to turn the odalisque's bland stare into a confrontation?

"Are there any cushions?" Viola asks, thinking of Ingres' composition. Franny fetches cushions and the cloth she asks for too. She sets those on the skinny bed in an attempt to set the mounded fabric against the angles of the nude. She unfolds her tripod, fastens the camera with its screw, inserts the first plate.

Eliza shivers despite the heat. Franny keeps a shawl to hand, but Eliza says go on, I'm ready, and lowers herself with Franny's help onto the bed. She rolls onto her side to show her back and, like the woman in the painting, turns her face towards the camera. Knobs protrude along her spine, and her ribs hang over the space where another woman's waist would be and nearly touch the blade of the hip bone. Her upper arm is yellow-brown with bruises.

Viola watches Eliza, waiting to see what hunger and Dalmeny itself and the palpable loom of the prison will bring out in the woman's face. Eliza finds the camera's iris and glares at it. She trembles from the strain of the pose but she will not flinch from the camera's inquiring eye. *Me*, she seems to say. *See me. You have not won.* This is exactly what Viola wants. She ducks beneath the camera's drape and meets Eliza's gaze through the lens. As she springs the shutter open and closed, Viola takes in a sharp breath. She has begun.

In the back of the room, Abigail stirs.

"Can it be my turn next?" she says.

Franny helps Eliza into her clothes while Abigail undoes her own. Her camisole pulled back reveals what seems a scar or new-cut wound over the ridge of her collarbone. Lines of raw skin shaped into letters. V and O. Confused, Viola takes it to mean LOVE, but Abigail tells her.

"*Votes*," she says. "I was planning to write *Votes For Women* and the last letters would have been on my face."

"You're lucky they caught you before you got that far," Eliza says. "Infection nearly killed her. And besides," she says to Abigail, "you began too high. You should have done the V between your breasts and then the entire phrase would have been below your neck." Eliza must sense Viola's shock, for she turns to her again. "More practical," she says.

"But why would you do such a thing at all?"

"They left me with a hairpin." Abigail says it with a smile.

Viola wonders if the girl is mad. To have cut into her own flesh and been ready to disfigure the face she shows the world. Or is this what happens when a woman cannot speak for herself? Must her words turn inward and against her? Is not Eliza a touch mad as well, to take such injury as common practice?

Abigail sits on the edge of the bed with her arms at her sides.

"How should I be?" she says.

Viola instructs her to recline. She will pose as the Rokeby Venus. But this image will have no cherub in attendance. Viola asks for a small mirror and it is fetched from another room. This Venus holds the mirror for herself and she angles it not to her own face but to the letters on her chest. Like Eliza, Abigail shows her back to the camera. She keeps her face turned, the mirror pointed at her wounds and sending the reflection to the lens. Viola brings the camera tight to the forms of skin and bone.

Once Viola is finished with Abigail and Eliza, three other women come into the room from other reaches of the little house. Florence, Molly, and Anne, each of them clutching shawls and rugs around them. Viola poses them as Titian's Danaë, Manet's Olympia, another Venus, this time from Giorgione. One by one, the women shed their clothes and show their scars and bruises. Anne coughs so much Viola takes only one frame. As she works, Viola tells herself don't gasp, don't wince. But beneath the drape she squeezes her eyes shut against the horror of it. These women are not soldiers, though their banners and badges name them so. They are the battlefields, cratered and ravaged. Whatever they do not destroy in themselves by starving, their enemy destroys by feeding. What army is this that turns the pain onto itself? What war that turns sustenance into vile attack?

She marvels at these women. Could she endure such pain, could she court it, for the cause? Does the cause mean enough to her that she would harm herself in ante to the wager? No. She nearly speaks the word out loud in the muffled darkness of the drape. Viola's father taught her illness knew no sex. Cut into a cadaver, he said, and find more that is the same between a man and a woman than is different. Then at the Slade, she saw the men granted more power, more success, and once her parents died it was almost in debt to her father's beliefs that she joined with the Pankhursts. But now that woman Tess was right to scold her. Viola would give up the fight before it came to damaging herself. Has she not given in already? She wakes each day in a home where Miner and Mary serve her, while these women starve themselves and endure what would amount in any other circumstance to violation, the feeding tube pushed into their very bodies.

She pulls out of the drape for air.

"Mrs. Heywoud?" Margaret Lyons cocks her head. She is ready to pose as Rubens' Venus, her long locks a perfect match for the figure in the painting.

"I'm sorry," Viola says.

"It can be a bit overwhelming," she says, "can't it?"

"Yes," Viola says. "It hardly seems I can match my efforts to yours."

"But as you said in Chelsea, you are a photographer. I believe in you, Mrs. Heywoud. You can help us change how people see us, and that will help our cause."

Viola answers her smile with a long exhalation.

"All right, then," she says. "Whenever you are ready, Miss Lyons. Let's have the Rubens."

Lyons hands her robe to Bellowes and perches on the bed with her back turned to the lens. She holds a mirror up to show her face. Where the Rubens nude has solid heft, Lyons is rake thin. Where the Rubens shows the shadows of a densely muscled form, Lyons' ribcage ladders up her back. With Lyons sitting upright on the bed as in the painting, Viola asks her to adjust the pose once, twice, to make the shadows deeper, then she springs the shutter.

"You see?" Lyons says. "Done."

"Yes. Perhaps we can do Tess next. Mrs. Bellowes?"

"Tess must rest a bit longer. No, I'm afraid we must stop now." Bellowes sends Franny to make some tea and bundles Lyons back into her wool robe.

Viola tries to hide her disappointment.

"I understand. I hope you will allow me to return soon."

She packs the camera away while Bellowes gathers up Margaret's clothes and goes with her to another room to dress.

In the drawing room, Franny pours tea and hands the cups around to Abigail and Eliza, dressed once again in their wool clothes and leaning towards the fire. They hold their cups in two hands and let the steam drift over their faces. A plate of biscuits goes untouched and Viola cannot understand why the women go on with their privation now that they are free. She realizes she is hungry, but she dares not be the first to eat.

"And now what next, Mrs. Heywoud?" Bellowes says.

"When do you think Tess might be well?"

Bellowes and Lyons exchange a glance.

"Tess is quite fragile, as you have seen."

"Yes, but she is perfect for Botticelli's Venus. I'm sure you can see it. It's the most important of all the Venus images. It shows the figure's very birth. To have a model who so strongly signals the original, and to make so stark a contrast with the painting's harsh ideal. And it's so familiar. No one will mistake my message when they see it."

"Your message?"

"Our." Viola's face goes hot. "Our message. Imagine a full gallery hung with nearly all the famous images of female nudes. At first it might look like a traditional exhibition. But a closer look reveals it is about the power women claim for themselves."

"I cannot promise," Bellowes says. "But why don't you try again in a few days?"

"I will," Viola says. "I hope that Tess recovers soon and that she sees how important the project is. How important *she* is." She rises to go and sees that Abigail's eyes are closed and the tea trembles in her hands. She takes the cup and saucer to set it gently on a nearby table. "I must apologize for having tired you. Thank you for allowing me to come today and do this work. And for all you have done and all you have endured for the cause."

As Viola leaves Dalmeny Avenue, she marvels at Abigail's joy, Eliza's defiance. These women are neither mad nor desperate. They are brave. She is not certain that she has that sort of courage. Is her chafing at rules and norms no more than a pose, something she feels only like the pain of those she photographs—one step removed, the idea of something, not the thing itself? Would she have truly taken the risks these hunger strikers take, the risks her men have taken, if she had been free to do so? Or would she have stayed low, stayed safe, stayed home, in secret relief? She has always thought of herself as brave and even bold. She chose art school at the Slade instead of Oxford or Cambridge. She chose the risk over the education one expected of a doctor's daughter. She chose the camera over the brush. She chose two men, not one, and of those two both strive for adventure. She learned to climb rather than be left behind. But what if in all of this she is at heart afraid?

The cab wheels around a corner at Sloane Square and Viola sees she will soon be home. She rights herself and sees again the images she captured in Dalmeny Avenue. She must join these women in their ambitions and their bravery. She must push herself further. Past the shame of giving in to Edward's wishes she not do so much as march. She must push too far—for is it not the point of pushing to exceed? And she will do this with her camera so that she can prove the force of a woman's will. It is not enough for her to push unless she helps break through for all of them.

13

89° 30'S

Watts steps into a sky of Wedgewood blue and curses this place that offers beauty with a fist. He breathes in and feels the knife edge that makes him cough. Heywoud's head seems bowed, the hand that holds the shovel resting easy at his side, and Watts hastens to join him in what small ceremony he enacts. He leans into the wind that spins wisps of snow up into dervishes. Heywoud lifts his head as Watts approaches, turns a masked and goggled face to meet him.

"We'll begin with the dog."

Inch by inch they pull its tether from the snow, ripping the hardpack like a sheet of paper. They follow the line, hand over hand, to reach the sledge that lies some twenty paces out, just half a rail angled up out of the ice. Heywoud leaves, returns with the shovel he dropped beside the dog. He digs and Watts clears away the chopped blocks of snow. They will place these later over the men's faces. They will balance them on points of noses, orbitals that frame the eyes. Watts sees an eternity of staring at a pane of crystals never melting, and he fights the spinning of the ice beneath him. These men are dead. It does not matter. They will not, do not, see. He pauses, hands and knees upon the ice, and tries to breathe without a cough.

They free the sledge and unpack all the boxes they can prize out of the ice. They find no flag and the work leaves them so fatigued that when they open a single small crate that contains no more than a box of biscuits and a herring tin they stop their search entirely.

"They were worse off than us," Heywoud says.

"We may be near a depot."

"There's nothing here for miles."

"Why did they die? They had at least something."

"Don't be a fool, Watts. Do I need to name the other ways this bloody place can kill you? Gangrene? Hypothermia? Do you want to strip the bodies nude and find the cause?"

"All right, Heywoud. But they were men like us. I'm simply wondering."

"I doubt they would have spared a thought for you." He hands the open crate to Watts. "Seal this up."

Watts' mouth waters at the sight of biscuits iced with sugar paste, a tin of herring. He takes the crate into his lap. He extracts the box of biscuits and with teeth pulls at the wrapper.

"What are you doing, Watts?"

"Hungry."

"Not now."

"Just one."

Watts tears a long strip of paper and tugs at it with mittened hands, grabs at a biscuit, bites. The sweetness hits his palate like a flash from a light pan and he laughs at the glory of the taste. He chews, eyes closed. He turns his face up to the sky and swallows. Heywoud bumps him, sits beside him. Watts opens his eyes to see Heywoud reach across him. Watts holds the package out then takes a second biscuit for himself.

It has been miles and days since they ate their last sugar. Watts gathers spit to form a paste he presses to the roof of his mouth. He sucks it with his tongue, rasping the slick surface to collect the sweet a little at a time. He curls his tongue and sends his mind to Viola, to his tongue inside her and the taste of salt. There is a pleasure in the feel of Heywoud at his elbow in the snow. Watts pictures kissing Viola, unseen beneath a camera's drape while Heywoud sits for his portrait. Watts would make Viola come and only he would know it from the shudder in her thighs. Watts squeezes his eyes tight at once to fight and feel the gathering of pleasure. Would it be so dangerous to seek release? He would freeze to death, cock first, like some Antarctic Priapus. Heywoud would raise a monument to him as an eternal torture.

He reaches for a third biscuit. Heywoud stops him.

"Not all at once. We have to build the cairn."

"Will we not search their pockets?"

"What for?"

"The flag, Edward. Nilsen could keep it in his jumper."

"You think that because you had your bloody pouch and your bloody notebook."

"I'm saying there are more places we should look if we want to be sure before going further."

Heywoud rises to a squat.

"The flag is here," he says. "I know it. But I am not going to rifle a dead man's pockets just to prove it to you."

Watts' lips crack when he winces.

"All right, Edward. We'll go on."

They close the box, fasten the crate with its strap of webbed cloth. They take up the blocks of hardpack and bring them to the bodies of the men. They squat and rise, fingertips and palms alive to new and deeper freezing. To touch here is to lose sensation. And yet they do not change their plan. They cover Nilsen and his partner as if to make a bed. Feet first, then legs, then hips and chest until they pull the covers block by block up to the dead men's chins. The dog is covered where he lies. Watts rushes through the work. He cannot bear to see the bodies disappearing. So he hastes to fetch the blocks that render them inhuman. He turns them into cairns.

Heywoud at the sledge takes the runner, more steeply curved and longer than English design, and steps a fulcrum while he wrenches up. The wood cracks loud and brings from Dagger three anxious answering barks.

He steps again on the broken runner's midpoint, shorter now and stiffer. His boot skids off. He stumbles. Heywoud sets the length of runner across his knee and tries to snap it but again cannot. Watts goes to him.

"Here." He takes the runner, tries his own strength with it. The cursed thing is like a rock, of wood they have no counter for in England.

"Let's use just the one."

"No," Heywoud says. "That's not a cross. We need a cross."

Heywoud seizes the wood from Watts and tries once more to step on it to snap it. His action drives the end into the hardpack. He curses, steps, slips on the wood, and falls.

"Edward, leave it."

"We said we'd make a cross so we will make a cross."

He is like Watts' sister's child, the boy crying frustrated tears over a hoop and mallet in the garden.

"Who are you keeping promises to, Edward? Nilsen won't care."

"I do."

"But why?"

Heywoud stops battling the wood.

"Are you not a believing man, James?"

"I suppose I'm not. Are you?"

"Of course. And so we must bury these men with a cross. If we give them any marker at all, it should be that."

"Fine," Watts says, and stoops over the Norwegian crate of food. He tears a slat from its top and takes from Heywoud the broken length of runner. This he drives into the snow at one end of the cairn. He turns the slat in his hands to find a weakness and, seeing the thin wood is made of fibrous bands, he pushes it gently over the runner's tip until it pierces. He slides it down so that it forms a cross of stubby arms, like something from a Norman church. St. Mary's in Southend where for an hour at sundown all the stones and markers bask in honeyed light. Watts steps back to admire his handiwork.

"How's that?" he says.

Heywoud's mask and goggles leave no bit of face that Watts can read. But the man's parka hangs loose upon his frame. His shoulders droop, tugged out of military posture by the haul of traces.

"It will do."

Heywoud stands at the foot of the cairn and bows his head. Watts does the same and waits. Church sounds here are creaks of ice, a sigh of wind, the flapping of a mitten strap.

"Amen."

"Amen," Watts says.

"Now get your camera."

Watts frames the standard shot of commemoration: cairn to the left, cross towards the center, lens pulled back far enough to allow a lower angle.

"We'll bring that to their king," Heywoud says. He throws the next words over his shoulder as he goes. "Not the dead. We've wasted too much time," he adds. "Let's go."

Ten months together in this blasted place and still Watts is surprised by Heywoud's shifts of mood. Pious one moment, elated the next, determined yet another.

"Come on, Watts," Heywoud calls again, and Watts joins in the packing of the sledge. Heywoud sets the Norwegians' box atop their own small pile and lashes it down tight. They shoulder the traces, tie in Dagger, fasten skis, and set off. Watts swears he feels the extra weight of Nilsen's herring, Nilsen's biscuits. He salivates at the idea, leans into the traces to replace the pang of hunger with the bite of straps into his shoulders. In Greenland they tell children that to whistle at the night sky summons the Aurora to chop off their heads. With Heywoud alongside him in the traces, Watts feels the knife edge of the sky over his neck. It finds his bristled skin, the chilblains where the tunic collar chafes. There. That is where the blade will slice.

Watts shoves his skis ahead one at a time and strains to ignore the hunger that coils in his stomach like a living beast. Pinprick dots of light dart at the edges of his sight. They arc and fall and disappear like sparks on Guy Fawkes' Day. He and Heywoud do not eat enough. They do not have enough to eat.

He lifts his eyes from the thrust and glide of his brown skis against the white and sees that the way ahead is overhung with thick gray cloud. They ski towards this featureless shadow as if to disappear.

"Look," Watts says.

"Another storm."

Another storm. They go into it, with each step fighting the urge to shelter. They do not speak, and even Dagger makes no sound besides a steady panting. The wind rises from the South and East. Watts hopes it does not push them off their course, hopes Heywoud will soon halt to read the sextant. Snow blows against them, blurs the edges of the view ahead. It is like skiing in an image whose photographer has left the lens unfocused. Or has set the aperture so wide the lens cannot grasp anything outside its focal center. Watts shuts his eyes. He imagines his body like a coast and signal fires along his legs and torso. Feet, knees, shoulders, wrists: one pain ignites another. He is ablaze with misery.

The pinprick lights return and he opens his eyes, tries to ignore the thirst and hunger. He and Heywoud have not eaten citrus fruit in weeks. Heywoud rations out scant bits of liver, seal meat, these mixed in their hoosh to ruin a meal that already disgusts them. Watts runs his tongue along his teeth, afraid to find the loose gums of scurvy. He has seen a man fight death for want of a lemon or a bite of offal.

He slides the skis out, one by one, for if he stops or slows he will not start again. He knows this, and the idea occurs to him as a pleasure. One thing clear, one thing in focus: he must not stop until the Pole. He cannot. Watts smiles into the storm. He feels his teeth move when the wind strikes them.

When Heywoud signals halt, Watts has no recollection of the previous hours. For all he knows, he has been standing in one spot, or speeding across ice at a great pace. It makes no difference to him. But Heywoud tells him it is time to stop, they have skied well, the continent has favored them this day with firm pack in spite of newly drifted snow. Heywoud removes his skis, erects the tent, leads him inside.

"Is this the night?" Watts asks.

"No. Just a rest," says Heywoud. "We'll press on. We are close now, James. 89 and 50. Less than a day's march. If it weren't for this damned storm, we'd even see it."

"See what?"

Heywoud laughs.

"Nothing. We'd see nothing, wouldn't we, James?"

"There's nothing there."

"Not yet."

A bell jingles nearby and Watts remembers Cornwall in the summers, the bells of pony carts along the strand, hawkers with ices, tea cakes, lemonade.

"Lemonade," he says.

"What's that?"

"Lemonade. Will we have lemonade at the Pole, Edward? Refreshing."

Heywoud's face nears his. The goggles like a second set of eyes upon his forehead. The dog's nose damp on his chin. Again the bells.

"My teeth," Watts says. He must communicate to Heywoud that this is not right. He must not die without his teeth. He has never seen a man that died of scurvy. Does he lose his teeth to the snow? Are his last words a mumble?

Heywoud strikes him in the jaw. Watts bobs to the right, sways up again, shakes his head clear.

"Oi."

"There you are."

"What did you do that for?"

"You were drifting."

Watts shakes his head.

"Not me. My teeth. Drifting."

Heywoud's fist, fat, mittened, thrusting something at his mouth. He dodges. Heywoud holds his head.

"Take it, Watts."

The face softens when Watts looks at it.

"Come on, James." Soft. "Don't die on me until I can kill you."

"Heard that," Watts says.

"I know."

Watts opens his mouth and tastes the thing Heywoud holds out to it. Not lemonade. Like bitter mud and dry like eating rope. He shakes his head again.

"Can't chew."

"You must. It's liver, Watts. You need it for the scurvy."

"Whose?"

"It doesn't matter."

"Whose?" He claps a hand to his mouth to catch the teeth he is sure are shot out by the sibilants.

"Kip's."

Watts gags on morsels he has taken in. His stomach rises.

"No," Heywoud shouts. "Keep it down. We cannot afford to waste it."

Watts groans and swallows but he cannot master the heaving of his stomach. He falls onto his side and vomits up a thin stream of brown liquid. Heywoud moves around him cursing. The dog comes near and crunches the frozen vomit between his jaws. One more for the list of things that freeze: sick.

"Go away," Watts says. "Don't do it." The name comes to him as if from decades past. "Dagger."

"You'll feel better now. Try some more."

Heywoud lifts him from the ice. He mutters something, brushes snow from Watts' cheek. Watts hears the pumping of the Primus and soon smells the sour scent of fuel ignited. The stove hisses softly, water churns into a boil, then sweet bergamot again and there is tea.

"Sit up," says Heywoud.

Heywoud cups his chin, tips the mug and makes him sip.

"Enjoy it," he says. "It's the last."

"Out of tea?"

"Fuel. We'll chew on tea leaves from now on if we want a cuppa."

"You sound like Lawrence. A cuppa."

"Lawrence will make us a pot of tea when we return."

"Yes, he will."

Lawrence, Tite, and the others at Shore Camp, waiting for them, playing football on the strand, hurling stones at albatross to spare their bullets.

"Do you think they lived, Edward?"

Heywoud tips the mug up. Watts gulps the tea that has already gone cold.

"Oh yes," Heywoud says. "They've laid some depots for us. For the return leg."

"We're on the last leg now."

"We are."

Watts wakes with a start and the smart of burning skin along his jaw.

"James," Heywoud says, and shakes him. "Stay awake."

"Stop hitting me."

"It's time to go."

But neither makes to leave the tent. Watts stirs within the bag and a patch of faintest warmth behind his right knee comes to cold. He dares not move again. What little heat he has rests in his posture: on his left side, legs curled inward, arms about his chin. If he moves even an inch, he brings some new body part to face the air. He will remain like this. They will find him like this.

He opens eyes to Heywoud inches away, the face turned up as if to call across a crowd. The mouth open. Heywoud's tongue will freeze if it has not already. There was a creature from a myth, a woman or a bird with tongue cut out. Some punishment she was compelled to serve. The mouth in drips of blood, a schoolboy's fascination, his horror now. Why does he think of these things here? Let him think instead of green light filtering through leaves, the song of birds. Streams, riverbeds, marsh grasses. A silver fish come to the surface of a pool, the pock of its mouth opening to take a fly. Watts sits up, fumbles for the camera that he cannot find. He will photograph this fish before it sinks back to the shadows.

The dog is whimpering. Watts reaches out a hand and finds the bony curve of Dagger's spine.

"Here, boy," he says, and pulls him close. His stomach hints a heave. "Heywoud," he says. "Edward."

Heywoud rasps a snore and wakes. For an instant Watts sees in him a peer, his friend, the face like his own as he imagines it, sleepy, confused. And then the lines assemble and once again Heywoud is leader, hero, star.

"I'm getting the sextant," Heywoud says.

Watts watches Heywoud rise and leave the tent. There is a stagger in his step.

Heywoud returns.

"89 and 55," he says.

Heywoud sits and hands him something, flashing like his fish rising to bait.

"Take some," he says, and Watts sees the tin of Nilsen's herring, laughs aloud at four fish on the label, blue-gray on red, stacked head to tail. Fish, fish, fish, fish.

"No," Heywoud says. "Eat it."

He removes a mitt to poke a finger into the congealed oil. He lifts a herring, rank, to slide between cracked lips. He swallows whole and takes another. If they survive, he vows to dine only on eels and herring, food for the toothless. He runs his tongue along his teeth. He has them yet.

"We've come a distance today," says Heywoud.

"How much longer?"

"Five miles."

"What do you think?"

"Less than a day, James. Less than a day."

Five miles. After eight hundred. After dozens of glass plates, five dogs, two men, five months at sea, the waves as high as steeples and the ship a folly thrown among them like an idiot's whim. Five miles to reach the end. And what will they do then? Will it be even possible to move once they have finished. Will they care?

Some hours pass and Watts awakes. Heywoud lies snoring, mouth agape. Watts steps outside to urinate. Dagger follows, lifts a leg. Watts goes to the sledge and digs out some biscuit, gives a chunk to Dagger who snatches it, teeth snagging briefly on his mitt. The dog snarls as he chews this food that Watts has given without Heywoud's license. Hunger has begun to change them all. Watts reaches beneath canvas on the sledge before he understands he searches for the gun, arming himself against the dog's certain attack. He pulls a mitten off, slides fingers under lashings. A tag of cracked skin on his index finger catches and gapes to a sharp sting. He glances where a gout of blood forms, sees it freeze, goes back to his search. He hears a noise behind him and he braces for Dagger's lunge, but it is Heywoud.

"Looking for this?" He holds the gun at his side.

"Dagger's not well."

Heywoud takes two steps towards Dagger, watches as the dog bites at a mat of fur beneath his leg.

"Don't shoot him, Edward. Not yet. Not now."

"Isn't that what you were after?"

"I was just looking. In case."

"He tried to bite you in the night."

Watts frowns.

"No, he didn't."

"Your hand. See where it's bleeding."

"That happened now."

"Dagger may try again. This way we're ready."

"I cut my hand just now. It wasn't Dagger."

"That's why I keep the gun."

Heywoud turns back to the tent. Watts looks down at his hand and at the lashing on the sledge where a dab of blood stains the canvas. Is Heywoud right? Did Dagger bite him while he slept? No, Watts cut his hand just now. The night's danger lay with the weapon, cold companion hidden somewhere among their pelts and fur.

Watts finds Heywoud in the tent, his expedition log open on his knee, the gun propped against his leg.

"How many plates do you have left?"

"Perhaps two dozen," Watts says.

"Save some of them for the return."

The return will take them weeks and they will travel with no dogs, for Dagger surely will not last. They'll dine on dogmeat, break their teeth on frozen hoosh, numb their lips and tongues with snow they hope to melt while swallowing. Their sores will open, cuts will chafe. Their frozen toes will undermine their balance and they will stagger in their skis. Save plates, Heywoud says. What will he photograph? A document of suffering for no one to discover.

14

23 January

Viola rushes up the stairs into the house, paying no mind to the ache in her ankle. She tugs her gloves off and tears the hat from her head, sheds her coat into Mary's arms. She races best she can down to the garden door and waits for Miner to bring the camera cart around from the cab she has just leapt from. While she waits, she fetches the notebook in which she sometimes records the timing for exposure or development and jots a quick note to Isabella. *Izzy you were right. My God it was glorious.* She strikes out *glorious* and starts again. *It was extreme indeed and I am already embarked on making the photographs. They will be stupendous. I am sure. Thank you, dearest friend!* She will have Miner send the note to Izzy in the evening post.

Miner appears with the case and she nearly knocks him aside in her haste to begin. It is the same as always. The darkroom neither knows nor cares what sort of images will soon be conjured in its space. The timing tank, the chemicals, the trays, the tongs, the clock. She goes through the steps in order, stilling her hands so that anticipation does not ruin the product. She must not spill a drop of one chemical into the other, must not leave a cover skewed or door ajar. She works smoothly, rising when she must from Samuel's wheeled stool, and readies the space for the developing and printing she is about to do. And again the process with all its steps is a great leveler. All are treated equal in the tanks and trays until she flicks the switch for the enlarger bulb. Then each image makes its claim, specific and importunate, each particular face—whether it returns the camera's gaze or not—saying in its own and distinct way *look at me.*

Viola slides the first plate from the wax-paper envelope she marked with grease pencil. She puts the plate through the series of baths, watching the timing clock at every step, until she can rinse it clean under the tap and set it in the rack to dry. She peers close and turns her head sideways to check the image. Eliza reclining. It takes her several tries to find the correct exposure. At five seconds, the plate is too dark, at three too light, even too light at four. Four and a half seconds beneath the enlarger light is just right to keep the whites white and the blacks saturated and details rendered clearly. Now that Viola knows the lighting of this body—the skin of each woman bearing its own particular tone, its own quality of light—she begins to print out photographs of Eliza as an odalisque. She flicks the enlarger bulb on for four and a half seconds on the timer and slides the exposed sheet of silver gelatin paper into the first bath. Eliza's face rises up from the developing tray with a look that is strangely accusatory, something Viola did not notice in the little room at Dalmeny. Eliza's gaunt form turns her reclination into a charge. *You did this*, the image seems to say. Viola shakes the final liquid free over the sink and clips the print to the drying line. She looks at it again and sees that there is something more. It is not a victim's laying bare of wounds—though they are visible on Eliza's arms—and it is not a pietá of suffering. There is something in Eliza's eyes—this is the beauty of the glass plate and its perfect precision—that Viola could not have even known to ask for. She seems, though reclining, poised to spring, ready to attack all who look at her.

From here, Viola goes on to Abigail and Florence and Margaret Lyons. Abigail's face shows the pain she still bears from the letters on her chest—as if she almost gasps with desperate need to finish the words *Votes For Women.* Florence's Danaë grips the bedsheet with a grasp almost fist-tight. This too Viola did not see through the lens, and now she wonders what else has she missed. Was her excitement or her shock so great that she failed to notice how the women of Dalmeny Avenue took charge? She understands now.

The hunger strikers did to her what she would have them do to those who will stare some day at the photographs.

The photographs are more than Viola could have hoped for. They are stark and clear and they buzz with a barely latent rage. Viola goes on, printing images of Margaret Lyons as another Venus, this time from a Rubens, and of Molly and of Anne. These will be her proofs and over time she will perfect them even more so that the silver gelatin prints turn light and shadow into living liquid. She settles into a rhythm. The more she prints, the less she needs to think as her every action seems to coincide with its idea. With her mind on nothing—or on all of it at once—she works like breathing.

A knock on the darkroom door startles her.

"Ma'am." It is Mary's voice. "It's gone past eight. I've brought you some tea."

"I'm in the middle of this, Mary. I'm not hungry."

"Either you open the door and eat what I brought, or I'll open it myself."

Viola groans loudly enough for Mary to hear and covers her supplies to protect them from the light. She squints in the corridor's glare.

"Here you are," Mary says. She has a tray of tea and toast with cheddar and she holds a small folding table under her arm. This she sets out now outside the darkroom door and rests the tray upon it.

Viola takes her tea while Mary watches with a supervising air. She must add more to her collection from Dalmeny if she can. She thinks of the girl Tess with the golden hair and of the fine Botticelli she would make. There must be others, too, and more arriving at Dalmeny every week, newly released from a prison that spits them out like so much gristle when they get too thin. *Fatten up*, the prison seems to say, *so I can swallow you*. And over and over the suffragettes starve, hoping this time Holloway will say *enough, you have won*.

She thanks Mary for the tea and returns to the darkroom and its soothing ruby light. The finished photographs dance on the line disturbed by the brief draft from the door. She pictures Edward in the little room, his eyes following where she points. Would she call the women by their names or by the poses they adopt or by the number of days they were imprisoned? What would he say, to see that this is what she has created? His eyes will need an education, trained more than a year to look at the simple geometry of ice and snow, at distant horizons and vast skies, and at the markings of his sextant. She must remind Edward how before they married he was eager for her art, how he loved to know what she had conjured from thin air, how it amazed him to see that such a thing was even possible and that the woman he adored could do it. There was something of poetry in how he spoke of it to her, in language beyond the common tongue she spoke with James. She must help Edward retrieve those words when he returns.

She uncovers the trays of chemicals and pulls the printing paper out once more and resumes her work. She takes up the negative for Abigail again and slides it into the enlarger. She wants to find a way to emphasize the letters she has carved into her chest. She tugs the enlarger head as low as it will go, making the image on the paper a little larger. There they are: V and O. She brings the enlarger head back up to its full distance and takes the burning tool from the wall. With the light on and the timer ticking, she stirs the burner in tiny movements at the edges of Abigail's scars. This makes the letters darker, but the skin around them darkens too. She makes a stencil from a piece of card and holds it above the image of Abigail's chest so the enlarger light shines through to darken what the woman wished to say. This print turns out better. The V and O are sharp and black. But Viola wonders at her satisfaction. How can she enjoy the message when the writer nearly died for writing it, when she was only saved to suffer further punishment and when the saving left her message mute?

15

89° 55'S

Watts leans into the traces and wishes he saw nothing save the ice under a moon. He wishes it were dark and that he skied in nighttime, for his eyes dart fitfully to scan what lies ahead. Is it there? Or there? He changes dread for eagerness with each glide of the skis. Twice Heywoud cries out and twice Watts speeds his gait thinking their goal in sight. But he sees nothing, and he wonders why Heywoud cries at all. Has he forgotten that to see a marker is to see defeat?

Heywoud makes them stop, retrieves the sextant.

"89 and 58," he says. "It's very near." His voice is high with elation. "We've only an hour more."

"Have you your watch?" Watts says.

"I'm counting paces."

Watts looks at him but earns no explanation for his puzzlement. He thinks of how he counts exposure in the darkroom, or how he counts the seconds of the shutter's slow release. So Heywoud, here, enumerating steps, a spare arithmetic for Polar calculations. How many pushes of a skinny ski fill up an hour? How many in a day?

"How many?" Watts says.

"One thousand, seven hundred, and seventy."

Watts falls into stride with Heywoud's skiing. Heywoud hums the numbers under his breath and soon Watts joins in the chant. Their voices rise together and they tally steps as if to name them brought some goodness into their possession.

"Seven hundred fifty-two. Seven hundred fifty-one. Seven fifty. Seven forty-nine. Seven forty-eight."

Watts stops. Heywoud continues and the traces jolt Watts forward like a doll. It is there.

The space ahead, where nothing has stood beyond the conjurings of their own ambition, the space ahead is suddenly not blank. It is the proof of an idea. It is a story they are told, a summons. *Come here. Come. I have been waiting.* A flagpole anchored by two guy lines. A pennant flapping. Red and blue and white, not theirs. Watts can hear the fabric crackle. *Come here. I dare you. See what others have done.* The dead man was Nilsen and his flag flies here at the South Pole.

They stand still, he and Heywoud, for a very long time. Watts feels his body flood with hunger, cold, exhaustion. They are all heavy with him now, companions he has carried all this way.

A movement to his right makes Watts take eyes off Nilsen's flag. Heywoud shrugs off the traces, tears at skis and boots to free them, runs across the ice. Watts shouts and starts to ski towards him, but his muscles blaze and the sledge is an anvil. He stops and watches Heywoud reach the flag. Heywoud sheds his mittens and with two hands takes the fabric and extends it. He brings his face so close to Nilsen's flag it seems he means to kiss it.

Watts removes his skis and covers the last distance to the Pole, slowly, gently. He wants to remember this. He must remember this. What did it feel like, Viola will ask him, and he will have to know. There is nothing. No new sensation, no strange pull downward from the earth's voracious magnet, no altered light or sound. Nothing. Were the rival's flag not here, they would know nothing of this Pole. They would ski past it.

His body shakes with sobs though no tears come. For more than one year he has measured himself against an idea so immense that he himself grew smaller every day in order to sustain it. And now he is a nothing to meet the nothing of this place. It is a hole he tumbles into. Feed his memories and photographs down into it. He will not need them any longer.

He presses mittens to his eyes and groans where he has fallen.

"Get up!"

Watts lifts his head. Heywoud stands beside him, looking down.

"I said get up."

"What are you doing?"

"Control yourself."

Watts comes to his feet.

"I was overcome, I think."

"I saw."

"I'm sorry." He says it like a question. Should he apologize for understanding what they've done, what has befallen them?

"Edward, how can you not be moved? This is the Pole."

Heywoud extends a hand. Watts takes it and they shake, Heywoud's left hand on Watts' elbow. It is a posture from a photograph. The victor laurelled. The treaty signed.

"Thank you, James. Congratulations."

"You too, Edward."

Heywoud pulls the goggles from his face as if to change the facts of what he sees. He screws eyes tight against Antarctic sun but will not look away.

"I'm sorry," Watts says again.

"Stop apologizing."

"I mean for this." He nods towards Nilsen's flag.

"Thank you," Heywoud says, and for an instant it is his friend's face Watts sees there, the friend who took his hand on the Mont Blanc *arête* and sighed with relief and gratitude to be pulled up to share the summit. Who blushed to learn that Watts' classmate wished to meet him, thought him dashing. Who said one evening that he feared she'd find him Watts' poorer copy. It was Watts who was the poorer copy. The lesser mountaineer, the less inventive climber, the less charming at a party. No one could endure like Edward Heywoud. No one could persist like him. No one, not Watts, could discard all other thoughts and hopes to foster one and only one idea.

"Thank you," Watts says.

The flag snaps in a gust.

"What do we do now?" Watts says.

"We plant our flag and make a record for posterity."

They return to the sledge and haul it the remaining distance. Watts sees now the rows of thinner stakes set by Nilsen as he measured. There is no doubt the Pole is here and they have come as if summoned by these markers. Heywoud must extract the flag that they have carried with some other end in mind for it than to keep company with its conqueror. A funny thing, to think that Nilsen can say he has conquered the Pole. As if he were some Cortes, William, Genghis Khan, to hold sway over populations. Nilsen rules over only the two of them, Heywoud and Watts, and these from death, and no one—no one in the world entire—knows his dominion.

Heywoud slides the flag from its envelope of linen and rests it on the sledge, creased strangely perfect like a soldier's trouser leg. He unfolds it, holds it down to keep the wind from stealing it. He gives this task to Watts while he himself unties the cords that hold a long stake to the sledge rail. It is a stake made special for this purpose and Watts marvels it has been there all this way, hidden in plain sight. As Heywoud works Watts stares down at the flag, fashioned from what looks like silk. The Norseman's cloth is canvas, homespun almost, faded already from who knows how many days already flying. Theirs is an elegant banner. Viola's doing surely. Here, she must have said. I had this one made special for you, Edward. It will photograph quite well.

Heywoud fastens the silk to the pole, though it takes time for frozen fingers to tie the knots required. He holds the flagged stake in two hands like someone going into battle and strides to the spot they and Nilsen agree makes the center of the earth's southern dome. He plants the stake a step away from Nilsen's. When the flag is up, Heywoud steps back and brings his boots together, standing tall, and makes a crisp salute. Watts follows, like a child caught out in church aping parishioners. Why do they do this? They are as unseen here as anyone in church who thinks God watches.

Heywoud fishes in his pocket and produces a thin package, blue with decorations of deep red. Cadbury's Dairy Milk. He leans on the sledge and unwraps the paper. He extends the bar to Watts.

"Where did you get this?"

Watts joins him and removes a mitten to snap a section from the bar. He chews the stuff and sighs at the familiar butter taste of the milk chocolate. This is better even than Nilsen's biscuits. What he swallows now is the most delicious food or drink he will ever consume.

"I've had it in my jumper pocket."

"You were saving it all this time? For here?"

"For this."

Heywoud places the remaining chocolate—more than half the bar—into his mouth and crumples the paper in his fist. Watts' mouth waters as he watches Heywoud chew.

"You're not the only one who hid the things he carried," Heywoud says.

Watts waits for Heywoud to say more, but the man stares ahead. They should erect their tent, or they should begin their journey home. At the thought of all the miles they must retrace, Watts feels his lungs squeeze and his heart jump. No, let them sleep one night before departing. Let them exist at the Pole for a few restless hours so that they can know it as a place and not a moment like all others that pass in sequence in their lives. Let it be *here* for them, not Heywoud's word. Not simply *this*.

"We must take our photographs," Heywoud says.

Heywoud tugs him to his feet and Watts begins to set the camera. With every trip he takes between the tripod and the sledge—carrying the crate of negatives, the drape, his photographing gloves—his weariness grows deeper. All these last weeks they have been breathing the thinner air of the plateau, and now his body clamors for something richer in his lungs. He dreams of breathing chocolate. Heywoud does not help him with these preparations, but squats on the ice, glowering at the flags.

"Will we not build the tent?" Watts says.

"We will start back once we're done. Preserve our rations."

Watts nearly drops the first plate as he slips it into the holder. He tries to ignore the fact of how much separates them from Shore Camp and from pots of hoosh boiled over fires from coal stored in the belly of their ship.

"Go stand beside the flags," he says to Heywoud.

Heywoud poses, does not smile. How can he, standing by a stranger's banner? Watts works the shutter.

"Another. Just in case," Watts says.

"You'd better get these right."

"I always do."

Watts steps beneath the drape to flip the holder, then releases the shutter once more.

He draws the holder out and sets it into the crate lid. Beneath the drape again, he lifts two fresh plates, curving callused fingers around the edges of the glass, unwraps their tissue and slides them into a new holder. The work makes him dizzy. He grips the tripod for balance.

"Keep your feet," Heywoud says. He stalks across the ice and steadies the camera. "Now is not the time to break the thing."

"Leave it," Watts says. "I've got it."

Together they stand behind the camera and look out at the two flags. The wind plays in the lighter fabric of the Union Jack, casting it open to the sun. Packed away for thirteen months, shielded from light of the Antarctic summer, it is the brightest thing that Watts has ever seen. The blue deeper and more brilliant to him now than any iceberg's azure form. The white far brighter than the white of ice that shades to faintest lavender or gray. The red more vivid than the freshest blood.

Before Watts can spring the shutter, Heywoud rushes to the Union Jack with a low grunt and grips the stake it flies from. He wrests it from the ice.

"What are you doing?"

"It's not right. I'll not have it there."

He seizes Nilsen's flag and yanks it too, and for a moment he holds one flag in each hand, wielding them aloft as if he were the planet and these two standards marked opposing poles of his own earth. Tugged by its guy wires, Nilsen's flag escapes his grasp and tumbles to the ice, and now Heywoud holds only one, the Union Jack. He plunges the point of its flagpole down between his feet.

"Edward, fix his flag."

Heywoud does not answer.

"Edward, fix it. Fix it now."

Watts rushes to him, grabs at Nilsen's flag and tries to plant it where it stood before. But the English flag usurps the spot and Heywoud, silent still, prevents him. They are face to face and the shaft of the pole between them like a gate and neither one will yield. Until Watts stops, releases his grip on the wood and steps away. His breath is heavy. Stars swim into his vision. He falls back against the sledge and wonders if the scurvy teases at his brain.

"What are you doing, Edward? Talk to me."

"Our flag was off the center. Why should it be when both are at the Pole?"

"But he was first."

"So?"

"He has pride of place."

"We both reached here. Why should only Nilsen have it?"

"Have what? Why would you want this place?"

"The fame. Why should only Nilsen have the fame."

"He won't," Watts says. "We will be famous, too."

Heywoud stands over him, blocking the sun.

"No one will bother with us."

"Nilsen is dead. It's you they'll interview, you they'll make the statues to."

"No. It will all be about Nilsen. They'll be asking me about Nilsen." He spits the name out. "Not unless we're first."

"But we are not. There's no *unless*, Edward. Look!" He points to Nilsen's flag where it lies on the ground.

"He is dead, Watts. It doesn't matter. We are the only ones who know."

"And we must be the ones to tell."

"Why? Why must we tell? We are *here*." Heywoud nearly growls the word. "And we are alive."

"We might die on the return."

"We might."

"Do you want to die with a stolen honor?"

"You're going to take a photograph," Heywoud says. "You're going to photograph the both of us with our flag. And not Nilsen's."

Watts rises to his feet.

"No, Edward. I'm not doing that."

"Yes."

"No!"

Watts rushes to protect the camera, but that is not what Heywoud wants. He stoops over the crate lid and lifts the holder that bears the two first images: him alone beside the English and Norwegian flags. He swings once with it and dashes it to shards of wood and glass against the sledge rail.

"You're mad," Watts says. "You've gone mad."

"Nilsen would do the same."

"Even if you're right, that doesn't matter. Edward, put the flag back up and then we'll take the photograph."

"I can take it by myself."

"I'll smash the camera."

Heywoud picks up the stake of Nilsen's flag.

"I'll smash all of your plates. I'll drive this stake into that box of yours. So you decide. Keep all your photographs, or refuse to take one more."

"What is wrong with you?" Watts' words come out in a whisper.

Heywoud heaves Nilsen's flag up with its guy wires, walks a few paces off and tosses it down. He returns and smooths the snow where the guy wires have left tracings.

"Is this because of Viola?" Watts says.

Heywoud stops and turns.

"How do you mean?"

"I don't know." Watts approaches him, places hands on his shoulders. "You are not yourself, Edward."

"My *self*?" He shakes free of Watts' grasp. "My *self* has man-hauled sledges more than one thousand miles over a hundred days and my self has nearly died of hunger and exhaustion and this fucking cold and my self did not drag other men to nearly dying for nothing."

"Edward."

Heywoud gasps for breath as he continues.

"If Tite dies it cannot have been for nothing. I am going home the hero of the Pole. Come with me if you want, Watts, or not. But you're going to take the fucking photograph or I swear I will smash your plates and I will kill you."

Raving or sane, Heywoud has the gun still in his parka. Watts must take the photograph. He can hurl it later like a discus out onto distant ice. It will catch the light as it flies, a hasty sun taking a day's arc in an instant.

"All right," he says. "Go stand where you like."

"Good."

Heywoud poses by the Union Jack, left foot propped on a block of ice and left knee bent. Watts steps beneath the drape and squeezes the shutter's bulb. He wishes nothing more than to be done with this.

"There," he calls.

"Make another."

Watts removes the plate in its holder and takes another from the crate. He sets it in the camera.

"Both of us."

Watts shakes his head.

"I'll not join you in this."

"We are both heroes now, James. Come."

It should not have come to this. It should have ended differently. The thousand days that they have journeyed scatter now into disorder, like beads shot from a necklace when the string is snapped. Watts has no choice but to obey. He extends the long lead of the shutter bulb and tucks the bulb into his mitten. He does not give fair warning when he squeezes, and the photograph catches Heywoud with left arm outstretched to wave Watts closer to the flag. Watts looks away, displeasure written in the press of his lips.

Heywoud makes him take three more. Watts ducks into the darkness of the camera drape and frames the image once, twice. Heywoud with a hand on the stake and the flag playing at the edges of his parka.

"Come on, man," Heywoud shouts. The voice comes to Watts muffled by the heavy cloth.

Inside the drape, his breaths build up around him like clouds ready to storm. He closes his eyes to listen better to the sighing of his lungs. He does not need his eyes to see Heywoud standing by the Union Jack, clasping the stake as if to hold to an elusive truth. It is Watts who makes the truth for them. Watts who makes the photographs that tell the story they will bring back to the world. He pops his eyes open with a click of frozen lids. In the viewfinder, there is Heywoud with his head high and the flag reaching for his face. The shutter bulb in Watts' hand is like a tiny bird stunned at a window's base and gathered up to save. He takes a breath and moves the camera on the tripod to change the frame of what it sees. All that is required is the shift of just one inch to the left—an inch after a thousand miles. And there it is: on the ice some paces off from Heywoud, the dark rag shape of the Norwegian flag. Watts squeezes the beating heart of the shutter bulb and takes the photograph.

16

24 January

In Ganton Street the next day, Viola rings the bell at Isabella's flat and rings again until she hears a window opening above. Isabella looks down at her, hair bundled in a colored cloth.

"What is the ruckus, Vi? For goodness' sake."

"Izzy, come down."

"Why? What have you got for me?"

"This."

Viola dances the portfolio at her.

Isabella groans and pulls her head inside. A moment later, she appears in the doorway to the building.

"It's practically the middle of the night," she says.

"Izzy, it's ten in the morning. Didn't you get my note?"

Isabella makes a show of squinting up at the winter sun.

"You'd expect better from the dawn." She leads the way towards the bottom of the stairs, her peony-printed robe waving out behind her. "You know," she says and looks back at Viola. "Rosy-fingered and all that."

At the door to the flat, she stands aside as Viola hastens through.

"Good Lord, Vi," she says. "Why on earth are you so—" She searches for a word. "Hearty?"

"I've been to the house," she says. "In Dalmeny Avenue. And I've got photographs."

"And I need tea," Isabella says and flings herself down onto the deep cushions of the settee.

It is clear that Viola is to make the tea, for Isabella has closed her eyes and wrapped her robe around her. In the kitchen, Viola lights the hob and sets the full kettle on the flame. She rummages in cupboards for a tin of biscuits, brings a half dozen out to Izzy on a plate.

"Izzy, you were right. It's incredible, the women there. They are—what did you say?—extreme. And what they've done. My God. I must show you." She spreads the prints out on the low pouf that serves as table. "What do you think? I need a critique. Like in our Slade days."

Isabella glances once, takes a biscuit, and then chews slowly as she sits up to look. Viola recognizes the scrutiny she has welcomed from her friend for years. They set their work out for each other at the Slade—Viola's paintings first, along with Izzy's, and then Viola's photographs to make Izzy sit up as she is now. Viola watches her for signs.

"Come on, then," she says, and Isabella nudges her turban up from her eyes.

"Well, this is interesting," she says finally.

"How?"

"It's the nakedness. Changes everything, doesn't it."

"The *originals* are nudes."

"Yes, but you've done something else here. They sort of flicker."

"Flicker how?" There is no trick of the light here, no sparkle made with something on the enlarger lens, no gelatin smeared for the soft focus Julia Margaret Cameron admires so much.

"Between the classic image and the new thing. This one." Isabella takes up the photograph of Molly as Olympia. "It's that famous Manet, isn't it? I recognize the neck ribbon."

"I used my hatband," Viola says.

"But you look closely and you see this woman has been struck or battered. She's a classic painting, and then, hey presto, she's something very much of our time."

"Exactly." But she senses Isabella is not satisfied. Viola perches by her on the settee and waits for her critique. Isabella lights a cigarette and exhales a puff of smoke. She draws another of the images closer on the pouf. It is a photograph of Abigail posed as Velasquez's Venus. The letters she carved into her chest show in the mirror that she holds.

"You have to look closely, though, don't you?" Isabella says. "If you're not going to think it's just another female nude."

"And that's a problem?"

"A bit. Like these scratches. Are they letters?"

"She cut the word *Vote*. I am working on burning them in darker."

Isabella shudders. A peal comes from the kitchen, the rising wail of the kettle.

"God, make it stop," she says.

Viola goes to the kitchen and snatches the kettle, its wail stopping with a final squeal. She should have known Izzy would find something.

Isabella is still examining the photograph when Viola returns with the teapot.

"It needs to be bolder, Vi."

"Bolder? How? Look at what you're holding, Izzy. The woman carved into her own skin. And I have captured that in my photograph. I've brought it out with the exposure. The same thing here." She waves a hand at Abigail's scars.

Isabella taps her ash into a dish.

"Are you going back?"

"To Dalmeny? I plan to, yes. I have more paintings I want to set."

"Which ones?"

"A Rembrandt Sabine and a Titian. And Botticelli's Venus."

"Botticelli." Isabella claps a hand on the settee. "That's the one."

"I know. I think so too." A laugh floats through her breath and she smiles at this shared discovery. "There's a woman in Dalmeny who is perfect for it."

"You put a hunger striker in that pose—"

"It's hard for that one to be anything but bold," Viola says. She pictures the painter's figure of the goddess, standing at full height and borne shoreward on her strangely large seashell. Any woman who would pose for the photograph would have nowhere to hide, her nakedness on full display. Viola takes a biscuit and curls her legs beneath her on the settee.

"This woman," she says through a full mouth. "Tess. She has a likeness with the Botticelli. But she also has this anger. If I can get her, her photograph will be the best."

Isabella pours out the cups and stirs plenty of sugar into hers.

"Well, good on you, Vi," she says. "I could never do what you're doing. I actually find all this rather horrible."

"What do you mean?"

Isabella holds the cup with both hands and lets the steam rise to her face.

"Hunger strikes, force feeding. Those cuts that poor woman made on her own skin. You can make good art from it. But it's not for me. Too gruesome."

"It needs to be gruesome, Izzy."

"Even the Pankhurst crowd don't like to think about it. They'd rather stick to throwing rocks and bottles. But the starvation. The feeding tubes. It's all horrible."

"But this kind of thing," Viola says, "is what will force Government to give in."

Isabella shouts out a laugh.

"They won't give in, Vi. Men will never choose to share their power. Goodness, is that what you're waiting for?"

"Aren't all of us? Why else do it?"

"We do it because we're finished keeping quiet. That doesn't mean we think we're going to win."

"I think you'd find most suffragettes would disagree with you. You don't get thousands marching in the streets simply for fun."

"Perhaps I'm not a suffragette. Are you?"

"You know I am."

She thinks back to when Edward asked the question, soon after James first introduced them. *My climbing partner, Edward. My friend, Viola. An artist and a suffragette!* Edward had feigned a prudish shock, but he had been interested. Did she believe in such demonstrations? Why did she wish to vote? What did she wish to say with a new freedom? She was surprised the answer had not been self-evident. How could she not want the vote and want to fight for it? Her childhood had taught her she was just as good as any man—as good a painter, as clever at the lessons her father set her at the microscope. Why would she cast that belief aside?

"I don't understand you, Izzy," she says. "You're the one who brought me to the ASL. I wouldn't have met these women in the first place if you hadn't told me they were so important. And now you tell me you don't think we'll ever get the vote."

"I did," Isabella says, sinking into the cushions. "They are. I don't."

"Don't be clever."

"Don't be angry."

"I'm annoyed." *With you*, Viola thinks. "I'm not angry. But I don't understand why *you* are not. Aren't you angry that a woman's husband speaks for her? That she cannot determine her own fate? That if she works, she is paid half what men are paid? I thought if you were part of the ASL, you must agree with all of this."

"Sometimes I do. And sometimes I am too busy working at half-rate to think about it. All this splendor," she sweeps her arm out across the little flat, "doesn't come for free."

"Yet you have time for the ASL."

"If I'm going to be a part of this movement that will never succeed anyway, I'll do so on my own terms." Isabella stubs out her cigarette in a dish.

"It's not just starvation for the sake of it," Viola says. "What these women do is a political act."

"When I first joined the League," Isabella says, "it was all sashes and posters. And then this hunger striking started and the League was in the thick of it. I tell you, Vi, they egg each other on in there, in Holloway. They join in because it's for the cause but before they know it, they're in a race against each other to see who is the most dedicated, who is the most determined to destroy herself for suffrage. It's all steeped in martyrdom. And that, in my opinion, is no way to claim the right to power."

Viola thinks of the way Abigail's emaciated stomach fell away as she lay down for her pose, the hip bone rising like a blade. There was a satisfaction in the young woman's eyes as she lifted her head ever so slightly to peer down at her nakedness. This is what Isabella means, this sense of justice in the deprivation.

"I agree there's something dangerous about it," she says. "But you cannot deny the starvation makes a statement."

Isabella waves the thought away.

"To say what? Look at us. We can endure suffering."

"Consider how important that is. The only suffering we are supposed to endure is childbirth. While when men go off and struggle and starve, we call them heroes."

"At least James and Edward are not starving on purpose."

"And I hope they are not starving at all, Izzy. But when they return and they have skin blackened and lost to frostbite, those marks will be proof of their bravery and their determination." A freighted silence hangs in the air. Viola shakes away the thought of her men wasting away in a frozen land. "The point is, women need to show that they, too, are brave. That they will stop at nothing and that they can do anything."

"Would you do it?" Isabella breaks the silence.

"Do what?"

"Starve, Viola. Would you go on hunger strike in Holloway Prison?"

"I'd have to get arrested first."

"Don't pick nits, Vi. It's a question. Would you, if arrested, go on hunger strike?"

"No. I wouldn't."

"Why not? If it's the way to show you can do anything."

She thinks of Tess' accusation at Dalmeny—that Viola cannot stand for the cause if she has not endured the worst of the struggle. But she knows what it is like to master the world—a small part of it, at least—with her body, legs and arms grasping bare rock to pull her to the top, to move through the air with confidence in her own limbs. She cannot starve herself, not even for this cause that she believes in.

"Because I'm better at photography than I am at starving."

They look at each other and laugh.

"So I reckon," Isabella says, "we neither of us are going to stake our bodies on this."

Viola turns to face her directly, waits until her friend's eyes are on her.

"But, Izzy, I'm committed to this project. If I do this right, these photos will show the power all turned around. It won't be the naked woman who is powerless," she says. "It'll be the man looking at the photograph." She waves her hands around to shape the scene. "He sees an image of a nude woman and he peers in close. He thinks he's looking at beauty, attraction, desire. But then he sees the scars and the damage, and he realizes he's trapped by the woman's stare. It's too late because the woman is doing two things. She's showing him the cruelty of his world, and she's making him the victim."

"You have a plan, then," Isabella says. "I don't know why you had to wake me at the crack of dawn."

"It was ten o'clock," Viola says, and Isabella allows another laugh.

Isabella lights another cigarette and for a while they sit together, smoke coiling around them in the drafty flat. Viola thinks of James and Edward—who would not even be allowed inside the house on Dalmeny. Still, they would both understand the hunger. They understand believing in something so much you whittle yourself away to nothing. They understand the way you feed yourself to it as if into a fire.

At home, Viola sits at the desk in the bedroom and writes a note to Lucy Bellowes.

> *Perhaps it is too soon, but if Tess is recovered, I would come as soon as possible to photograph her as Botticelli's Venus. I can prepare the room while she continues to rest and I will be mindful of her health. I will not burden her overlong.* She adds a line of persuasion. *Tess will make a very striking Venus and I do feel that the effect of that photograph in particular will give much power to the entire collection.*

She sends the note by afternoon post to Number 12 Dalmeny Avenue. She hopes not to exhaust Bellowes' tentative support, but she needs the Botticelli, needs Tess with her yellow hair and that look of exhausted fury on her face. She can already see the exhibition in her mind, with the Botticelli at the center, presiding over the sisterhood of Viola's inspiration.

17

83° 30'S

A shadow forms against the snow, a shape long and low, too low to be a man. A dog, a giant dog. Like something from a fairy tale. The fearsome guardian, eyes large and glowing, muscled haunches beneath sleek fur. The dog with eyes as big as round towers. But where is the tinderbox it guards? Heywoud will find it. Heywoud will shoot the dog and lift the box lid and they will have fuel and fire and hot water for their tea.

The dog is not a dog. It is further away, a bigger thing, and they have traveled close enough to see its size. It is a camp. There is a Union Jack. It is their depot.

Watts' knees go to buckle. He stares at the dark mass until they have labored close enough to see the edges of the wood picked out in rime, the black oilcloth tacked to the hut roof, and the corner where the wind has torn the oilcloth free. No larger than a garden shed, this depot brought in pieces and assembled there in hope to be refound in desperation. They undo their skis and traces. Watts presses against the wall and tugs his mittens off to know the depot is no figment. The textures are a marvel: splintered planks, sleek oilcloth, rime like pebbled leather.

Heywoud tugs at the door but it is blocked by driven snow. Heywoud on hands and knees and Watts beside him. His mittens on again, he digs and scrapes. They stop, lean back against the hut. Breathing scrapes their lungs like sandpaper. Watts lies down on the ice and makes a cushion with his arm. They do not need to go inside. It is enough to think of food they left there weeks ago. Pemmican and biscuit and marmalade. There was a time when there was marmalade. He sees it just the other side of the weather-battered wood. In the hut's dark, a bowl of marmalade glows orange.

Heywoud shakes him, pulls him to his knees. Heywoud digs a hand beneath the door edge and tears up at the wood. He can blow it down. He is a wolf now. He can destroy the depot to get in. Heywoud huffs and puffs through cracked lips and kicks at the door. Watts joins him. He must be useful to survive. They lie on their backs and kick until the door shatters the jamb and they fall back on the hardpack.

They crawl into the hut. Shelves, two crates, a canister of fuel. A lamp suspended from the ceiling. Heywoud lights the stove, attempting thrice with forgetful hands before the depot Primus sputters flame. Tea and lime juice from a tin. Then pemmican and hoosh that slides soft and warm down cracking throats. Here is what they need to stay alive.

The depot is unchanged inside since their departure months before. A battered *Ivanhoe* lies on a shelf where Heywoud left it to take Shakespeare with him to the Pole instead, though never once has Watts seen Heywoud read it. A tin of Bovril holds down a sheet of paper on which Tite left a message for his future self, not knowing he would be dispatched: *Keep on and make your mother proud.* And beneath it Lawrence's looping hand: *Get milk.* There are no signs of Tite and Lawrence on a northbound journey. Watts tells himself this means the men sped past in better health than he and Heywoud. He does not allow the thought that they are lost and dead. Watts folds the note and tucks it in his pocket. If Lawrence lives, they will laugh about the errand he forgot, and if Tite lives he will pretend annoyance. Here there is powdered milk and he and Heywoud stir it into second cups of tea along with cubes of sugar from an iron-banded box. Six for Watts and five for Heywoud. The tea is sweet enough to make his eyes water.

18

25 January

There is a letter from Lucy Bellowes in the next day's post. Viola opens it in the foyer, already smiling at the prospects of the day, but then she lets out a little cry.

"Is it Mr. Edward, ma'am?" Mary says.

"No, Mary."

She reads on. Bellowes is terse. Viola cannot come to Dalmeny. No one can. Constables are arrayed around the house and in adjoining streets on suspicion of a planned attack on Holloway Prison from the women's safe house. She wonders if the women were feigning weakness when she left, if they still had the strength to make themselves a threat even from hiding. She does not doubt the women's power to conspire.

You can imagine, Mrs. Heywoud, that this blockade poses quite a problem. Some of the women here today are quite ill and we cannot obtain provisions for them. You may do as you like with the photographs, and I can only hope that you will use them in service to the movement. But I am afraid all of these disruptions have cost us dearly and we cannot continue your association with us.

Viola's eyes sting at the implication that her visit has to do with this new attention on the house. She knows she was not followed to Dalmeny, and the location of the house is well known already to all the constables who dotted the surrounding streets. She must find a way to show them that her presence there can be a help to them and not a threat.

"Mary."

"Yes, ma'am?"

"I am going out. I'll need my camera case."

"Yes, ma'am."

"And please gather up some bread and cheese for me to take."

While the cab heads north through Mayfair and through Camden Town, she prepares the argument that she will make to Bellowes. While the women are under suspicion, she can move freely, and has brought them provisions that they surely need. There is only one more photograph left for her exhibition, never mind the Titian and the Rembrandt. She will pose Tess as the Botticelli and then she will be finished and will never trouble the safety of Number 12 again. She has to take that one last photograph, needs that image to give context for the rest. With Tess and the Botticelli, her exhibition will give voice to the movement's defiance.

She will not tell Bellowes she is in a hurry, that she cannot wait much longer to complete the set. She will not say she must have everything in place before Edward returns, before the newsmen can think only of the Polar hero and spare little time for the hero's wife. If she is ready, if the collection is prepared and hanging in a gallery, Edward will have no choice but to understand. Her involvement with the cause, the nudity, the stinging challenges she mounts to the very world he wishes to return to—all of it. He cannot stop her if the thing is already done.

In her haste, she tells the driver the exact address rather than conceal it, but as he turns the corner from the Holloway Road into Dalmeny Avenue, he brings the motorcar to a sudden stop. A constable steps out into the street and signals, palm out, baton at his side.

"This is as far as I go," the driver says. "You getting out?"

Number 12 is quiet, but she thinks she sees a curtain pulled back in the front window. Someone is there who surely will agree to speak to her. Someone will take the basket of provisions she has brought.

"I'm getting out," she says.

She wrangles the camera case and the basket out onto the pavement. The constable calls out to her.

"Where you going?"

"Just there, constable."

"Nobody goes in. Nobody comes out. Orders."

She moves past him, ignoring the baton that he will surely not use in so calm a moment. As she reaches the path through the small front garden, a second constable steps in front of her.

"Nobody," he says.

The door opens and Lucy Bellowes stands in the narrow gap.

"Mrs. Heywoud, go away."

"Mrs. Bellowes! Please let me in."

The constable comes closer.

"You go in, you don't come out again," he says.

"Do you hear, Mrs. Bellowes? I am willing to come in. And I have brought some things for you. Some bread and cheese."

"We will not have you here, Mrs. Heywoud, and we certainly cannot keep you."

"This is not my fault. Let me come speak to you."

"We have nothing to discuss," Bellowes says. "And can you not see your presence here this moment puts us in even greater danger? Please take your things and return home." She seems ready to say more but then purses her lips and makes a tiny nod before closing the door. Viola watches the house for some sign of greeting or regret but the curtains remain still.

"Sorry," the constable says.

She glares at him but sees he is sincere.

"I can help you with that," he says. "What you got in here? A body?"

He tugs the case to the corner of the Holloway Road and stays with her until she hails a cab. All the way home, she burns with humiliation at the scene that plays over in her mind. The door to Number 12 barely open to her as if she bore contagion, Bellowes pressing her lips together in distaste, the constables wincing in compassion. Even their kindness now echoes for her as a pity she rejects. Again her face heats with the shame of it and she realizes now that she can never return to Dalmeny Avenue. She must forget Tess. And yet Viola needs a photo of the Botticelli. The birth of a new Venus, defiant and strong. She must find another model, and she is loth to delay completion of the project. But if it cannot be the body of a hunger striker, then who can portray the defiance and resistance that she must evoke?

The idea comes with a shiver as she arrives at Margaretta Terrace. Why not photograph herself? Why not take the role for herself of the new woman born into this new world? She is, after all, a suffragette like them. If it is true they are in the same fight, then does Viola not belong among them? She calls for Miner to return the camera case to the darkroom, and she goes upstairs and begins to shunt aside the bedroom's smaller furnishings. The armchair and side table go against the windows and the desk chair goes to a far corner. She brings the Midg out from the wardrobe and sets it on the other side table she has now turned into a tripod. The shutter cord reaches across the room, long enough for her purposes. What remains is to fashion the backdrop as if she were in Dalmeny Avenue. The fire screen will do, and a sheet tugged from the bed. There is enough blank wall between the wardrobe and the bedroom door for her to work with. She sets the pleated screen against the wall as Botticelli's giant scallop shell. The bedsheet wrinkles beneath it to suggest the beach and the chair rail of the wainscoting will serve as the horizon line of waves. Her composition will dispense with the figures to the left and right of Botticelli's goddess. There is no zephyr here, there are no nymphs. There will simply be Viola standing naked.

She surveys the scene she has created and winces at its fabricated nature. In Dalmeny, the starkness of the little overheated room gave the impression of a stage set. The contrivances of sheets and cushions seemed in keeping with the mood. Here, in Viola's own room fully outfitted, her preparations have an amateurish look. For a moment, the entire project seems like playacting, the foolish indulgence of a woman too timid for the battles of the actual world. If that is true, then she must be even braver. It falls to Viola—to her naked body itself—to give the photograph the power it must have.

She undresses, laying her clothes on the armchair she has pushed into the corner. With the camera facing her on the table, Viola is conscious of her nudity—her navel that knots outwards, her knees that come to narrow points, the swayed violin shape of her waist and hips. She has been so long away from the mountains and the fells that her body has lengthened. There is more grace to it now than strength.

She takes up the shutter bulb and steps into place before the fire screen. Like the Venus in the painting, she leans slightly towards her left, her right arm across her breasts, her left over her pubic hair. She holds the bulb in her right hand, with the cord trailing around behind her and then along the carpet to the camera. If Tess were sitting for the image, Viola would use the woman's golden locks as a screen for her modesty, just as in the painting. Her own hair is too short to offer cover. She turns her head to stare her camera down. She thinks of the photographs she has already taken, of the women's deeper anger she discovered only in the darkroom. Where is Viola's own anger? She looks at the center of the lens where the glass goes dark. She sends her thoughts past indignation at the limits on a woman's freedom, beyond the injustices of the day, to the aches that fuel her heart. Yes, she is angry. Angry at Edward and James for leaving her behind, at the dawning knowledge they will never again be equals. She is angry, too, at Edward for all the ways he tries to save her when she craves a risk. And she is angry at Bellowes and the house that would not let her in. She glares at the black circle of the lens as if to say to anyone who will see the photo on a gallery wall *you cannot keep me quiet, you cannot hold me back from the ends I seek. Here. Look. This is me alone, and my own power is all that I require.* She squeezes the shutter bulb hard enough to crush it.

That night she writes a letter to Charles Aitken at Whitechapel Gallery. She sits at the desk in the bedroom, moved into its proper place now that her camera is put away. *I have some photographs that I am sure will interest you.* She tells Aitken that she studied at the Slade and that she can bring the images in two days—a decision she makes as she writes the words—and signs the note Mrs. Edward Heywoud. He will recognize the name. She taps the envelope against her palm, watches the ink's silver dull as it dries. Should she at least wait until she has developed everything and printed the final perfect images before she writes to him? No, she has little time to squander, with Edward surely on his northbound journey now. Let her ambition send the note out like a grappling hook and she will pull herself along it.

19

83° 29'S

In the depot, Heywoud sits upright in his sleeping bag, writing in his log. If Tite and Lawrence live, will Watts be weak enough to lie to them? To say that he and Heywoud reached an unclaimed Pole, that they found the Norwegians dead with their flag tucked atop their sledge?

"Can you do it?" Watts says.

"Do what?"

"Go ahead with saying we were first."

"I have to," Heywoud says.

"You can still tell the truth, Edward."

"Leave it, Watts," he says, continuing to write.

"I won't say anything about what happened with the other flag."

Heywoud claps the log shut on his pencil.

"Will you stop? Do you think the men's widows want to know they died for nothing? How does it make their lives better, to know that we failed?"

"Edward, we can't lie."

"That's rich, James, coming from you. How many times did you look me in the face on the same day that you'd slept with my wife? How many times did you come straight from her bed to meet me?"

"This is more important. This is history, not our little lives."

"My life isn't little to me. And even if we wanted to give it to Nilsen, we can't. We have no photograph of his flag."

Watts sees again and hears the shattering of the glass and wood against the sledge rail and the look of shock and fury on Heywoud's face at the swing of his own arm.

"Edward," Watts says, "if you just tell the truth and let me have my photographs, I will leave her. I will refuse to see her ever again."

Heywoud lunges at him.

"You have the gall to offer my wife to me. You bastard."

Heywoud throws him to the floor and his breath is rank on Watts' face. He swings at Watts with fists softened by mittens but the blows still land solid on his head. Watts lets himself be shaken against the depot's canvas floor, and the thought crosses his mind that Heywoud will succeed in killing him. When he punches back, Heywoud falls away. He rises slowly to his feet and pulls his goggles on. With eyes blackened to coals by the slit glass, he turns to face Watts from the door.

"Don't you ever talk to me of honesty. You're not the good man here."

Heywoud lets the broken depot door clap shut behind him and Watts watches the shadows play upon the wall as the lantern sways. Five minutes pass, then ten. Watts steps outside and the wind strips him of his hood. The sun dazzles him blind. He has come out without goggles. He scans the hardpack through his fingers and cannot see Heywoud anywhere. He shouts. Heywoud comes around the back side of the hut.

"I took a crap," he says. "The wonders of a good meal. My ass is numb."

When Watts returns inside, he finds the lantern extinguished and Heywoud lying in his bag.

"Know this, Watts. I'll kill you anytime I want. You are only alive because I need your help to haul."

The hut smells of acetylene from the lantern fuse. Saying nothing, Watts pushes into his own bag, the fur already frozen stiff from his brief absence. How could Heywoud get in his so quickly? The bag must be stiff as a coffin now and Heywoud willing it to thaw before he freezes.

20

1 February

The weather is fine for the first day of February, so Viola walks to Sloane Square with her portfolio of prints from Dalmeny Avenue beneath her arm. She takes the Underground and climbs the narrow stairs up to Whitechapel Road. But she can barely leave the station. A market packs the pavement with stalls and awnings. Every gap between the stalls is filled with shoppers, carts, and hawkers. The air is thick with smells—of dried fish and roasting corn and charcoal braziers—and alive with shouts for jellied eels and onions and fresh eggs. A boy skims his finger over a canary's head. A woman selling tiny roots like human figures knots a red scarf at her throat. Reality's particulars. If she had brought her Brownie she would take those very images now.

She grips the portfolio tight and plunges into the throng until she comes to the end of the market. There where the crowd has thinned, she goes on past shopfronts and a pub and finally reaches the Gallery. The building dominates the street, in yellow stone far brighter than the grim brick of its neighbors. A large archway forms its entrance, set off to one side as if to mock the notion of a center in this modern time. Two wide doors open directly to the pavement with no fence or rail to keep the people out. Viola straightens the portfolio under her arm and goes inside. She expects the hush of a museum but instead finds groups of people in loud conversation before large paintings on the lobby walls. Landscapes and farming scenes, a woman bracing her back from the ache of harvest. The visitors point and comment and jostle each other aside. It is little different from the clamor of the market.

A hatless woman in a colored waistcoat crosses towards her from a desk and asks to help.

"I have an appointment with Charles Aitken," Viola says, raising her voice over the din. "It's quite loud," she says.

The woman smiles.

"We don't follow conventions here at the Gallery," she says. "We believe art is a part of daily life. Our visitors can speak freely."

She leads the way down a book-lined corridor to Aitken's office, where he rises from behind a heavy desk. Viola has glimpsed Aitken across a room at the Slade, but only now does she see how tall he is, how his long nose and longer chin together with that height give the impression of a long-legged bird. He wears pince-nez with a chain that loops to his lapel. When he removes them after taking her hand in greeting, Viola sees the mark on the bridge of his nose from years of peering through the small glass ovals.

"I am honored, Mrs. Heywoud. Though I confess I am a bit puzzled as to why you would choose us."

"I'm sorry?"

"For your husband's portrait, yes? When he returns?"

She notes his choice of *when*. Since he thinks she offers what he wants, he plays the optimist.

"That is not actually why I've come," she says.

"Good heavens." He puts the pince-nez on his nose again, searches his desk for a notation. "Have I made an error?"

"Perhaps I was not clear in my letter," she says, though she knows she was deliberately vague.

He motions her to sit, then notices the portfolio Viola places at her feet.

"I assumed you had a photographic portrait of your husband and for some reason wished it to hang here and not at the Portrait Gallery. I was all set to deter you."

"Mr. Aitken, I was a student at the Slade. Professor Brown knows me as Viola Colfax. You may have seen some images of mine lately in the *Observer*." He shows no sign of recognition. "I am a photographer," she says, "and I admire the mission of the Gallery. I have some photographs that I hope you will exhibit."

"Ah."

In that syllable and in the way he lets himself fall deeper into the cushion of his chair Aitken tells her everything. He believes her to be an amateur, a lady photographer who wanders parks and picnics with a Brownie. He has not listened to her talk of the Slade and Brown, but heard only her request, her statement that she needs something from him.

"I'm certain, Mr. Aitken, you'll see that they fit with your work here."

She reaches for the portfolio. But now she thinks of the Botticelli and cannot bring herself to add her naked form to the collection. What if the image cancels out the others rather than make the stronger point?

"May I?" she says.

"Of course."

She brings it to his desk where stacks of books vie for space with piles of paper. She waits until he clears a spot on the leather blotter and she opens the portfolio. The images are upside down for her as if she were looking through the camera. Right side up for Aitken. The first is of Eliza. He sets the pince-nez on his nose and bends over the print and then pulls back. He clears his throat and glances at Viola and then looks at the print again.

When he speaks, he sounds vaguely irritated.

"This is intended to be like Ingres?" he says. He removes the pince-nez.

"Yes," she says. "The odalisque."

"I see. And instead this is—" He looks to her for a reply.

"A hunger striker who was released from Holloway."

"Ah," Aitken says again, but this time he bends closer to the photograph. "An injury," he says.

"Her ribcage was bruised while she was held down. To be fed."

He lets out a sigh of disapproval—of Eliza or of her jailers?—and turns to the next print, of Abigail as Rokeby Venus, with the contrast adjusted to emphasize the letters she carved into her chest. Viola waits.

"Are those letters—" He trails off.

"Yes, she cut them into herself."

He looks up at her.

"*Votes for women*," she says. "It was to say *Votes for women*."

The shock of it seems to make him curious, and he reaches for the pack of prints on his desk and fans them apart like so many cards. Molly, Florence, Anne, and Margaret Lyons, each of them bearing obvious wounds and bruises.

"I can see that your collection intends to make a case, Mrs. Heywoud. But we are concerned here with art, not advocacy."

"These photographs are modeled on paintings by Ingres, Velasquez, Titian. Surely you would call those art."

"But you aim to persuade the viewer about suffrage, do you not?"

"All the best art is persuasive in some way."

"The best art is universal in its message. Years from now, the cause of suffrage might well be forgotten and these photographs will have nothing more to tell us."

"If my work becomes irrelevant that will mean suffrage has succeeded."

He gives her an indulgent smile.

"There I cannot believe you, Mrs. Heywoud. You strike me as a young woman who would never wish her work to be irrelevant."

Viola's cheeks grow hot but she continues.

"What you do here in Whitechapel Gallery is political," she tells him. "You open doors to the poor. You depict modern forms and modern images. Do you not support the suffrage movement, Mr. Aitken?"

"We are a public institution, Mrs. Heywoud. I rely on Parliament for my funds and there are many in Parliament who oppose your cause." She begins a challenge but he raises a hand. "Regardless of my own views," he says, "I must not irritate my sponsors, or else the gallery will have to close."

"You aim to be of the current moment. These photographs speak to the current moment."

"We also aim to stay within the Academy," he says, and she lets her exasperation out in a burst of air. "We look for draftsmanship," he goes on, "technique."

"I have technique, sir. As I said, I have trained at the Slade and I can assure you I know how to work with light and shadow and with all the manipulations of the modern darkroom."

He has settled into his opinions. He has reached a point from which it will be easier to go back than to go forward. She must pull him on. She takes the photograph of Abigail and flips it onto the desk.

"Mr. Aitken, what you're seeing here is already around you. These," she slaps her palm down on the images, "are from a prison that all England reads of in the papers. Everywhere is anger and pain and women clamoring for what they want."

She stops to catch her breath. He does not rush to silence her.

"It's there," she goes on. "So we must photograph it. If you exhibit these, people will pack your galleries. I know it. Do you not see what these photographs do, Mr. Aitken? For centuries, women have appeared in men's paintings as nothing more than objects to be stared at. Naked, passive, doing nothing more than simply being beautiful. Look at the women in my photographs. They are the ones in control here. They use their bodies to claim power, to claim a voice. They've fought a battle, sir, and they are proud to show their wounds."

"Well," Aitken says with a little shake of the head as if a gust of wind has blown. "You are quite persuasive, Mrs. Heywoud."

"Then you'll take them?"

He tips his head. The pince-nez catch the light and for a moment she cannot find his eyes.

"I'm afraid not. And you yourself have given me the reason. These works, compelling though they are, are indeed political. I cannot take the Gallery in that direction."

He leans back in his chair to dismiss her. As if her photographs were not there at all, not spread out on his desk, not humming of where they might soon hang upon the gallery walls. She might try Grafton Gallery to see if Fry will take the work. But she does not want Fry with his academy and scholarship. She wants Whitechapel Gallery, where Gertler and Bomberg had their show.

"Wait," she says. "There is one more photograph I can show you."

"Please," he says with a sigh. "Go on."

She pulls the Botticelli from the pack.

"I was to use another model for the pose. But I was unable to photograph her. The police cut off access to the hunger strikers' safe house. Only a doctor can go in."

"Mrs. Heywoud, are you going to let me see it?"

He holds his hand out, waiting. She hesitates to set the photo out, but knows that she has saved the best for last.

She lays the Botticelli gently on the desk and braces for Aitken's reaction. He returns to his chair and makes a little gasp. His eyes widen and she can see he fights the urge to snap his gaze to her. She bites her cheek to keep from saying something as his face turns dark red. He removes the pince-nez and looks neither at the photo nor at her. Viola's own discomfort lessens as she watches Aitken's. His gaze skids off her face and darts over the bookcases that line the wall, as if he has walked into the office and surprised Viola herself undressed.

"Mrs. Heywoud," he says finally, "this is you."

"It is."

"I know the pose, of course."

He hums and Viola assumes he requires convincing.

"The Botticelli Venus is an essential statement of female beauty," she says. "It shows you how to read the exhibition. It tells you I am turning conventional views about women on their heads. It's aggressive and it's a confrontation."

"I see." He leans forward. "Now we have something to discuss." He looks at her. "You are a brave woman, Mrs. Heywoud."

"These hunger strikers are brave, Mr. Aitken."

"No," he says. "You stand here and show me a photograph—not even a painting, ma'am, or a watercolor, but a photographic image—of yourself nude. There are few women of society who would do such a thing."

"I don't take your meaning, Mr. Aitken."

"Simply that I am impressed. And that I believe that you have missed the very point of your own work."

"I do not need you to tell me what my art means to say, Mr. Aitken."

"Well, I would observe only that your exhibition says much more with the inclusion of this photograph." He taps a finger on the print. "You see, with you in the collection, it's no longer about suffrage. It is about how you have made yourself both object of the art *and* its creator. It is about you."

"It is not about me," Viola says, but she is lying. Aitken says aloud what her own thoughts have murmured. "It is about the cause. And I have not suffered like the others for it."

"But here," he waves a hand over the prints arrayed on the desk, "you establish a connection, a solidarity, between the hunger strikers and you, a well-to-do woman. You show us Venus, the very ideal of female beauty, now turned into a fighter. With you in the photograph and not some anonymous model, you tell us that women will not be passive—as you yourself said—but in control of their own lives."

"I promised the women of the Artists Suffrage League that my photographs would help the cause."

He shrugs. He gives her a smile and it is all she can do not to reveal her growing hope.

"If you only use hunger strikers," he says, "the collection is about them. It would be an exhibition one could easily dismiss. *Ah, hunger strikers, poor souls. Ah, hunger strikers, hideous women.* Either way, your collection would be about this group in particular. But if you include yourself, the collection becomes something else entirely. It is about *women.*" He stresses the word. "And it says exactly what you want it to say."

She waits a moment. Aitken speaks of her as an artist. He champions the power of her work. He sees that she has something she wishes to express.

"You will accept the collection?"

"Yes, I will," he says, and he tips back in his chair. "You can make your political statement, Mrs. Heywoud. And I can have my art."

Her excitement sweeps away any lingering modesty. She will be exposed on the gallery wall. But she is indeed to have an exhibition—exactly what she wished for. Her name will be on the posters for the Whitechapel Gallery. They will speak about it at the Slade and in all the other galleries in London. She will catch Gertler and Bomberg and she will far surpass them. She allows a smile to spread on her face.

"Do we have an agreement, then?" he says.

"We do."

He brings his chair down square to the floor.

"Well. All right, then, Mrs. Heywoud. We will mount your exhibition."

She holds back the relief that threatens to burst out of her.

"When might that be?" she says.

"I have a schedule to adhere to. We have Twenty Years of British Art coming up." He waves a hand. "Fry, Burns, Sargent. That lot."

All men. And all of them painting characters from myths and ballads. Even Aitken does not sound particularly interested in what they have to offer.

"And when will that be finished?"

"Not until the middle of May. We can mount your collection after that. Shall we say June?" He consults a calendar on his blotter. "The twentieth."

"That is so far away."

"I have commitments I cannot break, Mrs. Heywoud. I imagine your husband will have returned by then?"

Viola looks up sharply at him to see: is this what he is counting on? He busies himself shuffling a sheaf of stationery and standing it up in its wooden rack. He is pretending he does not much mind which way she answers.

"That is our expectation," Viola says. "Yes."

"Well," he says. He gives her a bright smile. "That will be a lovely boost to our attendance."

Even for her own exhibition, Viola must share the stage with Edward. Even now Aitken considers her the explorer's wife. What if there came a time when Edward was known through her? Edward Heywoud, husband to the photographer Viola Colfax.

She agrees to meet Aitken again in June. The date is so distant—three months away—she cannot quite believe it will arrive. He walks with her into the corridor and Viola goes on alone to the lobby where she comes to a sudden stop. Somewhere here, somewhere in this white-walled room, her images will hang. The space will be entirely hers. Her photographs will glow like windows to a surrounding world. One day in June, she will stand here with Edward and with James and she will watch them take it in. Her place, her creation, her Pole.

21

78° 10'S

They heave the sledge over a ridge of ice angled so sharply that they fear their skis will snap. Each time they cross a ridge, the skis become brief bridges, tips and tails resting on frozen snow, center and all the weight atop their boots suspended in air. Hours ago they entered the sastrugi, frozen ripples whipped from the hardpack by the winds that beat the sea ice. It is a sign they need no sextant to confirm. Shore Camp is near. Embarking on their journey months ago, they went from shape to shape like beachcombers—here is one like an anvil, here another like a baby carriage. Tite had teased Lawrence for the home life that awaited him. You'll look down into that pram and see the milkman's face. Now Watts is sure the ridges have grown in their absence, the peaks steeper, the troughs deeper. And every photograph he took is now an anchor. He could have left the negatives where he made them, one by one, a trail of glass to follow from their wilderness of cold.

Heywoud descends the north side of a ridge so high that Watts cannot see him. The sledge rests on the south slope nearly upended and Watts leans all his weight upon the rail to keep it from gliding back. Heywoud's mittened hands appear and seize the runner tips. Watts cannot hear what he is saying, but he lifts the stern as he feels Heywoud pull down on the bow. The sledge teeters on the tip of a sastrugus. The ice at the peak of the ridge crunches beneath the weight and this is lucky for the sledge will slow. Watts clambers crab-like along the sledge, never letting go, until he joins Heywoud on the north side and together they guide the dead weight down. When he has regained his breath, Watts raises head and shoulders from the ice. Sastrugi stretch ahead of them for miles.

They see a ragged flock of birds in the far distance. Watts thinks he dreams but sees in Heywoud's face the proof of waking. Heywoud climbs a ridge and fires the gun into the air. He is laughing. He looks down at Watts and laughs. These are the first living creatures he and Heywoud have seen since Dagger and they herald the society of men. Watts watches the gun, waits for it to point at him. Now Heywoud will shoot. Now that he knows he is already safe.

Four men ski from Shore Camp to find them. Not Tite, not Lawrence. Watts and Heywoud are made mute by their fatigue. They lie on an empty sledge brought by these four to ferry them. Their heads judder across the smaller ridges of the ice-sheet edge, their eyes stare at the seabirds' dart and wheel. Watts makes Not-Lawrence and Not-Tite understand he wants to take a photograph. They stop the sledge and follow his instructions to produce the camera. In his hands, it feels a stone. Five days have passed since he last placed his eye behind the lens. He frames the sledges, Heywoud standing, the men kneeling on either side. In the photograph, Heywoud will be a blur from the sway of his exhaustion.

Rectangles of black against the white. One large, two small, and smaller shapes like errant marks of paint across a canvas. Then three more men beside the sledges, then Lawrence near him but not Tite. Lawrence limps with Lulu at his heels to tuck a shoulder beneath Heywoud's arm. A man whose name he has forgotten helps him down, says something to him. All Watts can think to do is ask him for some tea.

22

2 March

Viola pours developer into her timing tank and sees the jug is nearly empty. She must visit the chemist soon for powders to mix into the solution. She could send Miner, but she prefers to do the errand with him, to be sure the chemist pours and sifts correctly. For now, she has enough developer for one more batch of plates, a group of seconds, as she thinks of them, images she knew were not quite right. The model moving as the shutter closed, a drape or cushion tipping out of proper composition. She will prepare them just in case. There may be something in the error that will now seem intriguing, something interesting that was before unseen.

She loads the timing tank with its dozen plates and sets to rocking the thing gently back and forth. Little waves slosh inside the metal and she closes her eyes to the ruby light and sees a ship on zephyr-gentle seas.

Mary shouts outside the darkroom's double doors and Viola nearly knocks the timing tank from the workbench.

"What is it, Mary?"

"Ma'am, you must come out."

"Hang on," she calls.

"Ma'am, it's a telegram. Please, ma'am." Mary sounds as though she is crying.

"Don't open the door," Viola shouts, and yet she wants to fling it open and rush out. Her hands tremble but she forces them to rock the time tank gently until the timer counts to zero. She pours the liquid from the built-in spout and sets the tank back onto the counter. She can barely breathe.

"Please, ma'am." Mary is sobbing.

"Did you read it?"

"No. Please come out."

Viola leans back against the high workbench in the darkroom, reaches behind her, switches off the ruby light. She stands in darkness. She hears her own breath and the creaking of her leather apron and, through the baize-covered panel and the outer door of oak, the muffled sound of Mary's sniffle. Tears rise. She looks around her at the absolute darkness of the tiny room and lets herself lose sense of up and down, floor and ceiling. She floats. She hangs. This is the last moment in which she will not know the answer to the questions she has asked for months. Are they safe? Are they both safe? If only one, which one? And the one question she does not think that she can ever answer: if only one, which would she choose?

She claps a hand over her mouth.

Mary whispers.

"Ma'am, are you all right? Are you coming out?"

Viola closes her eyes, to be for a moment longer both up and down, widow and wife and lover, artist and subject, camera and image. She finds the doorknob in the darkness. She squints in the corridor light but does not need to see for Mary thrusts the envelope into her hand. The paper is thick, the flap stiff. She pinches the telegram between thumb and forefinger. She slides the paper out, unfolds it, reads.

WE HAVE WON THE POLE. ALL SAFE AND SOUND.

DEPART LYTTELTON 7 MARCH. DARLING HOME SOON.

Viola reads and reads again.

"Ma'am?"

"They are alive," she says. *All safe* it says.

"Did they reach the Pole?" Miner is standing on the stairs.

"Yes, Samuel." She looks up at him and laughs. "They did."

Miner makes a growling noise and squeezes a fist.

"Good man," he says.

Viola reads the telegram again and catches the sob that rises in her throat. Only now she understands the worry that has hung over her for months. Only as it lifts does she sense how thick the pall of fear that has wrapped around her, fear that she would be widowed, orphaned again by this new loss, that she would be left utterly alone. Once more she reads the telegram, the words typed onto tapes pasted across the paper. *All safe.* What does he mean? Surely Edward has not brought back every man and dog. Some creature has perished, surely, or has returned unsound. Viola sees a team of men maimed like Miner descending the gangplank to the shocked throngs of Cardiff harbor. Edward would tell her if James had not survived. He would send a second telegram.

She imagines him at the post office, ceiling fans batting away the high summer of the southern port, printing out his message, blushing as he adds the final line. The telegram clerk's mustered seriousness as he reads back for correction—*Darling home soon*—the telegram an awkward billet-doux between two strangers, clerk and customer. Edward has included one admission of his private life: darling. Could he not have added one more? Could he not have said "James and I both safe and sound"? Is James no different to him than the men and dogs he labels *all*?

"When did he send this?" Miner asks, and Viola darts her eyes over the paper. Top left corner: 2 March 14:02. She laughs. It is just past 9:00 in London. He has sent it from the future.

She cannot fathom this, when for more than thirteen months their lives have been measured not by pages in a calendar but the distance on a map. How many miles to the southern continent, how many to the Pole, how many degrees latitude must they be crawling every day. How many miles could one man ski in a day? Edward told her before he left. But what knowledge did he have save from rehearsals in Svalbard and Alpine plateaus? He gave a number as if Antarctica were a machine and he could work it.

"How long, Samuel, until they're back?"

"They say it takes three months, ma'am. I've never made a crossing like that."

Miner's crossing was to France, and then by train to Chamonix. When he crossed back months after the Mont Blanc climb people stared or looked away.

"June," she says.

This is when Viola weeps. The word sends her thoughts ahead to Cardiff's Bute Dock and summer heat and the cling of muslin to her back. No breeze finds her through the crowd pressing behind her, all come to wave their flags for the explorers. She spies them at the rail. Both. Their faces are creased like shoe leather but they are whole and strong.

"It's all right, ma'am," Mary says. "The time'll go fast."

She must answer Edward. It has been more than a year since she received a letter from him, sent home with the depot ship soon after they reached ice. Her messages to both the men fill notebooks she has stuffed into the backs of dresser drawers.

"What time is it?" she says. From the cuff of her sleeve she pulls a handkerchief and blows her nose.

Miner consults a pocket watch.

"Half nine," he says. He holds that secret object of his in his other hand and slips it back into his pocket.

"I need to send an answer," she says.

The timing tank in the darkroom is secure and the glass negatives safe in their holders. She fumbles behind her for the apron strings, the thick paper of the telegram crackling in her fist.

"Mary, fetch a book for me."

"Which one?"

"It doesn't matter." She is halfway up the stairs with Mary trailing. "It must simply look as though I'm going visiting."

All the stately passage of hours and days and now this rush, this exhilaration of haste. It matters not at all to her that her message will likely miss the man or men it goes to, that her words of love will reach a telegraph office in New Zealand as her husband's ship leaves port for home. She must send her message all the same. She is glad for the urgency, glad to enter the cresting stream of seconds and minutes and to leave behind the track of endless miles. But *June*. Three months. It is so soon and it is hardly enough time. They will arrive, she realizes, within days of her exhibition's opening. James will appreciate the work, but she sees Edward shocked and fuming.

Viola puts on coat and hat and gloves and strides through the front door, taking Beaufort Street to the post office on the King's Road. She pulls her hat down low lest she be recognized and questioned. Should someone ask, she can invent a relative whose ill-health must be told to distant family. She knows the shock of such a message.

The clerk slips her a paper on which she must write down her name and Edward's and the message she desires to send. An address is required. She draws from her bag Edward's telegram, unfolds it, and copies the address: Lyttelton Telegraph Office Norwich Quay Lyttelton Canterbury New Zealand. *Dear Edward,* she begins, and cannot continue. Dear Edward, how is James? Did you protect him from the cold? Dear Edward, I am so happy for you. Darling, I cannot wait for your return. Dear Edward, I long to see you. Dear James, I ache for you. Dear James and Edward, boys, come back to me.

DEAR EDWARD. I AM SO HAPPY YOU ARE BOTH SAFE

AND I COUNT THE DAYS UNTIL YOU ARE HOME AGAIN.

I AM VERY PROUD. VIOLA.

She slides the paper back across to the clerk.

"Do you want to keep the extra words?"

"Beg pardon?"

"Extras. Like the *I*s and *You*s."

Viola hears letters not words, vowels she cannot spare.

"Of course," she says. "All of it. Just as I wrote it."

The clerk shrugs and taps a pencil to the words one at a time, murmuring, counting. Their meaning is of no interest to him.

"That'll be one shilling and seven pence."

A small sum though Lyttelton is so far away. She pays the clerk.

"When will it arrive there?"

"Right away. Long as the post office is open."

She points to the address.

"Southern hemisphere," she says when he returns an empty look. Viola sees the clerk does not know Lyttelton. Surely he knows New Zealand.

Viola calculates her message will arrive near midnight. Will it catch them? Let their ship await a favorable morning tide and let a telegraph boy in New Zealand find Edward at his lodging, at a desk, with expedition logs laid out before him.

On her walk home, she waits to let a tram pass and sees a newsagent's hoarding pasted with a new front page. An extra edition. HEROES RETURN FROM POLE. HEYWOUD VICTORIOUS. She stops on the pavement barely aware of jostles. She cannot take her eyes away. It is a photograph she knows, taken of James and Edward when they left, arms clapped on shoulders, hands raised to wave, and their faces smiling with the joy of embarkation. Viola has let out a cry, it seems, for two women turn towards her. She catches a flicker of recognition in their eyes, and then a man points. A crowd forms from nowhere and begins to call her name and Edward's. She should have realized. She was a fool to think hers was the only telegram from Edward. He will have sent one, of course, to the Royal Geographical Society and no doubt even to someone at Harrods. She turns for home, but as she reaches Margaretta Terrace, a group of men come rushing towards her. Newsmen. They press around her and a flash pan ignites so close that she can smell the powder burning. She pushes on towards the house. "Mrs. Heywoud! Mrs. Heywoud," they shout over one another. She hears a litany of *hey, hey, hey*.

She rushes past the house to the Embankment and leans out over the wall as if to hide behind it. Below her is the gray murk of the river where a breeze blows against the ebbing tide. Freshets curl back against skiffs and tenders that ride the current. She thinks of that photograph of James and Edward waving, of how the ship sailed on a rising tide that day more than a year ago in Wales. She could have sailed with them then, as far as New Zealand, or even simply joined for one week's travel to Madeira where they made their first port. Edward did not invite her, fearing for her safety should there be storms. Nor did she ask, already sensing there was more adventure for her here in London than as the captain's wife on board a ship. Now she wishes she could join the other way, meet in Tenerife or Rio, to reach them sooner, to see them with the tinny air of the Antarctic in their breath, fresh from their conquest.

But this is folly. How can she meet them both together after all these many months? How can she speak to them when she still holds the secret she has kept from Edward all this time? Is it a secret still? She could tell Edward the truth now with a new telegram. She could warn him he returns to an unfaithful wife. She flushes at the thought of such bold honesty. But James will bear the brunt of her confession now. She imagines Edward in New Zealand, her telegram crushed in a fist, declaring he will abandon James forever on the world's far side. She sees the ship sailing for home and James forlorn and shameful, lost to her as Edward will be too with this new knowledge. So many months together on the ice, they have a tighter bond than hers with either. They return to her as different men from when they left and she does not even know the changes. What if neither man wants her now? What if she has held to them both so tight that in Antarctica the traces snapped and she is the one left on a separate shore alone?

23

32° 37'N

Watts holds a halyard and the ship bucks beneath him. The others rush to the bow to see the green bluffs of Madeira swim up from the swells. Gray clouds snag at the peaks. The port city of Funchal clings to what little flat land there is between shore and headland. Red-tiled roofs surround the white and gray stucco tower of a cathedral. There are colors here. Watts has seen only the blues and blue-grays of the sea these seventeen weeks. Salt crystals coat his palm and he thinks for a moment they are ice and that he only dreams the ship and waves and smell of sweat from men working in hot weather.

Heywoud and the men will go ashore—Heywoud to buy provisions and to send another telegram, the men to fuck and drink. But Watts' legs are useless for land now, and useless for sea, too. He has given up what muscle he had left on this last journey. He possesses only bones and skin and when he walks on deck and lets go of a halyard or a cleat, his limbs jerk as if dangled by a master's string. At night when he lets trousers fall from too-thin hips, he sees hair returning to the patches where the traces rubbed him raw. He is not certain if this pleases him. What does he have now to show for nearly two years' journey but these marks upon his body? As they have sailed north, Heywoud has again grown solid. He buttons his waistcoat now in front of Watts and Watts can see the buttons pulling at the cloth. Watts is a ghost. Too strong a gust sweeping from Funchal's mountains could send him over the rail into the sea. How many times as they sailed around Africa's point and up along its western edge did he grip stays when others—even Lawrence with his limp—strolled the decks? How many times did he remain below for fear the wind would catch him? Watts lay in his berth ignoring bells for breakfast, lunch, and dinner, listening instead for the wind's whisper: *Thief*, it said. *Liar*. But not *coward*. A coward would eat. A coward would take ease from what was offered.

Heywoud returns from port next day with provisions for the final week of sailing. Watts sits on the bulkhead and watches hungover men load baskets of oranges, lemons, and limes into the hold. Eggs nestled in straw. Rabbits in crates. Cuts of beef wrapped in oilcloth and packed in ice. Bottles of port from this very place. Bile rises in Watts' throat to see it all, the stuff of dreams within their Polar tent. Over these chops and loins he and Heywoud clacked their teeth in frozen sleep. At these limes and lemons they pursed their lips. Watts watches a sailor lift a rot-brown lemon from the crate and toss it overboard. On the ice it would have made a meal of days.

At dinner Heywoud lifts the rule he set at Shore Camp. From now on Watts is to have full rations. And have a bit of shandy, James, he says. You need it for your teeth. Watts runs his tongue over his smile and feels the canines shift. Scurvy. He declines. He rises from the table. Heywoud shouts after him, but Watts lifts a hand and continues out. He hears a hint of panic in Heywoud's voice. Why will the man not eat what will save him? Watts does not tell him. What would he say? That he cannot bear to make his health sign of the other man's success? Or that he cannot bear his own good health? Both are true—and neither he nor Heywoud deserves the prize of his well-being.

One day in port and they set sail again, for six more days, to Cardiff. The ship rides lower in the water now, loaded with food and drink they barely have the time to use. Where they have come from, that place where they lost themselves and so much more, they would have journeyed six days with just the crumbs left in the hold and called them bountiful.

24

6 June

Viola waits for Isabella on the front steps of the National Gallery. She has received another telegram, this one from Madeira and with Edward's news that they arrive in six days' time. Her every glance into the fixer bath to watch a photograph emerge has brought a ghost image with it too—of Edward and James at the rail of their ship, or rolling in their berths in an Atlantic storm. She tries to set herself between them, tries to see herself with them in London once again. But now the secret she has kept from Edward feels a stone across her chest. She needs Izzy's company to clear her mind. After weeks in the darkroom, she is desperate to lift her head and look at something else besides her exhibition prints. She needs to stand so close to the canvases that she can see the brush strokes and conjure the hand that swept the paint. She can imagine the palette daubed with color, the specks of pollen or dust that found their way into the paint as if to germinate some later day.

Izzy's tall form strides towards her, holding an umbrella aloft in a slanting rain.

"Oi," Isabella calls. "Only for you would I come out in this."

Their hats brush together and the silk on Viola's brim makes a small sound like paper tearing.

"Only you would walk in this instead of taking the Underground."

Once up the stairs from Trafalgar Square, they fold their umbrellas and shake them out onto the honeyed stone floors of the portico.

"Come on, then." Viola takes her arm. "Let us see some art."

"Ah, yes. Lovely thing, art."

Up a short flight of stairs, they enter the first room in the museum and move through the British galleries and then the French. They pause at Gainsboroughs and Constables, linger in the next room at a large Poussin. They peer close to look at details—a little dog, a baby crying—and stifle laughter when they are scolded by the guards. They come to a wall of maritime paintings, ships at harbor with masts rising into leaden skies. Viola's mind goes instantly to Bute harbor eighteen months ago when Edward's ship sailed and the crowd stood five deep along the dock. How much greater fanfare will there be for the returning conquerors.

Isabella steps suddenly before her.

"What's the matter, Vi?"

"Nothing."

"I've been saying the most outrageous things about the guard in the corner and you've not even noticed."

"The truth is," she says, "I thought coming here with you today would distract me. But it's not working. Edward and James are only one week out from Cardiff."

She drifts to the banquette in the center of the room.

"Surely that's good news," Izzy says, sitting beside her.

"It is. Of course, it is. But," she says, "I will have to tell Edward about James."

Izzy looks at her sharply.

"Why on earth would you do that? You've gone along fine so far."

"It shouldn't have been a secret in the first place, Izzy. If I really meant what I was saying then, if I really believed I should be able to love two men at once and that the three of us could keep our lovely friendship, I would have—I should have—told him."

"James is part of this as well."

"Neither of us told the truth and it was cowardly. If I have learned anything, Izzy, from these women at the Dalmeny house, it is what true commitment to your beliefs looks like. Oh, I say all the right things, don't I? I'm very Continental about it. Two men at once, free love, no one unhappy or bothered." The guard coughs and Viola goes on in a whisper. "But I've never staked myself on it. No, I've been a coward. I must tell him all of it. James, the photographs, the exhibition, all of it. When they return, I will tell him."

She jumps from the banquette as if Edward were in the next room.

"Hang on," Isabella says. "Before you become too righteous, darling, have you considered what Edward will say?" Izzy steers her to a corner. "He would divorce you. You'd go to court. James would be named the guilty party. And you would have no money. Have you thought of that?"

"I have my parents' flat in Belsize Park."

"You would simply evict the tenants? And then how would you live? How would you buy your food, your darkroom chemicals?"

"I could sell the flat."

"You'd best be certain it's not in Edward's name, if you're planning to do that."

"I'd live with James." Viola tries to step past her.

"James and poverty," Isabella says. "Very romantic."

"When did you become so practical?"

"When I saw my banker. Stay with Edward and you'll have security."

They move aside to let a couple pass.

"The landscape man is sweet, but do you really think I'd choose him if it weren't for the cash?"

Isabella gives the word a cockney twang. Viola laughs, but Izzy takes her arm and leans in close.

"But it's no joke, Vi. With my landscape man, I have security. With Edward and his money, *you* have security. You have choices. Without him, you don't."

"You are telling me to go on lying."

Viola shifts away and they go on in silence through a series of rooms, past Bronzino and Correggio and Tintoretto. They arrive at the Dutch, a room full of landscapes with cloud-heavy liquid skies. Viola stares at a Van Ruisdael on the opposite wall. The painter has set a man and woman on his stormy strand, embracing in tryst or reunion. Izzy joins her and stands close.

"I don't know what to do," Viola says. "I can't lie to Edward and yet I cannot let James go. And I don't see how I can be honest and love them both." She turns to Izzy. "You've never understood that I do love Edward."

A guard steps forward.

"Mind the paintings, ma'am."

Isabella tugs Viola away from the wall.

"You're right. I don't. The man is utterly unlike you. He's stiff. Strict. He hasn't got a creative bone in his body."

"I don't care about that. I like Edward's ambition. He knows what he wants."

"The bloody Pole."

"Not just the Pole. Always. The top of any mountain, the route up a cliff face. He knows. He's certain. I like that certainty in him."

Viola's breath catches. How to explain to Izzy that there is something in each man that she loves deeply? It is a kind of perfect love to have the heart doubly anchored and tethered so, fixed and secure.

"You don't know what it was like, Izzy. How beautiful it was, to be with them both on all our rambles and our climbs. It was such bliss. To be with them both and love them and know they both loved me. It was perfect happiness." She lets out a rueful laugh. "Can't I have that again?"

Izzy reaches a hand up to Viola's cheek.

"Darling Vi. If Edward knows, he will put you out on the pavement. You either go on lying, or you end the thing with James. You either are divorced and left with nothing, or you remain the wife of Captain Heywoud and you go on with your art and with the suffrage fight."

"And what does that look like? How can I be sure Edward will allow all that? He had already insisted that I limit myself. Now when he discovers what I've been doing, with Dalmeny. I don't know."

"Tell him it's my fault. If I hadn't introduced you to the ASL, you'd still be photographing marches."

"It is not so simple."

She looks at the landscapes on the walls around her, takes in the shadows that mark time and travel, the leaden clouds and upturned leaves. If she is to be brave, if she is to be honest, she must not hide things from Isabella.

"I have to tell you something more," she says. "Do you remember the Botticelli?"

Izzy looks around as if to see the painting transported there.

"The Venus. Yes."

"I did it."

"What do you mean, you did it?"

"I made the photograph of it. With myself as the model."

Isabella draws away from her.

"When was this? You were going to use one of the Dalmeny women."

"It was weeks ago, and she was ill."

"And after?"

"Dalmeny was under police blockade. And Bellowes would not let me in." Viola's face warms again at the memory. "She forbade me to return."

Izzy's frown deepens.

"Why?" she says.

Viola wishes for a breeze to stir the humid gallery.

"She said I caused too much trouble for them, that I was willing to put them at further risk just to complete my project. But, Izzy, I did nothing wrong. Once it was clear I didn't have a model, I had to use myself. I wasn't going to hold up the entire exhibition for one photograph."

"Have you told Bellowes?" Izzy says.

"She still won't speak to me."

"She will not be pleased with this. Not at all. Unless you plan to get yourself arrested and then go on hunger strike and do the photo again between now and then." She lets out an indignant laugh, and before the guard can even think to hush them, she takes Viola by the arm and hustles her out of the room. "What did you do? Skip a few meals and then manipulate the photo so you looked like them?"

"Izzy. Stop." They have reached the octagon, where visitors brush past them from the room's four doors. "The show is different now," she says. "It's a bigger idea. It's a better way to make the case for suffrage. It shows that all of us are in this together, and what happens to one woman in this fight happens to all of us."

"Well, that's grand for you, then, isn't it?"

Isabella spins around slowly, as if to take in the paintings on the eight walls will help her understand. But it is Viola who speaks first.

"Didn't you just tell me I should go on lying? Didn't you just try to convince me I should hide the truth of who I love for my own benefit? Now all of a sudden it matters to you that I keep my categories straight, that I hold to the strictest definitions?"

Isabella shakes her head in disappointment.

"I introduced you to the hunger strikers because I thought you could make good art that would show the world the truth of what they suffer. And instead you have allowed your vanity as an artist and as a *model* to cloud your judgment."

"I hardly enjoy the thought of being nude on a gallery wall. This has to do with the politics, Izzy. About how women are confined and limited despite the truth that they are powerful and strong."

They have come back around to the front of the building, into a room near the portico where the sigh of rain beneath the wheels of motorcars in Trafalgar Square seeps towards them from the entrance. There is a large painting by Velasquez, the Rokeby Venus, alone on the back wall.

"Bloody hell," Isabella says.

"Just stay for a moment, Izzy."

"No. You stay. I've had enough of Venuses." She gives Viola a joyless smile. "I'll see you at your exhibition."

Viola stands there, pretending to gaze at the Venus, her face burning from sadness and the shame of being left behind. After a while, she walks out to the portico and sees Trafalgar Square is slick with rain. She opens her umbrella and descends the front steps to join the traffic circling Lord Nelson's column.

25

12 June

The day of the men's return is as hot as Viola has imagined it these many months. She descends in Cardiff from the morning train from Paddington. The locomotive ticks and clicks behind her and carriage doors slam shut as a few passengers depart. No one appears to be boarding for the train's return to London. The place has a deserted feel and Viola fears that Edward's ship will have sailed into the harbor without fanfare. Bertie takes her elbow to proceed and, turning, she sees the hoardings. *Polar Hero Arriving at Bute Dock. Edward Heywoud Returns Victorious to Cardiff. Cardiff Harbor Ceremony for Antarctic Explorer.*

"Good God," she murmurs. "Is the entire town already there?"

From the cab windows as they drive to the harbor, she watches as shop-fronts and signposts pass, bristling with double consonants. No number of trips taken to Snowdonia with James and Edward taught her to pronounce the Welsh. Llewellyn. They pass a greengrocer's by that name, the word beginning with something like the sound of a breeze.

Bertie grips her hand and she sees him staring at the line of motorcars and carriages and omnibuses their cab has joined with. The day is bright and humid. The heavy lignite smell of coal wafts into the cab. Men, women, and children weave among the vehicles, and many of them carry small paper

Union Jacks on sticks. Something in Viola's stomach shivers and her hair feels as if it must have stood on end. She takes a long breath.

"Yes, dear," Bertie says. "Breathe."

Only now does she realize she will see them, touch them. She will hear James and Edward speak. The thought of their breath near undoes her. For more than their bodies' feel or than the sight of them, it is their voices that will make them real. Edward's rumble and James' hoarse baritone—as if he is always just come from shouting at a pub. The jostle of her head resting on a chest. The warm air of their words.

The cab comes to a halt.

"God, Bertie, why is it so slow?"

He leans out of the window and calls to the policemen standing before a gate that blocks the road. One of the men comes to stoop by the window. Bertie tells him something, he glances into the cab at Viola and tips his cap. He returns to his colleagues and they swing the gate aside to let them through. Now Viola sees the newsmen, the photographers with their box cameras swiveling this way and that to catch a view. The car drives along the channel of Bute Dock where eighteen months ago Viola gripped her stole around her throat as rime hardened on the ship's stays and halyards. As the car inches through the crowd, she sees the ship's masts and Edward's expedition pennant. She reaches for the handle of the door.

"Slowly, my girl," Bertie says, his hand on hers. "You will have all your lives together now."

"I know," she says, but does not know this to be true. Edward has won the Pole, but he did not leave his ambition there. He will need to summit other peaks, to visit other remote places. McKinley next, or Borneo, or Kangchenjunga. But what if he brings from the Pole a different future for the two of them—he in an armchair with a rug around his feet and she tending when he shivers at the cold that never leaves him? What if the Pole has finished it for him and he craves hearth and family, Viola with a child in arms and someday another at her skirts? What will he say when she explains that that is not what she wants? She squeezes the handle of the door but does not move to open it. Now he has returned, they must fashion a new way to be together. There may be places Viola wants to go where Edward cannot follow.

She cranes her neck to peer through the motorcar's front window, but the crowd blocks her view. She pictures the bulk of the ship and Edward and James at the rail searching the mob for her, the one figure pushing through to reach them. There is no doubt in her mind that she will go to Edward first. If they are both at the rail, she will go to Edward first, and not only for the sake of what is proper. She holds both men in her heart equally. But now it has to do with loyalty, devotion. Edward is home. He is returned, yes, but he *is* home. He defines it. And this moment as these strangers watch the car come to a stop at the end of the dock in a town on the west edge of Britain, home is what she wants.

Bertie opens the door for her and she steps out to a cheer from the crowd and the rattle of the paper flags. She smiles and lifts a hand in a wave and Bertie takes her arm. The ship bobs in the channel, tethered with heavy ropes like a wounded beast. Too small to be majestic. Too scarred to be pretty. It was always an ungainly vessel—she, Viola supposes she must call it—made for the harsh duty of breaking ice in the North Sea. Now its hull is scarred and gashed and the colors of its pennants have faded to wan pink. It tugs at the bollards as if without the ropes it would skulk away, ashamed to have been brought among so many so much finer. Viola cannot quite believe this ship she is about to board has ventured to world's end. It may as well have traveled centuries as miles.

"Mrs. Heywoud."

She turns. A newsman takes her photograph.

A man in a Navy uniform approaches and a small cadre of older men adorned with club rosettes draws near. Explorers. Britain is full of them, adventurers of the Hindu Kush or the Great Rift Valley or Lake Victoria. They fall in behind the Navy man to form a little retinue.

"Where is Edward?" she asks the man.

"Captain Heywoud is just here, ma'am. He will meet you in his cabin."

"Bertie." She wants to ask him why is Edward not here to see her at the quickest moment?

"It's all right, dear," he says. "Go on."

Then she is up the gangway and onto the deck where sailors with weathered faces stand at attention. A tall man, a giant with a black-headed white dog at his heels, comes to take her to the cabin. She cannot hear him for the blood pounding in her head. He knocks on the cabin door, bends down to the dog with the curled tail, and Viola sees it is missing a leg.

The door opens and she sees him instantly. Despite the beard and the creases of weather and the dark color of his battered face, and his shoulders and chest that do not quite fill out his coat, she sees him. Edward. She takes him in her arms and feels the slightness of him, smells the mildew in his clothes. He is there with her. He is not disfigured. She holds him tight and pins his arms by his sides. His hands are light on her waist, as if he does not trust that she is real. She goes to kiss him. He leans away and she takes his hand and kisses the rough knuckles.

"It's really you," she says.

"Viola, sit down."

"I'm not sitting down," she laughs. "You've been gone a year and a half and I will not sit down."

She presses his bearded cheeks but he extracts himself.

"Sit, please," he says.

"Edward." She attempts another laugh, then thinks a reason for his strange behavior.

"Oh, God," she says, "where is James?"

"James is alive. I told you in the telegram."

"Is he here? Will he come see us?"

The word rings in her ears. *Us.* How easily it comes back, this word that means so many things to her with these two men. But of course: Edward must know. He has discovered the affair.

"Viola, please sit."

But she will not sit down. She is certain now. James, in a throe of frozen agony, has confessed. James warming himself at the Primus has revealed the woman that he pines for.

"Edward, let me explain."

"Explain?" he spits the word out. "There is nothing to explain."

He paces the cabin, three steps and a turn. His gait is stiff, his knees bony and jutting in the heavy trousers.

"I am in a quandary," he says. "I have returned from eighteen months in the world's most miserable place and here is my wife and I should by rights be overjoyed. She embraces me, she kisses me."

"Edward," she says. She takes hold of him. "Please stop."

"I can't, Vi," he says, but he does not resist her. "Vi." When he says her name a second time, his voice is hoarse and choked.

She sweeps the hair up from his eyes. The skin at hairline's edge is palest white and damp with sweat. He takes her hand and holds it in a tight grip that grows tighter.

"He told me," Edward says. "I found his notebook and he told me. All this time on the ice and on the ship, I planned what I would say to you. I thought I would be angry, seeing you. I *want* to be angry."

"Edward, please, I am so sorry."

She repeats the words her very acts have rendered meaningless. Edward. I am sorry. What is her apology to him when she has wounded him in ways she should have known would come? What intimacy does his name convey when she has shared intimacy with another man? She should have known the sorrow of this moment—not just Edward's but her own. She should have known the discovery of the affair would feel nothing like the airy philosophy of her idea. The joy she felt in loving both of them is gone. She was a fool to think Edward would ever share it.

She starts to tell him that she loves him still.

"Don't say a word," he says. "I've waited seven months since that day on the ice to speak to you and you will not interrupt. You never stopped," he says. "You left him, you met me, you married me"—his voice rises to a whispered shout and he glances at the cabin door—"and you never stopped seeing him."

"It's not like that, Edward."

"He confessed it to me. He was writing to you. In his sketchbook. Out there on the ice he was writing back to you."

She sees a flash of something in his eyes that is not quite like hurt. Is it guilt because perhaps he did not write to her and he is jealous of the lover's greater dedication? Or will he produce a greasy packet for her now, saved up for this reunion? She would like those letters, would like to know she played a part in his ambition, in his heart.

"You have nothing more to say?" He looks across at her with the importunate look of a child.

"I loved you both," she says. "I love you."

"How can you say that when you've betrayed me?"

"I should have told you the truth. That was my betrayal."

"You knew it was wrong."

"I didn't know how to explain it."

How could she have made him see there is in each man a different thing that pulls against her vision of herself? She has not practiced this. She does not know what to say and so she chooses the truth now, inarticulate and vague.

"I love each of you differently."

He laughs.

"It's the same act, Viola, no matter who you do it with."

"Please don't make this crude."

"I wasn't enough for you," he says. "You had to find more."

"It's not a question of enough." She goes to him. "You were and are the full measure of yourself. And so is James. One doesn't cancel out the other."

He sits in the low chair, a giant in its spindly frame.

"Don't philosophize with me, Viola."

"I'm trying to be honest with you."

"That's impossible. Honesty is not with us in this room. We are long past honesty."

She loses him for a long moment as all energy drains from his face.

"What do we do now, Ned?" she says.

"He was my friend, Viola. He was my best of friends."

"Can he not be that still? You have endured so much together."

He shakes his head as if to cast a pain away.

"It's too late now. I had you both and now—"

"You have me still, Edward." She takes his face in her hands and turns it up to her. "It was never about giving you up. It was about loving you more because the three of us were still together."

They sit silently for long enough that Viola notices the gentle dancing movement of the ship, hears the muffled sound of voices from the dock. She tries to see the cabin angled and heaving in an angry sea and Edward sitting, sleeping, writing, thinking on his way back to England and to her. It seems a punishment that one can only reach the vastness of the Southern Pole through captivity in this dark prison. It is like climbing a mountain in a coffin.

Edward clears his throat.

"We've taken too long," he says. "The people want their heroes." He opens the cabin door and gives someone an order on the other side before closing it again. "Here is what you are going to do," he says. "You will greet Watts warmly when he joins us on deck. Neither you nor he will speak to anyone. You will stand with me and greet the dignitaries." He sets his peaked cap upon his head, the brim low and level so that it shadows his eyes. "Come."

He places a hand on the small of her back as the door swings open, and for an instant she is entering a drawing room, a restaurant, a gala, turning to smile at her husband who escorts her in. Further along the narrow deck is James. He looks at Viola with the large brown eyes of a Byzantine. Despite his beard, his mouth is prominent and when he smiles at her his teeth seem large and loose, too long now for his jaw. His hair, once thick with dark curls, is straw-straight and dull. She has seen this kind of face before, in female form. It is the face of Dalmeny Avenue. She goes to him, but Edward's hand on the small of her back seizes a fistful of her dress. He pulls her away from James, as if she were a dog nosing something fetid on the street. She stares at Edward and he nods outward and she sees then the men arrayed on the deck and Bertie and the Explorers and the crowds on solid ground beyond and, knowing what is necessary, she stands still. Viola stands between the men, waving to the onlookers, as Edward's arm circles her as if she were a conquered possession.

They step out onto the narrow deck and a cry goes up from the crowd. A brass band plays a fanfare. Edward leads them to the bow of the ship where the crew is arrayed in ceremonial order, Bertie and the Explorers in a row in front of them. Viola searches for faces that betray some sign of the Pole. Among these leather-faced men surely are some who journeyed at least part of the way with Edward to his goal. *All safe and sound*, his telegram said. Who were they *all*?

Someone calls out and it is a voice she recognizes. A newsman from the *Observer*. He winks at her.

"Sum it up for us, gentlemen," he says. "What was it like?"

A second's silence, then James' hoarse and reedy voice.

"I've never seen anything so beautiful."

She feels Edward tense beside her at James' defiance.

"More beautiful than Wales?" says an official, to laughter from the Cardiff retinue.

James' eyes are on Viola, and Edward stares ahead, lips pressed together, nostrils flared. He seems to be deciding what to say.

"Edward," she murmurs to him, and then he sends his voice out over the crowd.

"There is so much that we cannot express save our great love and pride for Britain. It is our honor to have set the Union Jack at the South Pole in the name of the King."

In the cheering that follows, only Viola hears James say in his newly reedy voice that he is ill from wanting her. She cannot help it and for an instant takes his hand.

There is a call for the Polar Party for a photograph to stand in a row before the expedition crew. Edward calls for someone named Lawrence and the giant man limps towards them with the three-legged dog at his side. They stand together, Edward, James, and this tall man and his lame dog and Viola cannot believe these three are sole survivors of the Polar Party. Lawrence removes his cap and stands hatless for the photograph. She does not know who he is mourning.

Photographers' flash pans pop and blaze as they capture the heroes together. One of the Explorers pins a rosette on Edward's chest to mark he is among them now.

Edward turns to Lawrence and to James and thrusts a hand out. This is the men's farewell, it seems. After eighteen months together at sea and on the ice, James and Edward and Lawrence are to part from each other with no more than a handshake.

"Where is that car of yours, Bertie?" Edward claps him on the back. Then louder for the newsmen: "We've had enough of skiing for a bit, haven't we, boys?"

Again the hand on the small of her back as Edward leads her down the gangplank to the motorcar and from there to the railway station where the little building Viola and Bertie came through this morning has been decorated now with flags and bunting. Through the station archway, Viola can see the train and a single carriage draped in blue, white, and red cloth with swags of the same colors at the compartment windows. A small crowd has gathered here, and they cheer when she and Edward step out of the car.

They are seated in their compartment when a dignitary emerges from the throng with arms waving. It seems there has been an error and they must wait for James who is to ride to London with them. Edward protests that he and Viola wish for privacy. But the dignitary will not be deterred. James is brought by a small group of the Explorers who hand him up into the compartment.

"It seems we are not finished traveling together," James says and takes a seat that faces backwards. He positions himself so that he is across from Edward, as if to face Viola is to claim connection where there should be none.

A signalman on the platform pipes three notes on his whistle and the train begins to move. Viola keeps her eyes on the brickwork of the station and then the railway cutting and the backs of row houses with their iron downpipes snaking to the ground. She cannot look at the men. There is something charged among them now. It is a new thing for the three of them to know that she has had them both. They have no secrets, any of them, and the knowledge of it mounts like pressure all around her. The clacking of the points swells in the car's silence, and Viola knows the miles that they must cover to this uneasy rhythm. She grows hot, unpins her boater to fan herself with its broad brim. Edward stands to push the compartment window down to its full opening. A scent of hay sails into the compartment and she catches both men sniff the air like dogs. Though they have been on shore in Lyttelton and in Madeira since the Pole, she sees them revel in the smell of soil and grass beneath a summer sun.

Edward clears his throat and leans back into the seat.

"There is to be a ceremony at the Royal Geographical Society," he says.

"That is wonderful, Edward." She attempts the cheerful tone of normalcy.

"I have talks to do, and presentations."

Only one week since the ship reached Madeira and his schedule is set. There must have been mailbags of summonses and invitations for him at first shore. *The pleasure of your presence. Do us the honor. Accept our award.*

"The RGS event is in three days," he says. "Viola, you will have to prepare the prints."

"What? James has his own darkroom."

"You will develop the plates, not Watts."

"Why?"

"Because this is my arrangement."

"Edward, this is nonsense. James took the photographs. James should do the darkroom work."

"I told you, Heywoud," James says. "She is right."

"This is your punishment and I'll not change it."

"His punishment?"

"He knows, Viola. We discussed this on the ice."

"What if I have changed my mind?" James says.

"Suddenly, Watts, you have found a spine to argue with? Because of her? Because she's watching?"

"Edward."

"Do not tell me I lack a spine," James says, with sudden firmness in his voice.

"No," Edward says. "I decided. Viola is to do our developing and printing."

"But, Edward, I must tell you my news," she says. "I am to have an exhibition. At Whitechapel Gallery." She glances at James for whom these words have meaning. "Charles Aitken who is the director there believes that I will make a name for myself."

"Charles Aitken," James says. "Well done, Vi."

"Don't call her that," Edward snaps.

"The exhibition is in eight days' time," she says.

"Then you can certainly prepare our prints before then."

"I have so much to do now in the run-up. Aitken has booked the press for my opening. Critics are coming. There is a hubbub already for my work."

And yet she knows that Edward has the greater claim. He holds a victim's right to recompense. She owes him at least that—some hours in the darkroom to put him and his achievements over her own.

"These gallery people know your husband has returned from the South Pole," he says, "which will be quite the boon for their turnout. I would wager they've made that calculation themselves. So you'd best work to get my photos done."

It is clear he expects no rebuttal. He is unaccustomed, it seems, to conversation that does not consist of giving orders. These months at sea have no doubt strengthened his Navy ways. This punishment of James that Edward levies cuts him from his own creation. Edward lets him see what he has made even as he expels him from the making of it. He turns James into a tortured man from a Greek myth, forbidden from drinking from the very water that he floats in. Viola has played her part in this. But must she help Edward bring Antarctica's cruelty with him back to London?

They ride on in silence while from time to time a passenger wanders down the corridor and glances through the inner window. She is surprised to see James falls asleep, jaw dropping open, sour breathing she can smell across the compartment. A piece of rainbow hovers above the Wessex Downs and she looks to Edward to tell him, but he, too, is sleeping. How can either of them sleep, when the very air of the compartment is a battleground? They pass through a band of rain. Mist sprays in and jewels Edward's hair. He leans his head against the glass and a small frown of worry picks at his brows. She sees the alterations in his face. New creases by his mouth visible even through his beard. White spider lines etched in the browned skin around his eyes. A flake of skin on his right ear, remnant of frostbite. She wonders why James appears so ill when Edward is merely scarred from a successful outing. She should have asked Bertie to look at James, to see him with a doctor's eye.

When the train slows at a level crossing, Edward starts awake. He clears his throat and looks out to their surroundings.

"We will be in the station soon." He leans forward and James wakes with the movement. "I'll not arrive in London without asking. Who else knew?"

"What?" Viola says.

"Heywoud, don't."

"Who else knew?"

"Please," she says and reaches a hand out to him. He flinches away. "It is too soon for this, Edward. Let us find each other again."

"It is not soon enough. We will be in Paddington in minutes."

"What do you want me to say?" she says.

"How did it begin?"

Viola takes a breath. It should be nothing to express what she has thought these many months and yet she thinks again how foolish she has been.

"I can't tell you that," she says.

"You can. And I am asking you. How did it begin?"

"Leave it, Heywoud," James says.

"No," he says. "I want to know the first time. When was it?"

She looks at James though she does not want him to answer. But his silence irks her.

"You were in Lofoten," she says, closing her eyes against the words. "To visit Nansen for training. James had stayed behind and I had asked him for help in the darkroom." She takes a long breath. "It was then."

His eyes widen and he falls back into the seat.

"That was six months before we left for the Pole."

"Yes."

"Six months in London you were seeing him."

"Yes."

Edward does not reply for a long moment. The train slows as it comes into outer London. Along the rail line now are cramped cottages and the hulking tanks of the gasworks with the reek of burning coal.

"You have not humiliated me," he says.

"Edward, no—"

"Stop," he says, and glances out at the brick walls of the railway cutting and the next words come clipped and quick. "You have not humiliated me because I choose to keep my dignity. You are my wife. He is my photographer. I am the hero of the South Pole. That is where we stand."

Viola looks at him and feels tears forming. In all that hardness, there is something tender in his trust that to declare something makes it so. This trust has made him endure and persevere. This simple trust in his own strength is what has made her love him.

At Paddington, they get into another car and travel south to Margaretta Terrace where a large crowd spills from the pavement onto the street. Constables hold the crowd back as the car pulls up. Viola recognizes one of the officers from a suffrage march, a small man with a boxer's agility. Out of the car, Edward and James tip their hats and make little bows to the people who come in small groups, neighbors and tradesmen, women with their children, emissaries from a world they think Edward belongs to. Even before the expedition, Edward was a stranger to it—one foot always striding towards a new achievement. Now Viola must invite him home as to a foreign country.

She pulls the men away and towards the house where she sees Mary and Miner standing just inside the open door. There is a catch in Edward's step—she feels it in his arm—but at the door he stands and waves once more to the crowd.

"Mr. Watts and I are proud to have won the Pole for England," he says, "and so grateful to be home."

An instant later, both James and Edward have fallen into Miner's arms. The three men stand in one embrace, rocking as if on board a ship. Mary makes wide eyes at her and they wait while the men press foreheads together. Some words pass between them but Viola cannot make them out, nor even which of them is speaking.

"Let's have a look, then," Miner says, when they pull apart. "Nothing missing?"

It is an awful joke and Viola wonders is it said in charity or anger. He makes to scan them up and down and they allow the game. They stand straight—even James pulls to his full height—and wait like soldiers for Miner's inspection. If they are shamed or saddened by the damaged man who finds them whole, they do not show it.

"Two heroes is what I see," Mary says. "And hungry, by the scrawny looks of them."

Mary bustles Miner away and shakes hands with James and Edward. She vows to have them fat within the week and departs for the kitchen to begin.

"I'd best go," James says. "Before she stuffs me like a suckling pig. Think the car will take me home?"

"It's gone," Edward says.

"Right," James says. "Then my long journey will end with a London taxi."

"I'll get you one."

Edward goes out onto the street with the speedy courtesy of someone who regrets earlier anger. James and Viola are alone in the foyer.

"Good God, Vi," he says, and wraps himself around her. There is nothing soft to him. He is all bone and sinew and the weft of his lapel is rough against her cheek. He squeezes tight and then releases just as Edward reappears.

"Constable found one for me," Edward says. "The perquisites of being a hero."

There is an antic brightness to Edward's actions. He is impatient for James to go.

The men walk together to the curb where the taxi waits. The crowd is smaller now, though two constables remain to guard the pavement. Viola watches as Edward holds the door open. He and James shake hands before James gets in the cab and goes away.

26

12 June

Edward closes the house door behind him and for an instant he looks lost, all forced cheer and urgency gone. She takes him by the hand and draws him up the stairs. He enters the bedroom like a mourner looking on at things that hold no sense but in the past. She sees him work his mind to bring these things into his life—or bring himself into the story of these objects. He sits down on the edge of the bed and Viola wonders if he thinks of her and James together.

"What do we do now, Edward?"

He undoes buttons on his coat and sets his hat beside him on the table.

"I don't know, Viola. I am tired. I am home and I am tired."

He falls back onto the bed as if he has not slept since he last left it. His feet dangle over the tall side and within seconds Viola hears the deep sigh of his breath. She retreats to a slipper chair by the wall and watches as he sleeps, his head cocked at an angle, his hands cupped loosely by his sides, the collar of his shirt still buttoned to the top. He cannot be comfortable. And yet how much better this than any bed he's occupied since New Zealand with a whore or mayor's daughter sneaking back to see him with the dinner and the speeches done. Viola knows these things, knows how to hold an inner doorknob to control the noise of its release, how to tell when the goodnight means not goodbye but come back. She looks at Edward's slack jaw and remembers his eyes smiling up at her over the hand he kissed at that first gallery exhibit. The man who was always prying James from the studio to climb mountains, standing before her tall and blond, trailing ambition and resolve. She remembers his delight and hers in the promise of their next meeting.

She tries to think how she will tell Edward about the Botticelli. How she can ever make him understand it is appropriate his wife appear naked before the eyes of artistic London? And yet she must explain. She must prepare him for the fuss and furor of the exhibition—for if she succeeds and if Aitken is right, there will be many voices raised in praise and shock.

A breeze stirs the drapes at the twin windows onto Margaretta Terrace. From the windows comes the hum of people still crowding the pavement, thrilled with anticipation for a glimpse of their hero. The room looks east, not a good painter's room. But the full sun of the long June day gives it a soft and even light. The light is perfect for a photograph.

She tries to resist the pull of the camera—it is an odd thing to do with a newly returned husband—but she wants to look at him with the attention of a photograph. She wants the concentration of the camera lens. What cuts and bruises will she see beneath his clothes? His body will be like Abigail's or Margaret's, marked by pain and struggle. Viola swings his legs onto the bed and goes to get her Midg from the cupboard. She kneels over him and scans his face. The only damage she can see is that small flap on his right ear, a tiny wound where the skin will keep on blistering at the slightest touch of cold. Edward must be careful, even in a London June, or he will lose the lobe.

Viola brings the lens close to his face. She frames an image of the wounded ear and jaw, and another image of the wrinkles by his eyes, the way they form a river delta and, at the meeting of the lids, a tiny gleam of water. She photographs the ridges of his palms, the chafed and cracked pads of his thumbs. His collar presses up into the loose folds of his neck where she can see he has not shaved. She hooks a finger behind the stiff fabric and tries to work the button for his comfort.

He bats at her hands. He sputters anger.

"It's me," she says.

She presses him back to the pillow. His hair is coarse from salt and sun.

"Edward, it's me."

He looks at her with wild eyes. Then he sees her, frowns.

"Was that your bloody camera?"

"It's all right," she says. "I only took a few."

"I was asleep, for God's sake."

"I've photographed you in your sleep before."

Images from their first months together, when the lens was another way for her to touch him. Arms crossed beneath his head, his boater tipped over closed eyes, his chest rising and falling beneath his summer linen. Then later, Edward posed at a cliff's base, a loop of rope crossed on his shoulder. Or smiling up at her, hands on a bootlace, forelock falling over his eyes. She wants to tell him of the images she works on now, how they are so much more than lovely memories of lovely times. How she does more than just depict the world; she changes it. But still it is too soon and she is neither brave enough nor foolish to invite his disapproval.

"Go back to sleep," she says. "I'm sorry."

"You've woken me now."

"Let me at least undo this. You can't be comfortable."

She undoes the button and slides the collar band from around his neck. She removes his tie. He watches as she frees his shoulders from his coat and shirt, pulls his vest over his head. He is deciding, she knows, between old love and new resentments. She tracks a finger over the line left by his collar. His skin is so white it is as if he is still dressed. His face and hands are leather-dark. She is deciding, too.

She reaches for him and he does not move, either to help or hinder. It is as if they have agreed to play that he is weak, that he cannot or should not stir unless she moves him. She turns him this way and that, runs her fingers over patches where some object has chafed the skin to leather: his ribs, his knees, his shoulders.

"From the traces," he says, when she looks a question.

"I thought the dogs did the pulling." She has imagined him upright as on a chariot pulled by loping Russian hounds.

"We became the dogs."

She kisses these rough spots of skin and teases with her tongue around the new contours of his body. And still he watches her and she can see that he is thinking did she do these things with James. How can she make him see that, yes, she did but that that other body has a different musk, a different taste?

She slips the pins out of her hair and undoes her jacket and blouse, unties her camisole. She flinches at the scrape of his calluses against her skin. He lifts his hand, but she presses it to her back.

"I like it."

This is how she knows he is truly home, like Odysseus returned and recognized by the dog for his smell or for the curve of hand on its fur. Edward's rough palms are proof of all his miles and his degrees of latitude. If he lacked half his face today, like Miner, she would know him by these cold-scraped hands. His hands search her, learn her. She moves against him, tumbles him above her. A crease of skin runs from her hip to her groin where the hip blade angles sharp. She wants to drive his eyes there, her eyes on him a lesson in how and where he must look. Let his gaze run from her nipples to her stomach and along that crease.

"Wait," she says.

He presses into her.

"No, Edward, wait." She sits up.

"What?"

"Let me get something."

"Something like what?" He laughs but she can see he is uncomfortable.

"A prophylactic."

"You're joking," Edward says.

"No."

"I'll not use a French letter with my wife. You shouldn't even know what they are." She sees the notion come to him. "You used them with Watts, didn't you?" he says. "Of course, you did."

She catches a hint of relief in him—that if they used French letters they intended for no child. He sits up in the bed.

"I don't know what I'm doing here," he says. "In bed with you after everything that's happened."

"Ned."

"Don't say a word. Do you not trust me?" Then more clipped, "Do you fear disease?"

"It's not that," she says. "It's pregnancy."

"What?"

"I can't do it again," she says. "I won't."

Blood in the darkroom and her with barely time to call Mary and pull herself upstairs. And then the sheets bloodied and Bertie summoned, bringing Alice with him since it was Viola with no mother to assist. Doors of the motorcar slamming shut below the window, then Edward in the room, eyes wide and fear on his face as she had never seen it and she not sure even then whose child it was. She watched him take it in: the mound of five months gone from her, the clammy pallor of her face, the muslin sheets on the bed because the damask were already soiled.

She is shaking her head.

"I am sorry."

As she says the words, she hears this is her deepest apology—for not giving him someone else to love. Edward makes a sound, something like a laugh, and she sees he is surprised by tears. His face darkens in a flush so vivid she can see it on his sun-browned cheeks. He bears her miscarriage in his heart, his grief there to be summoned up again. He swipes at his eyes as if to clear ice from eyebrows. She repeats her words.

"I'm sorry, Ned. I have had time while you were away to think on this."

"I thought we agreed. And Bertie told us that you would be well," he says. "It will be all right this time."

"I'm sorry, Ned. I changed my mind."

"You changed your mind?" He says the words as if each one is preposterous.

"I feel differently now."

"What is wrong with a child, for God's sake? What is better than a child?"

"I understand that for you a child is lovely. You want a son to be your heir and legacy. For me, a child takes away the kind of legacy I want."

"What other kind of legacy could you possibly want?"

"As an artist. Surely you know this."

He tosses the thought away.

"I knew it when we met. But—"

"But what?"

"But we married."

"Why should that have changed anything?" she says.

And yet she knows it did. He worried for her, kept her from climbing high, from carrying her heavy camera. Soon as they moved to Margaretta Terrace, there was Miner and the camera cart and everyone watching to be sure she did not do whatever Edward deemed too much. Each moment spent with James became a freedom and that freedom a new pull to an old love.

"It did change things," he says. "You wanted a child then. We tried. We almost had one."

"Edward, I can't." Her voice is loud enough to make him start. "You don't understand. You can't understand. I can't feel *connected* that way. I can't be pulled apart that way, the way a child pulls on you."

"You're not even making any sense. Besides, a nanny would take care of the child. You would not be *pulled*." He uses the word with distaste.

"I'm sorry, Ned. I thought about it all the time you were away. Losing the child. The pain of it. The thought that I could lose another. And then I realized that if I hadn't lost the child, I would have lost everything else. I would have had to stop everything. My photographs, my work for suffrage."

"You want to be an artist."

"Yes."

"Then be an artist and a mother."

"I told you. I simply can't."

She thinks of her stomach rounded and taut, her cheeks full and her breasts heavy. She cannot inhabit that body. She cannot be an artist and move through the world in that form.

He goes to the wardrobe and pulls on his dressing gown.

"This is intolerable, Viola. I cannot tolerate it. I cannot understand it."

He spins around.

"Was it those suffragettes who made you think this? Was it Isabella?"

"It was none of them. I made up my own mind."

And yet she would not have made her wish a certainty had it not been for what she saw in Dalmeny where a woman's body found a different kind of power.

"All the time that I was on the ice, I thought about coming home to you to try again, to have a child. And now you tell me this."

He sits heavily on the slipper chair across the room.

"You're wrong, you know," he says. "I didn't want a son. Not a son. A daughter."

"Oh."

The thought of him with a little girl makes her nearly toss her resolve away. With such a man—a hero with the sweetness to want a daughter not a son—could she find a way to be a mother and an artist both?

She wraps the sheet around her shoulders and perches on bed's edge.

"It will be all right, Ned, with just the two of us."

"And him? What about him?"

He asks the question not as challenge but concern, as if the two of them must care for James now that his life is bound with theirs.

"Were you ever going to choose?" he says. "If I had not found out?"

"I don't know."

"You could have room in your life for two men at once but not room enough for a child?"

"I don't know, Edward."

"You can't embark on a grand idea without knowing the cost. Which of us would it have been?"

She has been a fool, to think she could explain to Edward something she cannot quite express herself. She has been wrong about it all. About herself especially. She is no acolyte of Bloomsbury. Her modern idea that she could love two men survived these last eighteen months only because they were a world away. Now they are both here she knows she cannot stay with both without causing pain to Edward. He is right that she must choose.

And still she cannot let go of the idea. She squeezes back tears.

"There will always be more than one part of me. I wanted a way for all of me to love and be loved. I still do."

"What does that mean? That I can't ever have all of you?"

"I suppose yes."

"You are my wife."

"You don't have all of me, Edward. No more than I have all of you."

So many months he gazed at ocean charts and maps in books by Ross and Weddell, newspaper accounts of Mawson's failed attempt and Shackleton's. He traveled away from her to the farthest north of Norway, to Lofoten and Svalbard, over and over again. Antarctica was like his lover just as much as James was hers. The look he gives her now is one of forced acceptance. He reminds her of a scolded child. She goes to sit beside him in the small chair, waits for him to make room, sets her head into the crook of his shoulder. Without thinking, she returns to this part of him, as if her body had a memory.

"All right, Ned?"

It is her part of their catechism, the one question whose answer brings them close after discord and separation. When he woke from dreams of falling—the shudder in the bed and his sharp cry the alarm for her too—or glowered at the fireplace, arms braced against the mantel, she asked him all right Ned and he would answer yes to make it true. But this time it is different.

"Will it ever be all right?" he says. "How can it?"

He is not defiant now, or angry. He does not move to get away from her. She feels his body sink into the cushion and she takes his hand. She brings it to her lips and kisses the knuckles. The drapes stir and the filtered light has mellowed to the honeyed shade of summer evening. In time, Edward goes to the bed and drops face down onto the coverlet. She cannot add to the burden of the day. She cannot tell him now about her exhibition. He is soon deep asleep, his breaths coming with the hum of speech. The room is full of questions, and all of Viola's words and worries have done nothing to find answers.

27

12 June

Barely an hour has passed since Viola crept out of the bed and left Edward there in heavy sleep when Mary finds her in the parlor. She has been attempting to jot notes for the commentary that will accompany her exhibition, but her ideas sink beneath her thoughts of how to explain it all to Edward.

"Mr. Edward is awake, ma'am. He is in the *kitchen*," she says. Viola can hear the girl's dismay at this invasion.

"Go on back to him," she tells Mary, "and I will be there in a moment."

She taps the page with the pen and skims her notes for sense. There will be brief labels for each photograph, and she intends to add the information about each striker—how many days in prison, how many days refusing food, how many times force fed. But she cannot decide if more is needed. An explanation of her purpose? A claim for what the photographs demand? She knows she must allow the images to speak for themselves—she must have confidence in their voices, in her work. She claps the notebook closed and goes down to the kitchen.

Edward sits in his dressing gown at the deal table with a glass of beer and a plate of bacon and potatoes. Miner sits across from him with his own beer, and Mary stands with her back to the sink, eyes darting from Edward to Viola.

"Mr. Heywoud asked for breakfast," she says. She makes a little shrug at Viola as if to explain. "And for Samuel to join him."

"Nothing for me, ma'am," Miner says, "but the drink."

Edward wipes his beard with the back of his hand and looks up at her.

"I've lost my ice eyes," he says, and for a moment she thinks he speaks of some new anatomy the Pole has grown upon him. As if he has evolved those eighteen months to become a different creature. As if he is no longer fully human.

"You didn't sleep long," she says.

"Too bright. You'd think I'd still be able to sleep in it." He shakes his head, drowsiness lingering.

Edward and James inside their tent, the canvas glowing from the constant sun, black lines etched in the orange of closed lids. Tiny creases at the corners of James' eyes from a squint he cannot lose. He will be lying now on his bed in Camden, eyes closed against the sun from his north windows, sounds of barges drifting in from Regent's Canal.

"I keep waking up hungry," Edward says. "It's been like this since Shore Camp. But no one can cook rashers good as these," he says and gives Mary a firm smile.

"Thank you, sir," she says.

Mary is chuffed at the praise but Viola sees that Edward's presence is a shock. His bulk in the kitchen, his heavy tread, and the rumble of his voice have in a few short hours made Mary clatter trays onto tables and press her back against the walls. Viola knows her discomfort. It will take them all some time to fit this new body in the house. Even the sight of his dressing gown jars now, the piping worn at the edges, the burgundy and gold of the stripes loud in the room's dim light.

"Will you want dinner, too?" Viola says.

"I'm always hungry. I don't know where it goes."

He spears two rashers onto his fork at once and chews them loudly. This, too, has changed. His careful manners are now camp-crude.

"Would you like something, ma'am?"

"Not just now," she says.

She sits at the table with him and Miner and watches Edward clear his plate. He takes a long swig of the beer and wipes his hand across his beard again.

"I expect, sir," says Miner, "it will be a good while before you feel full up again. If the Alps are any guide."

"Of course," Edward says.

He scrapes his chair back and stands, and Miner comes to his feet in deference. Mary bobs a curtsy when he thanks her for the food.

"Edward, I must speak to you," Viola says.

She follows him up to the bedroom. She watches the familiar way he hangs poised on the balls of his feet for an instant with each step. Eighteen months away and slogging across a continent and his feet remember the rhythm of the treads.

He stands at the window and peers down to the twilit street.

"Still a few people there," he says. He cannot hide his delight. "I should go speak to them. Give those newsmen some information for their trouble."

"You can't. The *Observer* has the exclusive."

"Well, where are they, then? Who else will they speak to about Antarctica but me?"

"Edward, I must tell you something," she says.

"Go on, then."

"Please sit down and pay attention."

"I am not a schoolboy to sit for a lesson."

Yet he perches on the bed, peering at her with impatience.

"It's about my exhibition."

"Look, Viola, I told you. You are developing our plates, not Watts."

"I will. But that's not it." She sits beside him. "I must tell you what the exhibition is about."

He lets out a puzzled laugh.

"All right. Is it one of those abstract things you used to take me to? Collages?"

She reaches a hand to touch his cheek. There is a sweetness in the words, so unfamiliar to him, coming from his lips. He is trying. In his way, he is attempting to belong.

"While you have been away, the movement—"

"This again?"

"The suffrage movement," she goes on, "has been changing. There have been many marches and protests against Asquith's government. Some of the women who are arrested take up hunger strike in Holloway Prison, to protest their sentences and to demand the vote. When they refuse to eat, the prison warders feed them by force. Like geese, Edward. Or pigs. It's horrible."

"It sounds quite horrible indeed but I don't see what it has to do with you."

"My photographs for the exhibition are of some of the hunger strikers staying in a safe house here in London."

He considers this and lets out a sigh. He shrugs out of his dressing gown.

"Ned," she says, and something in her tone stops him. "The photographs are nudes."

He pauses, then hangs the dressing gown inside the wardrobe. When he turns back to her, he is composed.

"All right," he says. "Though they must be rather ghastly to look at. You've already done this with no thought for what I think, Viola, so I don't know why you ask me now. I only need that my own photographs be finished for my lecture."

"One of the photos is of me."

"What? Why? Were you arrested? Were you jailed?"

He spits the words out with urgency, as if he were planning how to aid in her escape.

"No," she says, "no, I wasn't."

"Then why are you photographed among hunger strikers?"

"I posed myself the way I posed the other women. It is complicated to explain but I can show you. I would like to show you before you see the photograph in public."

His eyes widen.

Here is the moment she has feared the most, the moment when Edward comes to full understanding of the consequences of her actions. The moment when he tells her he will demand of Aitken that the show be cancelled. She tucks her feet up beneath her on the edge of the bed and hugs her knees.

"I see," he says. "And you are recognizable as yourself?"

"Yes."

"I see."

"It is an important exhibition, Ned. Whitechapel Gallery is the place to present your work if you want to be taken seriously. And I have something to say with this collection. I know you have worried about my participation in the movement, but with my art I am able to do something important."

He looks about him as if for a place to settle but stays rooted where he stands.

"How could you believe I would allow this?" he says.

"I am not asking your permission."

"You cannot go on with this."

"Edward, the gallery has scheduled the show. They have printed pamphlets. There are to be critics there, reviewers."

"I don't care. How can this be so difficult for you to comprehend? You are not an art student anymore, Viola. You are the wife of a Navy Captain and hero of the South Pole." A blush deepens the leather of his face. "You cannot appear naked in public."

"I'm not going to change my plans, Ned. I told you because I didn't want to keep it secret."

"That's rich."

She swings her legs down from the bed.

"We are beginning again, Ned, now you have returned. I want to be honest with you now."

"You want to be honest." He scoffs and moves away from her. "All right," he says, turning. "Fine. Go on and have your exhibition. But you will give me something in return."

"I am to make your prints," she says. "What more would you have me do?"

"You will not see Watts. Not unless I am present."

"Edward."

He shakes his head.

"You will not see him except at our events and speeches."

"He is my friend, too, Edward."

"He was your lover." He snaps the words. "And your only reason to see him now would be to go on with your affair. Is that what you want? Because if it is, I can spare you the journey home from Camden. I will lock the door to you. I will sue for divorce."

His eyes betray a moment's panic that his warnings turn reality and he must push her from his life.

"You won't do that. You cannot. With all the newspapers waiting, you cannot afford the air of scandal."

"Do you threaten me?" he says.

She thinks of Isabella and her talk of money and court cases. If Viola is wrong now, if Edward chooses to risk the scandal she lays out for him, she will be left with nothing.

"We are threatening each other, Ned."

He sits heavily on the little divan and drags both hands over his face.

"What if I refuse to make your plates?" she says.

He looks up at her sharply.

"You wouldn't."

"I could. If you don't let me see James."

He cocks his head at her.

"Is that what you want? You would put James above everything, Viola? Without my name, you will never have the access that you seek. You would sacrifice your debut in the most modern gallery in London so that you could go on with a man you will live with in poverty, divorced, disgraced?"

She takes her breath in sharply with the strange satisfaction that he has understood what she has hidden from herself. He knows her ambition because he has his own. He knows what tempts and what delights her. In that single breath she realizes it is James she will give up and not her art.

"I didn't think so," he says. "You will stay away from James and you can have your exhibition and you will print my expedition plates."

He knows her eyes are on him, but he will not look up. She goes to the wardrobe and flings the door open and begins to undo the buttons of her shirtwaist. She hears the creak of the chair.

"Where are you going?" he says.

"My darkroom."

She tosses the shirtwaist onto the bed and puts on a linen blouse without a collar. She drops over her head a loose smock with pockets sewn onto the front.

"If you're going to assign me the task of printing all your photographs, I must begin. The sooner I finish yours, the sooner I return to mine."

She goes down through the house to the ground floor. The boxes of Polar plates are still in large crates deposited yesterday outside the darkroom. She calls for Miner to come help her, and he knocks down the stairs in his uneven tread and takes a crowbar to a crate lid. Inside, the smaller boxes of Polar plates nestle in sawdust. James has numbered the boxes, but there are so many—perhaps fifty boxes of a dozen plates each—how will she ever finish? She sees now this was from the outset Edward's way of punishing them both at once. James to be separated from his own creations, Viola to be burdened with this Herculean task.

"Bloody hell," she says to Miner. "No sense in bringing them all inside the darkroom. There'll be no room left for me. Help me find the last ones, Samuel. The highest number. James has marked them." The boxes are numbered in wavy script in grease pencil.

"Take the lowest number, too."

The start of the journey, perhaps photos of the ship at sea, and albatross, perhaps a whale.

"We'll get there soon enough." If she goes backwards in the plates, she will be unwinding time. The men will grow healthier and younger with every box.

Miner helps her bring ten boxes into the darkroom and stack them on her counter. Edward expects her to toil here, alone, in darkness, for what he knows will take her days to do. Her guilt is not deep enough to let her accept all this without resentment. She closes the darkroom doors and turns on the ruby light.

She opens the first box—the oldest box—and flips through the stiff envelopes until she finds the earliest plate and the date written in grease pencil: 10 October 1909. There is James' hand again, though here it is jagged, blocky, and she imagines him gripping the pencil in thick gloves, hands frozen and fingers numb, even in this first month of the expedition. She slides the plate from the thick waxed-paper envelope. In the darkroom's ruby light, she can see it is pale green, shaded darker in some parts, lighter in others. The latent image hangs in the emulsion, waiting for her to bring it out, to turn it black and white.

Holding James' plate by its edges, she sets it into the time tank and adds the others from the box. When the timer rings, she takes the plates one at a time and slides them into the fixer bath. The images are mostly black, the silver halide gathered thick where light has struck. When the fixer is finished, she takes up the first image and sees against the plane of black an etched figure of white. From the carriage of the head and shoulders, she knows that it is Edward. She takes this one to the sink at the end of the workbench and rinses the extra emulsion from the plate. She tells herself that she performs a task. This is not art and she must do this work as if she were a stranger in a shop. She puts it on the rack to dry and moves on to the next plate.

When she has developed several boxes full of plates and they sit drying in the racks like so many dishes in a scullery, Viola prepares to make the lantern slides that Edward will need for his presentations. She places a fresh plate on the base of her enlarger and sets the first developed negative directly onto it. She sets the timer, turns on the enlarger's bulb, waits one, two, three, four, turns it off. Again, she sets the glass into the baths, developer, fixer, water, and this time the image that forms is positive. A man, Edward, standing on the blinding white of ice. But she has exposed the plate too long and Edward is too dark. His body is undifferentiated, a black oblong, and the face edged by the fur hood a murky circle. Viola gets another fresh plate and this time shines the enlarger's bulb for just more than two seconds. Now when she pulls the plate from the fixer, she can make out the mitten-holder looped around Edward's neck, a strap crossing his chest to keep the lengths together. She makes out the whites of his eyes. She has found the right exposure—just two and a quarter seconds—to get the image right.

She develops another lantern slide and her breath catches when she sees it: Edward and the flag. Her anger at him falls away and she is both proud and relieved at the simple fact of him. There is her Edward at the Pole. He called himself the hero of the Pole and here he is. Even in parka and boots and bulky trousers draped with gabardine, she knows him, knows the way he weights his right hip and slopes his shoulders. Beneath the black disks of his snow goggles, she knows the dark of his eyes and the steady way that he has always looked at her. James has taken the photograph and must be standing behind the camera looking at the grim expression on Edward's face. Viola knows not to look for jubilation. Only when the peak is low, the summit simple, does she see smiles and happiness. Where success is hard-earned, their victor's features look like anger.

She cannot stop gazing at the plate. Her mind plays the terms of it over and over: Edward, Pole, flag, Edward, Pole, flag. James has set him slightly to the right side of the image and the composition sets Edward in context of the vast and empty space. She imagines she can look through that clear-sharp glass to the moment itself, through time and space to find herself standing by James and with her finger on the shutter. Push in and snap the shutter closed and open. Push and make the camera blink to snatch the image like a gulp of time. What is the word for such a thing? It is not there or here. It is not there or then. It is all in one word. Now? That, she thinks, is what the camera does that paints could never do: captures the now and renders place and instant one and the same, together. Here is Edward, at the Pole now, holding the flag, now. And she in her Chelsea darkroom bringing him to life now so that others can see.

What must he have felt, and James, to reach the place he strove for. To touch the one place in that vast continent that marked out his arrival. Before they left, Edward explained to her his system of navigation and of mapping a quadrant to be sure of the very center. It seemed impossible, though he explained in detail, that even careful measurement could solve the problem of Antarctica's immensity. It seems to her still to be the purpose of Antarctica, to be the very definition of the place—to be so large, so vast, so featureless to overwhelm all human regulation. Light changes there.

Space too. How is it possible to measure when the tools of measurement and the men who wield them become so altered? She peers at Edward's face. She knows it is the cold and pain and hunger that lend such a strange set to his expression, but she lets herself imagine that he knows he is the point from which all measures come.

She looks again at the image of Edward and the flag and Viola wonders why James chose the composition. It is an infelicitous alignment, especially for so critical a photograph. Edward is neither in the center nor in a position that adheres to the rule of thirds. This must be an artifact of his emotion, that he was so moved by their arrival at the Pole that he let go his judgment as an artist. Perhaps she should crop the image for the lantern slide. She can adjust to make the image find its balance. She sets the plate aside to consider later on and takes up another from the rack.

It is an image now of both of them, again with the Union Jack beside them. They have removed their snow goggles—surely for no longer than it took to make the photograph lest they sear their eyes. She can see the determination on Edward's face, and on James' face a set to the jaw she knows to be a sign of irritation. It is as if she were reading the photographs in order and here is James annoyed at the mistake he has just made in the photograph of Edward. She can imagine him thinking then he should have framed the image differently and now here is one plate he has carried all that way and will carry home that bears an error. She smiles at her invention, likes to think of so human a response in such a brutal place. She wonders, if she were to read every plate in order, would she spy the moment Edward learned of the affair? Would she see in his eyes a fall from trust to betrayal, a new pain where there was only cold before?

28

16 June

Edward and Viola take a car to the Royal Albert Hall where the Royal Geographical Society will honor Edward's achievement. Miner rides with them as guardian of the camera case and sits opposite Edward to face backwards. Inside are all the plates Viola turned into slides for the magic lantern. The ride to Kensington takes only minutes. On another day they might have walked the journey, but it is clear they must arrive in cavalcade. They pull up to a crowd of faces and cameras shoving at the glass. Edward opens the door and shouts instructions to someone behind. He thrusts an arm into the car, wiggles his fingers, ducks into Viola's view.

"Come now, Viola. Let's be quick."

She steps out onto the pavement and the noise rushes in around her. It is like the furor of a suffrage march. But this crowd is made up mostly of men. She makes out only a few broad women's hats among the men's homburgs and bowlers. All around her there are cameras, flash pans, calls and yells. She cannot gauge if these are thousands or tens of thousands, more than for a march on Parliament or fewer. Edward moves ahead and instantly the gap is filled with newsmen and their cries rise like those of some sort of bird. "Captain," they shout. "Captain!" Their voices peck at the air.

Edward is waving to Miner who has followed with the case. The crowd makes way for this man in a strange mask and for the cart he pulls. Viola looks for James but cannot find him. She takes a few steps up towards the Hall's entrance to see over the crowd. A sea of Union Jacks, made of paper like the ones in Cardiff. One of the newspapers included the flags in the morning edition—quarter sheets printed in color with a baton to roll up for a miniature flagpole. Still no James. A dignitary frees Edward from a gang of newsmen and brings him up the steps to her. Other dignitaries descend from the entrance.

"Captain Heywoud," they say. "Mrs. Heywoud."

Inside the Hall it is near chaos. Men shout and wave arms in the air. Flash pans make their small explosions and fill the hall with smoke. People drape over the balconies at every tier. Viola is taken up by yet another dignitary from the Royal Geographical Society, a wiry man with leathery brown skin and an air of the tropics. Ahead, Edward is being brought up to the stage. She sees no sign of James until the wiry man leads her to a place in the front row. James is standing by a seat on the aisle.

"Am I to sit here?"

But the wiry man departs and she does not care to know if her seating is Edward's desire or someone else's error. She takes her seat by James who remains standing to shake the hands of those who recognize him. James is no star like Edward, whose photograph has graced the papers many times for routes and peaks and for discoveries published in the scientific journals. He stands near with his back to her in his white tie and tails, his sleeve cuffs newly starched, the trousers pressed, though James cannot compete with Edward's Navy epaulettes and braid. The wool of James' trousers is just inches from her knees. She reaches out where no one sees and runs a fingertip along the crease.

There is a break in the attention to him and he turns to her.

"You're here," he says, in his newly hoarse voice.

"Why aren't you on the stage?"

"Part of my punishment. I am not to speak at our engagements."

"And I am not to see you except at places like this."

She does not tell him the bargain she has struck.

"With Edward watching."

Edward stands on the dais among Explorers intent on conversation.

"I don't know when I will see you next," she says.

"Then we must say everything now."

He turns to smile at her and she sees the sallow color of his cheeks beneath the weathering.

"What did Penelope weave while Ulysses was away?"

She frowns at the comparison. She does not like to think herself besieged or having to undo her work to keep her freedom.

"Tell me," he says.

"There is so much. I joined the suffrage marches, and I've had photographs in the papers. Then Izzy introduced me to these women who go on hunger strike when they're in prison, to protest for the vote." Now it is she who is Ulysses, she who tells her stories of adventure, whose every word announces who she really is. "There is so much more. Come to the gallery, James, and I will show you. The show is in four days," she says.

"Whitechapel Gallery, Vi. That's really something."

"I know," she says. "But I have so much to do and now I'm printing yours."

"It's all right," James says. "The darkroom is not the place for me these days. Too dark."

"You always liked to be there." His curls glowing in the ruby light and the shadows on his face like something out of Caravaggio.

"That was when we were there together. It's too small and cramped. Just the thought of it and I can't breathe."

She tries to picture him out on the ice with only Edward and the other members of the southern party, and that a crowd numbering only four. What must this crowded Hall seem to him, to Edward too, after so many months of isolation. The yips of dogs now turned din of motorcars and omnibuses, whistles and shouts. The spread of white now crowded with the busy press of colors.

She is about to tell him that she understands, about to tell him how she longs to be alone with him, when Edward's chair scrapes back and he goes to the lectern where the Society man extends a hand in invitation. The Hall breaks out into applause and cheers.

Someone switches on the magic lantern positioned on the stage and the lights are dimmed inside the Hall. A large screen is wheeled out and Edward coughs, waiting for the Society man to align the magic lantern lamp upon the screen. Thousands lean forward in their seats and the Hall fills with the rustle of fabric. An image glides up and down and across the stage so that for an instant the seated dignitaries are illumined with the figures of men in parkas and a sledge. Weathered faces glance like ghosts across the shirt-fronts of the delegation. Edward coughs again and this—this act of nerves, this frailty—reveals him to her all at once. Her Ned. He holds the room of thousands in his hand but to her he appears suddenly diffident and anxious. Now for the first time she is afraid of all the time and space of all his travels, all the dangers he has faced and overcome. It is a blessing that he survived. That he did so and succeeded is a miracle, and there he stands to set his achievement out before them. James pulls his hand away and only then does she realize she reached for it.

Edward has things to say about each image. He gestures to James and Lawrence when their faces appear upon the screen, and James and Lawrence, from front row and from back, in frock coat and in Norfolk jacket, nod in gratitude. When Tite appears in an image, he sets his hand on his heart and speaks of the depth of the man's sacrifice. The crowd murmurs its sympathy. Icebergs. Shore Camp. Dogs. This is the Ross Sea. This is the Barrier. The screen shivers with motion as the delegation fidgets on the dais to get a closer look. Viola has done her work well. The images are crisp and clear, the contrast exact. The crowd is mesmerized by what the slides depict, but also by their beauty. If there were no punishment behind the thing, these slides would be a perfect expression of the three of them: James to take the images, Viola to develop them, and Edward to tell their story. But she recognizes anger in Edward's face as he goes on with his narration. This is Mount Erebus. This the Beardmore Glacier. And then the Union Jack and Edward, and the room leaps to its feet. They cheer. Someone begins to sing and the rest join in. He is a jolly good fellow. No one can deny. Men thump the floor with canes. They pull James up and smack him on the back.

But he can barely crack a smile, keeps staring at the screen that shows the photograph of Edward and the flag. There is Edward's grim expression and James invisible behind the camera. She thinks for a moment again that she should have cropped the photograph for a more pleasing image. The hubbub dies down—one of the Society men is cajoling them to quiet—and Viola sets a hand on James' shoulder. His eyes snap to her and she sees his face has gone sallow.

"What's wrong, James?"

"Nothing," he says. His smile is tight. "Brings back memories. That's all."

"What is it?"

"Nothing, I said."

He jerks away.

The audience has reclaimed their places. Edward looks down at her expectant, annoyed. She settles back into her seat.

On the stage, Edward points to where the screen now shows an image of sastrugi, the frozen dunes of wind-whipped snow that force the sledge nearly on end to climb through. He looks not at the screen but at Viola, not at Viola but Viola and James. He has seen them whispering. He watches now as she leans away and sets her hands in her lap. His face is cast again with that sadness and anger she saw when she told him she would go to James.

When it is over, there are cheers again. James is summoned, and Lawrence and another man join Edward on the stage. The Society president, Lord Minto, comes to take her arm.

"Mrs. Heywoud," he says, leading her up the short flight of stairs to the stage. "Please do us the honor."

He takes her to the lectern and sets before her on the sloping wood a sheet of parchment, beckons her to read. The room hushes at her first words.

"Let it henceforth be known that the Royal Geographical Society honors Captain Edward Heywoud, James Watts, William Lawrence and Angus Tite for their brave exploration of the Antarctic Regions, and honors Edward Heywoud and James Watts for their heroic achievement of the Earth's southernmost point."

Viola is nearly drowned out by applause and cheers and stomping on the wooden floor. Minto calls the men forth one by one and sets over their bowed heads a broad ribbon. Bronze medals the size of saucers hang on their chests. Lawrence stands a full head taller than the others so that the president reaches nearly overhead to give the man his prize. Minto ties a ribbon around the rolled parchment and gives it to Viola.

"Mrs. Heywoud," he says to the room, "we owe a debt to you for your patience. You have tended home and hearth so that your husband could explore the ends of the earth. You have done your wifely duty so that he might do his hero's duty for England, for Britain, and for the King."

When the ceremony has finished, she and Edward are led through the clamor of the Hall to the portico that gives onto Kensington Road. There she sees James standing separate on the steps. No one is speaking to him, no one is photographing him, and he appears like a man lost. Viola sees from this distance how gaunt he is. His jacket hangs loose across his shoulders and the collar of his shirt gapes at the neck. She calls to him.

"What are you doing?" Edward says. But before she can find an answer, he turns her down the steps away from James. "Smile, darling," he says, and turns her towards the nearest photographer's camera.

They return alone to Margaretta Terrace, where Viola follows Edward from the car into the hall and past Mary's worried face. The girl can sense no doubt the mood behind the briskness that bears her employers up the stairs without stopping to hand her a hat or coat or pair of gloves. As the car moved south through Kensington, Viola held her tongue about Edward's behavior on the steps. She is not chattel to be turned this way and that. Edward sat in a stew not seemingly diverted by the medal's heavy weight around his neck. She pursues him now upstairs, skirts in her fists so she can speed him to the bedroom's privacy. He goes ahead as fast as she can chase him.

Before she can upbraid him, he wheels around.

"Did you think no one saw?"

She thinks for a moment that he speaks of her hand tracing the crease of James' trousers.

"Did you think no one saw you lean together, whispering? I forbade him from speaking at our engagements, but that did not mean he could sit with you."

She sees now this will always be between them, more obstacle now that the secret is clear than when they lived around it.

"Like lovebirds," he says. "Sat together like a couple."

"That was not my doing. One of your people."

"Who?"

He steps closer. The medal swings out as he leans.

"I don't know. One of your minions."

He glares at her and she can see he feels the medal's weight, wants to remove this thing that has suddenly become ridiculous.

"Every one of those Society men has been a hero," he says.

"Hero or not, it was one of them put me next to James."

"You couldn't keep your hands off him. I'm right, aren't I?" he says, and there is miserable triumph in his voice. "And to think," he says, "I wasted breath telling you I was trying to be kind. Accepting your exhibition."

He yanks the medal off and drops it on the desk.

"I saw you take his hand. I stand there telling the world that I've achieved something and I look down and see my wife sharing the moment with another man."

This. This is simpler.

"That's not what it was at all." She crosses to him.

"I know what I saw."

She shakes her head.

"It's because of you I took his hand. I was afraid for you."

"You'll notice I have survived."

She thinks of trying to explain and in the end she leaves it.

"At the next speech simply seat me by myself," she says.

"Oh, you're not coming to the next speech."

"Don't be ridiculous."

"I'm not."

"Edward! The press will eat you alive. You cannot not bring your wife. You need me as much as you need James."

He snatches up the medal and shoves it at her.

"Do you see this? They gave this to me. Because I nearly died to carry that damned flag to that godforsaken place. I looked a good dog in the eyes and shot it. I ate its flesh. I sent Tite away to die because he would have slowed us down. I became a monster for this medal so I'll give the speeches any way I like."

They have been through this before. There is something Edward loses in his conquests and she cannot even see the place it has been taken from. There is no easy scar, no wound to heal. But every time he wins something he lets something of himself be usurped and then despises the part of him that so easily gave in. She can tell him that she understands the cost and that she will help to make him whole. She can explain that she knows the temptation of surrendering one's self to make a bargain. She can set a hand against his cheek and tell him look, look at me, Ned. I am here with you. But he is furious and rigid now, not the man whose act led her to take her lover's hand in sympathy but that monster of his own invention.

At night, when Viola gets into bed beside him, she lies on her back, eyes open, too aware of their evening argument and of his breathing and the mass of his body on his side of the mattress. Her thoughts reclaim the day's events as images—the crowds, William Lawrence at full height, Edward's single cough. Only three days he is back and she pines for the spread of her limbs, the level of the bed beneath her. Now his weight makes a dip that rolls her towards him but she does not want to touch.

29

17 June

Viola goes down to the kitchen in the morning after a restless sleep. She drinks only a few sips of the tea that Mary makes for her. She cannot shift her thoughts from James. Four days after their return, and months since their ship left the Polar coast behind, and he still seems to suffer. Despite exposure to ice- and sea-reflected sun, his skin is sallow and the crescent folds beneath his eyes shade purple, as if he has been punched. While Edward nearly fills out his jackets once again, James swims inside his clothes. But most of all, she cannot stop thinking of the way he stared up at the screen and jerked away when she asked him why. There was more than a lopsided composition to bother him.

Edward is out to visit the Norwegian embassy and offer a victor's token to King Haakon. He will be out for several hours and so Viola leaves the teacup on the deal worktable and goes to the darkroom. She seals herself in behind the muffling doors and finds the plates she used to make the magic lantern slides. She brings this box up to the workbench. She knows the images by heart now. A group of men—that giant Lawrence, and the other man she now knows as Tite—sitting by a meal, with dogs at their feet. Edward by a cross and cairn. Edward and James by the Union Jack and Edward alone. Edward flanked by Lawrence and Tite, the three of them crouching like holidaymakers on a beach. She picks up each plate and holds it to the ruby light, peering into the negative, knowing to see white where there is black and black where there is white. She is long trained in these inversions. She can look at an image and see the opposite that makes it true. She peers at the negative of Edward and the cairn. They have built it from blocks of ice and stuck into it a cross that leans to one side. She sees now the cross is made of rough-hewn planks, their jagged ends searing through the shaded tint of the sky. Viola does not like to think of what lies inside the cairn but knows this must be Nilsen, frozen to a statue, unable to bend or shape into decorum, unyielding to the actions of decay. The man will lie there—though to lie suggests a different place than that he is condemned to—for eternity, unchanging in the strange unmoving violence of Antarctic cold. This could have been her Edward, her James. Thank God that they are here and James is only ill.

She holds the plate up to the light once more to look again. She reaches for the magnifying glass among the tools hanging on the board, a tool she uses to see where to dodge and burn a print when it requires manipulation. But she sees nothing that would make James worry. She falls back against the door and closes her eyes. She has stared so long at the ruby-illuminated plates that her eyes' darkness glows with ghosts. She pushes herself from the door and takes up the plates again, one by one. She holds them quickly to the light and sets them down. She mutters. "Not this one," she says, and again, "No." She lifts up the plate depicting Edward and the flag, holds it to the light. She brings the magnifier to bear again but now everything is too big. She can make out only that there is a dark shape on the ice far to Edward's right, in the corner of the image. It is only James' lopsided composition that has brought that space into the frame. She peers at the shape again. A dog or a cover for the sledge or something else flung or dropped.

She drops her apron over her neck and ties the strings around her waist. She sets into the enlarger the negative with that dark speck, switches on the light bulbs, adjusts the height of the enlarger head until the corner of the image is focused clearly on the enlarger base with the dark shape at its center. She turns the bulbs off, slides a fresh sheet of paper onto the base where the image will once again project, and switches on the bulbs: one, two, and off. She slips the paper into the developer bath and waits. The image darkens, as if rising from a depth, until she sees it clearly: Edward and the Union Jack. With her bamboo tongs, she sets the paper into its baths—stopper, fixer, rinse—and plucks it from the final bath to clip onto the drying cord that runs across a corner of the darkroom.

The shape on the ice is still unclear. She must go on. She takes a sequence of photographs to enlarge the details of the background a little more each time, until the background objects have come clear. It will be like an exploration going forward, moving deeper and deeper into an instant captured from the past in a place a world away. She should not be doing this. She has her exhibition prints to work on and the manifesto she must write for Aitken and only four days in which to do it. But she knows this image has something to tell her.

She prepares the camera and aims the lens at the stand where she secures the print with clothespins. A bright light illuminates the stand so that she can make a photo of the photograph magnified as if through a telescope. She takes the new photograph and sets the negative into its baths until she has an image. This she sets on top of a new sheet of paper and again she brings the enlarger into focus. Again she prints the image out onto a new sheet of paper, and again she slips the paper into its succession of chemical baths to make a print. She clips each print to the line and stands beneath them, peering, to make out what she sees. There is something. There is more than a dark shape on the ice. She presses hands into the small of her back, squeezes her eyes shut. The sudden shifts from dark to light as she goes from print to camera have confused her vision. She does not know what she sees. Is it a trick of the Pole, that place where they say compasses forget their obligations and point only down as if to indicate themselves?

Again she sets the print in the holder. Again brings the camera close to photograph a detail. Again prints the photograph and photographs it. As she works in smaller and smaller portions of the image—zooming in to make Edward larger and yet larger—she begins to see. What began as a speck in the background has now been magnified into a shape, a form.

With each new photograph, it grows clearer and darker, clearer and darker, as if moving towards her in the light.

And then she sees it. But this cannot be. This cannot be what James cringed to remember, and this cannot be what appears in the print before her. She looks closer still and closer. She brings the magnifying glass to her eye again and there is no denying that on the ice to Edward's right, discarded as if by accident, is the white-outlined dark cross of the Norwegian flag. Viola shies away and drops the magnifying glass onto her bench. Perhaps this is simply a flag that Edward brought with him to the Pole. Perhaps it is a testament to his intended kindness, to fly his rival's flag with his own. But there is no photograph of such alliance. The Norwegian flag—Nilsen's flag—lies as if tossed aside. She peers through the glass again and sees the faintest trace of a line beside the flag. She sees the stake it flew from.

She covers her mouth. She goes to James' box from the Pole and rifles through those negatives, looking for another image she thinks she remembers. James and Edward standing side by side, the Union Jack between them, and James' lips pressed tight as if against a wave of nausea. Before she can see if the black speck appears there too to tell a troubling story, she stops and slips down to the floor, sits with her skirts tented before her and her back against the wall. She pushes her hands into her hair. Surely there is an explanation. Surely she does not understand what she is looking at.

The workbench is littered with photographs. Someone entering the room would think them pieces of a puzzle. A shoulder here, a forearm there, a field of ice, a flag. Together they seem to make an image: the explorer successful at the Pole. But Viola sees now that is not what it is at all.

Edward will return soon from the Norwegian king. She pushes herself from the wall and gathers up the photographs, looks around the room for a place in which to hide them even if their meaning is not clear. Where to put them? Where to put the plate? Edward will need it for the prints she must keep making, for the newspapers and for his admirers. James will need it for the exhibitions he will surely have and for the book he will no doubt publish. She looks about the darkroom as if for some equipment she possesses that can make this right. The original negative is beside her on the workbench. She could destroy it and silence the whispers that rise up around her now. She could print a new image and burn away the speck so that its blemish never showed again in public.

And she may be wrong. Surely there is an explanation for what appears to be amiss. She will say nothing yet. Perhaps it is a simple defect in the lens that takes the shape of Edward's greatest fear and he is innocent of usurpation. She sat once with a student of Madame Blavatsky and wanted to believe the lignite smell and wisp of steam could be the spirit of her father. If ectoplasm can show in a portrait, then why cannot a man's real fear produce a ghost?

Viola returns the glass plate exactly where it should be in its box. She takes up the new plates she has just made and slides their box into a small gap beneath the darkroom floor and the workbench where its base is elevated to allow a drain. She slides the sheaf of prints there along with the box, stands back, makes sure that they cannot be seen. She folds the camera away and pours the chemicals into their bottles. And as she does all this, she tells herself again that she is being skittish. Edward and James can explain. Surely it will all make sense.

She thinks of those last strides and seconds of possibility, the last moments when Edward might still have come in first. There must have been a glory to it, something stronger than fatigue. It must have been a delirium of expectation, to keep the body moving in its rhythm while wanting to dash ahead and reach the future. And then the sight of the flag, a red cloth in the near distance. To realize that he had both arrived and lost in the same instant. What would she have done in Edward's place and with the rival dead some miles behind? Would she have been strong enough to set her flag beneath the other and turn for home? Or would she have done what Edward may have done? Would she fling the Norwegian flag away or set it gently down, and take the rival's fame? With Nilsen dead, what harm could it have done?

30

17 June

Edward is at his desk in the study, his jacket draped over the back of the chair, his shirtsleeves rolled to the elbow. The dark skin on his hands makes him appear stitched from pieces. He turns at the sound of her skirts rustling and she sees his eyes are moist.

"I'm writing to the families," he says. "I am set to meet with them this week."

"I've brought the tea," she says, so that she will not have to speak about the men whose lives may have been lost in a false journey.

"Do you know," he says, "I lost three. Tite from the Polar Party. Mac-Burney and Jones from Shore Camp. Jones was not even meant to come. Carried stores into the hold for us. Said he had no job and could we give him an adventure."

She pours the tea the way he likes it now, thick with milk and sugar.

"At Shore Camp, the fool took a tender to go touch a berg and it calved just as he reached it. We lost the tender, too."

"You'll find something kind to say of him."

"They want to know what it was like, how their son or husband died a good death, a noble death. What can I say? It was scurvy for MacBurney. And the cold killed Tite." He seems to shake himself and looks up at her. "Did you want something?"

223

"It's about one of the photographs," she says. "Of you at the Pole. One of the ones you showed at the Society."

"I have four more letters to write, Viola. Haakon kept me longer than I thought."

From the scent of whisky on him, she suspects he followed Haakon with a visit to his club.

"There's something odd about one image."

"You'll have to show it to me another time."

"Do you remember anything strange happening with the camera?"

He sighs and screws the cap on his fountain pen and sets it down. "When?"

"At the Pole," she says. "At Ninety."

"You'll have to ask Watts about the camera."

"I want to know what *you* say. Tell me. What happened at the Pole?"

"I took a reading and planted the flag. I've explained what it was like."

He turns back to his writing. She stills his hand on the paper. "Edward, stop. You cannot write your letters until we speak of this." She squeezes his hand as if he would break free of her, as if they fight now for the shape his ink will take across the page.

"What happened at the Pole, Ned?"

He tugs his hand away and leaves an errant line of ink on the letter.

"I told you," he says, as he fusses with the nib. "We were nearly dead with cold. We didn't do a dance, Viola, or make a snowman. We took our photograph and got the hell out of there to come home."

"And that's all? Nothing else?"

"We ate some chocolate to celebrate. Cadbury's."

"Ned."

"Viola." He looks at her. "You have been working very hard on your exhibition. You have been staring at those nudes so long."

"What does that have to do with anything?"

"How can you trust your sight?"

"My eyes are fine. I spent hours and hours in the darkroom while you were away."

"You've simply mistaken a speck or a piece of lint in this photograph for something else."

"I saw something there on the ice."

"Come now, Viola. You're being hysterical."

At this, this damning word, she stares at him and feels a surge of new anger. In all their disagreements over what she should and could take on—whether to march, to climb, to protect the womb that bore and could bear another child—not once did he reduce her to so base and hurtful an idea. That he has done so now is both a sign that something is profoundly wrong and a goad to greater confrontation.

"You're a liar," she says, her face burning, afraid for him and for herself. "You lied, didn't you, about the Pole? I know," she tells him, because in that moment and in the question she asked to which she already had the answer, she has come to understand everything. "I know."

He begins to say something and she sees he will again try to dismiss her.

"Stop," she says. "There's nothing more to say. I know what you did." Her eyes grow wide at the shock of her own words. "I saw it when I made the photographs. I saw the other flag. What happened, Ned?"

He has no reply.

"Why was the Norwegian flag lying on the ice?"

He falls into the corner chair.

"They were dead, Viola," he says finally. "They were already dead. It didn't matter."

"They got there before you." She says it as much to confirm the fact as to rebut him.

"But they died on the way back."

"They were still first."

"We were first to go and return."

"Oh, Ned. That's not what you're being celebrated for and that's not what you're saying to the world."

He shakes his head.

"You don't understand," he says. "You can't imagine what it was like."

"You lied, Edward. You lied."

She fights a sob and looks across to see that he, too, is nearly crying.

"What part of what I went through was a lie?" he says. "The cold? The suffering? The man-hauling and skiing and starvation? Was that not real? And to discover that all the time that I was planning the journey and thinking how I would be parted from you, you were sleeping with James? Was that not real either?"

"Don't turn this into my fault."

"We went, Viola, and we came back." The words are choked and straining.

"You couldn't have been sure of that when you took the photograph. Had you died—"

"But we didn't."

"Had you died, they would have found your bodies and Nilsen's and all your photographs and plates and they'd develop them and they would know the truth. The same way I do."

"They'd never find our bodies."

"You found Nilsen's."

"Do you understand what kind of miracle that was? In all that ice?" He shakes his head. "We had to do it. He was dead." His voice comes in a hoarse whisper. "Why did he do it? The fool."

"Who?"

"Watts." He snaps his head up sharply. "He did this. We had moved the flag away. It was not meant to be in the photograph. He could have aimed the camera where I told him. But he had to go against me. That damned flag. I carried it with me all the way back to shore as if it was a thing I loved. I burned it somewhere in the Southern Ocean. Threw the ashes overboard. That bloody flag was the only thing in the way of my achievement. That was the only thing, Viola, that could ruin my legacy."

"I would not claim someone else's achievement for my own."

His body stills and Viola realizes he has been in endless small motion since she returned to the room, picking at his clothes or his own hands.

"Have you not already claimed the achievement of another with your photographs? You may not be lying, Viola. But you assume a place at the head of these women who have sacrificed their bodies, while you take your photographs from a safe distance. I know full well you do this for yourself as much as for your cause. But I do not begrudge you. I know who you are, Viola. You see," he says. "It is not so simple. It is not simple at all."

"No," she says. "It isn't. But, Ned, you can't go on this way."

"Why not?"

"Because with every lie you tell, you become angrier."

"You are the only one who knows," he says. "You and Watts."

"And look at him. The guilt is killing him."

"Listen to me, Viola. If the truth comes out, we will be ruined."

"But you will live your entire life in a lie."

"If I admit what happened," he says, "there will be no money. None. Nothing for you and me to live on. We will be disgraced, ousted from all circles. No one will send me on an expedition ever again. No one will want your photographs. This is the situation we are in."

"You put us in this situation. You could have come home and told the truth. Surely, there would have still been funds for that."

"For being a noble failure?"

"For reaching the Pole. Which you did."

"This is a pointless conversation, Viola. You know as well as I do that I did not go and come back to have simply gone and come back," he says. "I didn't go to the Pole for a journey. I went to be first."

"I know, Edward. But this lie." She pushes hands into her hair. "I wish I had never seen that bloody speck in the photograph. We could have gone on together. I would have never known. We could have moved on, from everything."

"And we cannot now?"

"I don't know, Ned." She does not want to tell him that the lie itself is not as troubling as the craven way he clings to it. There is something about his actions that is desperate.

"You know you cannot prove anything," he says.

"What?"

"If you wanted to tell the truth," he says, "it would simply be a matter of your word against mine."

He does not know that she has made the detailed prints. He might destroy the plate she made them from, but they remain her proof. They show the flag discarded on the ice, its blue cross outlined white on a red field clearly visible in the grayscale of her enlargements. But would she ever show them to expose his lie?

"You should have asked me, Ned."

"Asked you what?"

"I could have helped. I could have altered the photograph, cropped it, dodged and burned the flag away. You assumed I was against you so you didn't even ask." How could she have denied him when her very own prints for the exhibition cast what is false as true?

"I don't know what I am supposed to do," she says.

He jumps to his feet.

"You will go on as planned. You will go on with your exhibition. There must be no sign that there is anything amiss. Do you understand that?"

She looks at him and tries to see in the new lines of his desperation the gallant face of the man she followed up so many cliffs and crags, the man who came to know enough to let her sometimes lead him. But it is too late now. It is all too late.

"Will you tell? Viola. Will you tell?"

"I don't know. I cannot be here with you now."

"What do you mean?" he says. "Where are you going?"

"I don't know." She is not lying. She knows only that she cannot remain in the house and cannot sleep beside him in their bed.

Alone in the foyer, she puts on her hat and linen jacket and takes up her bag. The latch clicks softly as she closes the door behind her. In the time it has taken her to descend the stairs and collect her things, she has decided where to go. She goes to the darkroom to retrieve the sheaf of Polar prints and walks out onto Margaretta Terrace where the streetlamps blind the sky for stars. At the King's Road, she waits for a taxi and gives the driver the address.

"Gloucester Crescent, Camden Town."

31

17 June

Viola stops the cab when it reaches Camden High Street and walks the short distance towards the canal and to the curve of James' street lined with large semi-detached houses. The street is hushed, as if she has traveled not a few miles but hours into deepest London night. She walks the passage beside the main house and emerges into the back garden where smells of rotting leaves and soil mingle with the night scents of moonflower and primrose. James' cottage is at the rear of the garden. A row of glass panes set in both eaves of the tiled roof sends a glow into the twilight.

She knocks at the door and a fox shrieks from somewhere in the shadows. She hears kits mewling and a rustle in the brambles.

"Viola."

James is wrapped in a tartan blanket that makes a triangle of his shape. "Come inside, Vi."

She covers her mouth with her hands.

"I don't know what I'm doing here. I shouldn't be here."

"Come inside," he says again. "Please?"

"James," she says, and the name holds all her sadness and her fear for what the men have done. He draws her with him down the short passage to the large room whose ceiling rises to the transoms. There is the stove like a creature squatting by the corner, the patterned rug, the easels and paints from before James took up the camera.

"Nothing's changed," she says.

"You didn't come while I was gone?"

She shakes her head. How could she have? It would have been no refuge from her longing. It is no refuge now. She spreads the prints out on a little table.

"What is this, James? What am I looking at?"

Each print captures a detail of the image of Edward with the Union Jack. There in a print of its own is that dark speck on the ice now magnified enough so they can both see clearly: the Norwegian flag. She whispers it again.

"What did you do?"

He sits on the end of the bed with his head in his hands.

"You saw something," she says. "You saw something at the Albert Hall in the photographs. And like a fool I went looking for it. God, I wish I hadn't."

He looks up at her with so much sorrow in his eyes she goes and draws him to her chest.

After a time, he pulls away and runs his hands through his ragged hair.

"We found the Norwegians dead," he says. "And we kept going to the Pole. We saw their flag. Edward took it down and put ours up. He wanted one more photograph. But I shifted the camera. I thought maybe if I had a photograph that showed Nilsen's flag on the ice, maybe I could show it to Edward later and convince him."

"Why didn't you?"

"The entire idea seems so foolish now. As if he would have sailed home and changed the story. What would he have said? *No, the telegram from Lyttelton was a mistake. We were never first at all.*"

"You could have told a newsman, shown the photo to the press."

"That would have ruined Edward. You know that. I couldn't do it. Besides, what would they say of me? Didn't I go along with it? Didn't I bask in the praise and the celebrations?" He picks at the coverlet. Outside, the fox repeats its shriek. "The truth is," he goes on, "I kept the secret because it was easier to go along. It was better. I could be a hero and be part of this story no one would ever know we had made up. We could tell the world whatever we wanted. We had the photographs. We were alive. The Norwegians were dead. That was all we needed."

She sits beside him.

"I hate my part in this," he says. "I hate that I chose to go along. Do you wish I hadn't, Vi? Do you wish that I had told the truth?"

The question is so stark that she lets out a gasp.

"Do you?" he says.

"I wish that there had been nothing to tell. I wish that what you did and the tale of it had been the same, no matter what it was. The same instant," she says. "So there was never any possibility of making the truth what you wanted it to be. It would be so much simpler that way."

"But that's never how things are."

"No, it's not. And it's a silly thing to say when I don't even wish it for myself."

She takes his hand and turns it over in hers. The tips of several of his fingers are waxy and hard from frostbite.

"What will you do, Vi? Will you expose us?"

How can she expose the men when her own exhibition depends on a thing that is not true?

"I don't know."

"You came here to ask me for the truth. What do we do with it?"

"I don't know." She thinks of Edward telling her he owes it to the men who died and to the living who risked so much. She wonders again what she would have done when faced with shocking proof someone had beaten her to her own hope.

"I think I came tonight to say goodbye to you," she says.

He rests a hand on her cheek and she turns to kiss the heat of his palm.

"You're burning."

"I am always cold."

He pulls her up to stand with him. They undress, almost with ceremony. Her hat and gloves, his shoes and socks, her bodice, his shirt. When he is naked she sees the hair on his shins has worn away and his buttocks are inverted bowls bracketed by jutting hipbones. There is about him something feral, like a wild child from Rousseau, strange product of the frozen land thrust into this Camden cottage.

He is so thin she is afraid that she will break him. He moves as if his bones are loose. But he tugs her shoulders, seizes her knee, her hair. He tears open the prophylactic and fits it on. He pulls until she has no choice but to pin him, bite him. She drops down onto him and watches his pleasure edge with pain. When he comes it is as if he does not want to, as if she has compelled him to give up a secret he would die to keep. She brings his head between her legs. Here, she thinks. Tell it here.

They lie together on the bed and though the air outside has cooled, a damp rises from the nearby canal. She pulls the sheet over them both.

"You said you'd come to say goodbye," he says.

"I did."

But she cannot bring herself to leave. Not only because she worries for his illness, but because the cottage is a kind of home. She goes to the sink with its skirt of printed fabric and fills an enameled mug with water. She brings it back to him and holds it up for him to drink. She tucks him in and sets the back of her hand to his forehead. He is still hot to the touch.

"I will ask Bertie to come and see you."

"I'm just tired," he says.

"You're rail thin. Edward is up and about as if he never left London and you are feverish and weak."

"I'll be fine, Vi. Right as rain."

"Don't do that, James. Tell me what is going on."

"Besides the fact that we are liars?"

He takes a deep breath and makes an effort to gather himself.

"Edward was angry at me," he says. "Because of you. On the boat he wasn't giving me enough to eat. No meat or limes or lemons. Not a gin and tonic to be had. Not the right stuff for scurvy."

Viola knows how a man can die on these expeditions for want of citrus and fresh meat. Edward is always careful to bring bottles of juice.

"Your teeth get loose." James pushes at his teeth with his tongue. "I've got them all though."

"Don't joke."

He shrugs.

"He started giving me the same as everybody again in Madeira. I didn't eat it."

"Why on earth not?"

"It was interesting. How much could I endure. How much did I deserve, after everything we'd done. It became my calculation."

She tries to hold his gaze but his eyes dart away. He tugs the bedsheet up over his chest.

"It's too late now, isn't it?" she says.

"For what?"

"To undo it all. It's too late to tell the truth."

He lifts his head to look at her and now it is her turn to look away. The pain they have all caused one another is so great the scar that it would leave behind outdoes the wound. There is no way to heal except by going forward.

"I don't know, Vi. Do you remember the place I used to tell you about?" he says. "The Broomway?"

His mind has drifted to the east as if moon-pulled. Near Southend where he grew up and where his mother lives now with his sister, the Broomway is a path across the glassy sands of a tide-washed sea. To walk the Broomway is to walk on water, to take up a space between land and sky and walk out to a sea with no horizon. James told her how he knew to read the route as if by body's memory, how others not so expert had drowned in the tide's stealth or suffocated in a quicksand. She wanted him to show her but he told her it wasn't safe, even for her who climbed cliffs and mountains. It was, he said, the most dangerous place he'd ever seen.

"I remember," she says.

"I can't stop thinking about it. At the Pole, you ski and ski and ski and sometimes you can't tell what is up or down, whether you've moved at all. It's like that at the Broomway. Especially on a cloudy day. Everything is gray then. Bloody awful for the camera." He laughs a little. "I'd been telling myself to be in the Broomway. Not to mind that we weren't being honest. Not to feel we had to make everything crystal clear. Be in the Broomway. It will be all right if you accept that nothing is ever clear." He brings the coverlet up around their ears so that their faces are tucked in a dim shelter. He presses his forehead against hers. "The thing is, I can't do it, Vi. It's no good because you don't know where you are. Can't get your bearings. You can't live in the Broomway. You can only pass through it or die in it."

She pulls her head away enough to see him. She thinks of her exhibition and the fact that she aims for exactly this unease. Can't get your bearings. That is exactly what she wants her viewers to feel when they look at her photographs.

"Yes, you can," she says. "I can."

Viola has her own idea of the Broomway as a shoal of cloud and silted sand beyond which lies a bank of blinding light. She does not mind that the maps say different. Her Broomway is a place to linger in to see its beauty. She looks out now at the cottage walls with their paper in rinds at the corners, the soot collected in the sashes. There is no mystery in this place. There is no future here.

"Come with me," she says. "When all of this is done."

"Where are you going?" She can see he doesn't expect an answer but the question sharpens something in her.

"I don't know, really. Does it matter?"

He sits up a little and the coverlet falls away.

"I am leaving Edward," she says, and the words make it true.

"What did he say?"

"I haven't told him yet." She touches his cheek. "I'm telling you," she says. "I will go sometime after the exhibition. If you like, you can follow."

She pulls the coverlet back up around them and they lie back and gaze at the transom windows until the moon, full this night, glides slowly past. It marks a rectangle of light so clear upon the carpet that it looks almost like a door.

While Viola lies beside James, the full moon crosses over the cottage and now she sees it, faint and blurred in the west-facing transom windows. It is still out in the full light of morning, a ghost moon in a light blue sky. She rolls to look at James who sleeps with lower lip tucked behind his teeth. This is a new expression for his face, surely an artifact of Antarctica. In the muffled quiet of the cottage, she lies on the bed and feels alone in a world as vague and blurry as that stranded moon.

She kisses him on the cheek.

"I must go," she says.

He reaches a hand up to her hair and rolls a lock between his fingers as she has seen him do so many times with rope at a crag's base.

"I'm hanging the exhibition tomorrow," she says. "Come help me."

He cocks his head as if he hears something else in her words.

"I'll come to the opening."

"I need to show it to you when we are alone. Come tomorrow, at seven."

She dresses and pins up her hair and kisses him once more. She takes up the prints and pauses on the carpet. She gives the room a look she knows is valedictory. She meant what she told him. She will go soon enough, though she does not know where. But she may never see the cottage or Camden or London again.

Viola returns to Margaretta Terrace with a sense of long farewell. She walks into the foyer and Mary's head swivels as she passes. Edward emerges from the parlor.

"Don't say a word," she says. "I could lie to you about where I've been but I'm not going to. I went to James." He bites back an exclamation. "I had to hear it from him too."

On her way down to the darkroom, she passes the workroom's open door and sees her framed exhibition prints leaned against the wall in an orderly stack, each one wrapped in cloth. She cannot resist the desire to look at them, with their public presentation just two days away. She flips through the frames, peeling back the cloth for each one to see the image. There they are, her creations, her women. Danaë, Venus, odalisque. And then the Botticelli. The old shock of it is gone. She is accustomed now to seeing her nude form and delights in the beauty of it, the imperfections that render it particular, the particularities that make it lovely.

She has a thought and spreads the prints out on the table—the six prints that, brought together as in a collage, make up one enlarged image of Edward and the second flag. She pulls the Botticelli from the stack and lays it on the table facing down, knocking cutlery to the floor with a ring she is sure will send the household running. She stills the forks and knives and listens. There is no sound of someone on the stairs. She takes a knife and slices the paper backing from the frame and then peels it away entirely. She scrabbles at Miner's work supplies and finds brads and a mallet. She tacks the six small prints, one by one, around the frame.

The prints leave a gap in the middle, in which she can see through to the image on the front. She straightens to consider it. It is a strange artwork she has fashioned, breathless, braced for discovery at any moment. Six fragments of an image of a man, and in the center visible the fainter image of a woman rising from the shapes of waves. She pulls a fresh length of paper from the roll that Mary keeps for packages and flattens it across the back. She pulls the paper tight so it is flush and smooth and makes a package of her own. No one can tell this framed photograph is different from the others. Let her hide the damning evidence inside, where Edward will never look, in case she must ever wield it against him.

32

19 June

Viola reaches Whitechapel Gallery ahead of the goods lorry in which Miner accompanies the crate of photographs. She starts towards the entrance and then is caught by the sight of the poster by the door. There is her exhibition, advertised. *Hungry Women: Photographs by Mrs. Edward Heywoud.* A smile spreads on her face and she does not even mind the fact that neither name that she was born with appears on the gallery's facade. The clock on St. Mary's tower across the road says it is past seven. There is no sign of James. But now the lorry has arrived, and Miner and the driver begin to unload the large crate of photographs.

Aitken comes to greet her, in shirtsleeves and waistcoat, his jacket shed since the Gallery has closed for the day. "Just think, Mrs. Heywoud. By this time tomorrow, you will be the talk of London. Are you quite prepared?"

"Of course."

He asks the question with so light a tone she wonders does he believe his words. Does he think instead that she will fail? Does he imagine her hounded from the place, his gallery walls stripped to the white once more so he can hang the work of a man?

Aitken leads her into the gallery where all the walls have been cleared of paintings.

"Your Venus," he says, with a wave at the main wall, to their right. "We will put your Botticelli there."

"Not there, Mr. Aitken. If you put me there, I am the first thing people will see."

"Quite right."

"But my face has lately been in the newspapers with my husband and everyone will recognize me. You risk turning the exhibition into scandal."

"When we spoke in February you insisted you were making a new kind of art, in which the subject turns the tables on the viewer."

"I did, but—"

"This is the inevitable consequence of that argument, Mrs. Heywoud. We *must* place your Venus photograph here. It can teach the viewer how to look."

She likes his phrase. What is her exhibit to do but teach the viewer how to look—and to see women as individuals, not ideals like angels or goddesses or saints. If the viewer can understand that, he can begin to accept the idea that women must determine their own fates.

"All right," Viola says. "I'll hang the Botticelli here on the main wall. But you must label it clearly so that people know it is the photographer and not a hunger striker. I don't wish to mislead in that way."

He smiles.

"Not in that way, but in other ways," he says. "Of course." He taps his pince-nez into place. "You'll find the usual equipment in the gallery. Miss French will show you where to go."

"Do you not have anyone to help me?"

"You have your men there with the lorry. And I must leave you as I've curatorial paperwork to finish."

"Mr. Miner is not appropriate for these photographs."

But Aitken is already making for the corridor.

"I am including some of your *manifesto*," he says as he departs.

Viola instructs Miner and the driver to bring the crate in from the car and set it down in the main gallery beside a stepladder and a box of tools. She sees Miss French pretend she is not taken aback by Miner's appearance.

Viola sends the driver away with a coin and goes to the door once more to look for James. She wanted him to be here, wanted to be with him at the moment all her avid hopes became reality. She lets out a long sigh.

"Something missing, ma'am?"

"No," she says. "It's all right." She turns back to the gallery and catches Miner working something in his fingers. He stuffs his hand into his pocket.

"What is that, Samuel?"

"Pardon, ma'am?"

"Your trinket. I don't know what it is but you are always toying with it."

As she utters the words she knows she has sprung out into new space. To question him about his talisman, to invite such private information—this exhilarates and scares her. Several seconds pass and Miner seems to be making a decision before he pulls his hand from his pocket and holds it out towards her, turns it palm up and uncurls his fingers. A metal ring dangling from a stub. A piton. A piton whose spike has snapped off in the seam of a cliff.

"Where is this from?" She comes close enough to see where a dot of rust pocks the piton's surface.

"France," he says. "Mont Blanc."

Her eyes dart up to his but she reads nothing. James told her once that when Samuel fell on Mont Blanc the rope snapped below Edward and he was saved only by a ledge in the crevasse he tumbled into. Viola sees climber and rope falling, piton ripped from the rock and sliding down along the tumbling rope, a hiss of iron against twisted fiber. Miner holds the thing on his open palm and Viola reaches out to touch it, as if she tests for a pulse still there within the iron.

"Are you going to need assistance, ma'am?" he says, and for an instant she thinks he asks of ropes and crampons.

"I suppose I am." She lets out a little laugh. "But I must explain something to you, Samuel," she says. "You know I have been photographing marches. And you know I have gone without you to Dalmeny Avenue."

"Indeed." He disapproves of the trips she took without him. How much more will he frown on the photographs themselves?

"The photos I took there are of hunger strikers. The photographs are nudes." She can see his effort not to reveal a changed expression. "And one of the two large photographs is an image of me."

Here he stirs. He moves just enough to make a sound of boot-sole on grit on the gallery floor.

"So you must treat this work with delicacy."

"Yes, ma'am," he says. He tugs at his muffler. She wishes she had her own cloth or leather for a mask to hide behind.

"Right. Then hand me the crowbar, please," she says and reaches out a palm.

She pries the lid free and, one by one, she slides the photographs out in their coverings. She instructs Miner where to place the prints according to her numbered map. He sets them on the floor and she can see he tries not to glimpse the images beneath the cloth. He leans the frames against the walls until the room is lined with bundles, swaddled like so many foundlings on the steps of a church.

"Now we must hang them."

Viola begins with the image of Florence as Titian's Danaë. She unwraps the photograph and looks at it as if in benediction. She gives the frame its length of wire and hangs it from the hook Miner has tapped into the wall at her direction. She comes down from the stepladder to assess the height and finds it suitable. The visitor will read the room from left to right and Florence will be first, Viola's new version of the Danaë no father's prisoner or victim of a raping god. The visitor will feel Florence's hungry gaze upon him and will ponder what is his own crime today. And on and on, he will look around the room, each photograph to serve as challenge and indictment.

"The bruises," Miner says. "Are they real?"

"They are."

"Bloody hell, that's not right."

"No, it is not."

She follows the Danaë with the odalisque and the Olympia. As she works, her thoughts fly out to tomorrow and to the room full of people and the newsmen Aitken promised. There could, of course, be no one, but she doubts an exhibition of nudes by the wife of Edward Heywoud will go unnoticed by either press or public. She glances out towards the entrance. James should have arrived by now. Will he not come to see her triumph as she has witnessed his—and his a fabrication while hers at least acknowledges its masquerade? But she cannot simply stop and wait, and so she goes on until only two of the small photographs and the two large Venuses are left to hang. Miner hands her the mallet and she steps up the ladder to set another hook. She tells herself she must ignore the very notion that James told her he would come. Let it be she never asked him. Let it be that she and Miner, Miner only, will finish the creation she began so long ago. From the first blink of the shutter in Dalmeny Avenue to what will be the final mallet tap into a Whitechapel wall, she has made this exhibition without James' help. Why need him now?

She hears noises in the entrance hall behind her and does not recognize the man speaking with Miss French until she remembers James' new hoarse voice.

"Look at you," he says.

"You've come," she says.

He gives Miner a distracted greeting as he stares at the wall of photographs. From her spot on the ladder, she watches him take them in with curiosity then admiration.

"I see it," he says. "I think I see it, Vi. It's good."

"You haven't even seen the best."

"Then show me."

She comes down the ladder.

"I'm glad you came. I want you to see this. Just us without a crowd."

"I'll step outside, ma'am," Miner says and it is almost with sadness that she sees him go.

"Come," she says to James, and brings him to the remaining photographs that lean against the wall.

"Titian, Ingres, Rubens." She counts them off. "You see what I've done? Classic nudes of women lying there to be stared at. But I turn it around. My women refuse to be a part of that. My women are in charge of what they let you see and they demand the right to speak for themselves."

"This is good," he says. "You were always good." He gives her a tight smile. "Now you're better."

She pulls out the large frame she knows from its muslin is the image of herself. She props it in front of her and carefully pushes the cloth down around it, front and back, so that it stands as if undressed.

He takes a sharp breath in. His head pulls back but his expression does not change. He looks and looks and looks and his pallor gives way to a high red in his cheeks. But he is not embarrassed. He is not shocked. It is something else that fuels the heat in his face. James' very posture seems now to sink and slacken.

"What's wrong?" she says. "Are you angry?"

He closes his eyes.

"Are you upset with me?" She does not know what she could have done to upset him.

"No," he says. He looks at her and shakes his head.

His silence irritates her now.

"What's wrong, then?" she says.

"It's good," he says finally.

"That's all? It's *good*?"

"What more do you want me to say?"

"It's me, for God's sake. Or say something about the concept. Say something about the light, the contrast, the clarity of the print. The *idea*."

"It is perfect, Viola. They all are perfect. Perfectly executed. And the idea is a good one."

"You sound as though we've only just met," she says. "What is wrong with you?"

James has not taken his eyes from the photograph and now seems to waken to Viola herself before him.

"Nothing is wrong with me. I suppose."

"This is good, James." She will not tell him how it came to be. That another woman was intended to be Venus. Her portrait is here now and she believes in it. "It makes the case for suffrage in an elemental way."

"How is that?"

"Don't you see it, James? The goddess herself makes the point. The whole idea of the feminine is a fabrication made by men. And now it's time for women—time for me—to invent ourselves."

"I see," he says.

"Then why aren't you pleased? It shouldn't matter, but it does, James. It matters to me what you think."

"Why?"

"Why?" she says. "Because you taught me."

But as she says the words, she knows she has moved far beyond that sentiment. This need to hear his approbation is mere habit. She knows she has surpassed him.

"Do you not understand," he says with a rueful laugh, "that with this photograph, with this exhibition, you have destroyed me?"

"What?"

"I knew you had become a good photographer, Viola. And I was afraid you were better than me. As long as I didn't know that for certain, as long as I had my photographs from the Pole, a place you could never get to, I could tell myself I mattered. That my work still mattered."

"It does."

"No." He shouts the word. "Your work is so much more intelligent than mine, Viola, so much more meaningful. And I am jealous of you. I hate you a little for it. Perhaps a lot."

"You can't compare the two of us, James. We are doing very different things. Your photographs are beautiful."

"That's my point. At the end of the day, I'm just a landscape photographer. And you—" He leaves the thought unfinished.

"James."

"No." He backs away. "I had left myself a little spot to stand on. A little piece of the globe that was mine, Antarctica, even after everything, after all the lying and the cheating." He taps his forehead. "But it's no good. I can't do work like this. I've never had the thought for something like this. I never would have understood it. But you did."

"That's nonsense. If everyone agreed with you"—she fights the smile of pride that curls her lips—"I would be the only artist left."

"Oh, the others will go on because they don't understand that they can't match you. I understand, though."

He turns for the door but she calls after him.

"No, Viola. My achievement is a lie. Yours is a kind of true illusion. *You* are an *artist*." He brings the words out one by one as if they are heavy. "I am just a fraud."

He gives her an apologetic smile and leaves.

For several moments pride and sadness pin her to the spot. She blushes to know James' praise is true, but grieves the loss of him. She wants to stalk the gallery with head held high and elbows jutting, but she sinks to the floor and rests her back against the nearest wall. She has held James and Edward to a standard of certain truth. Their conquest of the Pole is false so they must tell the world what really happened. But who is to say what is real, when they can show a fake image that the world believes? She looks out at the women on the wall and wonders if it is enough to ask that question, if asking what is real absolves her from the charge she aims at Edward.

33

20 June

Viola arrives at the gallery before the doors are open to the public. Aitken lets her in, glances left and right along the street, and closes and locks the door behind her. He looks for newsmen—whom he wants—and for protesters—whom he desires only if they draw more newsmen. Word has spread, he tells her, that her photographs are shocking. What he hopes for—and has reason to expect—is curiosity enough to fill the gallery, and for newsmen and critics to report success. He assures Viola he will defend the exhibition should need arise. She takes little comfort in his late warnings and reassurances and worries when time comes he will retreat to his old caution.

She goes from photograph to photograph in the gallery to check the placement is correct, the lighting from the room's high skylight adequate and even, with the help of the electric bulbs. Her Botticelli pose hangs flush against the wall. Only someone who knew the smaller photographs were attached inside would notice a faint shadow line around the frame. Her heart leaps into a rush as she looks at herself presented there. Suddenly the image is absurd, foolish, the product of a woman playacting with meager props. If it fails to seem like art, it will be just what Aitken warns her of. It will be prurient. And she will be present in the room as visitors gape at her nakedness. And what will the women of the ASL think of her pose, and of their own? If they are angry at her? What will she do? She must explain and hope the scale of the exhibition makes the message land with force. She takes a breath but it is not enough. It is as if she has been shifted to the thin air of a summit, as if she may tumble from a ridgeline with an entire valley town arrayed to watch.

The exhibition is set to open in minutes. Edward will be here soon, and James. Isabella and the others from the Slade set: will they come? She thinks of Morton and suddenly wishes more than anything that he were here. He knows something of fame—from Muybridge and his images of motion—and he would surely give her solace. He would know what to say to someone who sees fame close enough to touch.

When it is nearly time for Aitken to open the doors, when Viola sees the dark shapes of early visitors in shadows against the glass, she retreats to a book-lined corridor that leads out of the gallery. She cannot bear it, cannot bear to be in the gallery until the space is full of bodies and no visitor can look with ease from her to the photograph, from model to photographer, and recognize the face in both. She drifts further and further from her gallery and towards Aitken's office and the other smaller rooms. She tries to ignore the noise but she can hear the doors opening from the street and people shuffling towards the exhibition. They shuffle, she realizes, because the room is too full for them to stride. She tells herself she is a coward. These are her photographs. This is the work that has cost her dearly. Isabella, James, Edward—she has hurt or lost them all because of these dozen images. To shy away from them now is to squander what connects her to these people. Since she has asked Abigail and Eliza and Margaret Lyons and the others to withstand the public eye, she must endure it too.

The room is packed four deep in front of every photograph. She stands alone in open space behind the crowd as one and then another face turns towards her. Someone begins to applaud—Viola cannot see who it is and wonders is it James—and a few others join. She recognizes people she saw at Isabella's party for the Daylight Comet. Two women in deep fuchsia and in blue with feathered hats. A tall thin man in a scarlet waistcoat. Isabella. Isabella has come, standing by the waistcoated man in a dress of palest green. Viola cannot read her expression, but that does not matter for Isabella is here and she, too, is clapping. A woman pushes towards her. It is Lucy Bellowes, with Margaret Lyons at her side. Bellowes, who said she would have no more to do with Viola. If she is here there is a chance to make amends.

"What have you done?" Bellowes uses no title, no honorific.

"I'm not sure—"

"What," Bellowes pauses, "have you done? You have no right to be on that wall with my Margaret and the others. You did not starve."

"Mrs. Bellowes, is this quite the best time?"

"When Tess chastised you I supported you," she says. "You were going to take the photographs and that was how you would involve yourself. Just that. Not more."

"I must explain."

"And then I asked you to stay away and I thought you understood. And now? Now you give yourself the same status as women who have nearly died for the cause? What were you thinking?" There is almost a concern to Bellowes' voice. "What possessed you to usurp that place?"

"I did not plan it from the start, Mrs. Bellowes."

"You did this on a whim?"

"No. I mean to say I have nothing but respect for all the strikers. I only included myself once it became clear there was no other way."

"I do not follow you."

She takes Bellowes by the elbow and leads her out of the room to the corridor she occupied before. She lowers her voice.

"The photographs from Dalmeny were not enough." She has a sense she sounds like someone finding fault with the strikers. "I needed the Botticelli and since I could not come to you, I had no choice but to use myself."

Bellowes pulls her head back.

"You would blame us?"

"No."

"Let us leave aside for the moment the fact that there should never have been a photograph of you among these others in the first place. You made an agreement with this Mr. Aitken and neglected to tell us." Bellowes looks at Lyons. "One suspects you knew you had done something wrong. I had you for a braver woman, Mrs. Heywoud." She takes Margaret Lyons' arm and turns away.

"I am naked on the wall just like the others," Viola says and Bellowes stops.

"You did not go to prison," Bellowes says. "Margaret did."

Lyons' face is altered since Viola took her photograph. The cheeks are full and pink. The bridge of her nose where an uneven bump showed through the skin is now rounded and smooth.

"The exhibit is made stronger, Mrs. Bellowes, by the fact that I am *not* a hunger striker but I, too, like all women, am a victim of this oppressive idea."

"You told us you would photograph these injustices to serve the cause. Instead, you used these women to create some sort of perverse art."

"Look how many people have come today. Everyone here sees what has been done to these women. To *all* women. Mr. Aitken has written a description that makes that meaning very clear."

"What have you risked, Mrs. Heywoud?"

"Pardon?"

"These women you use in your display have risked their lives, their status, their safety. You include yourself among them. What, I ask, have *you* risked?"

They look at each other for a long moment. Viola can think now only of what has made her safe. She is a married woman still, and she exhibits even now under her husband's name. She has his status, his fame. She has done much these last days to preserve them. And yet, she has lost much. The notion sweeps in around her like a tide and she fights a sudden sting of tears. This is no day of triumph for her—not while she knows the lie she is a part of. Not while those she loves are absent from the room and those she admires denounce her as dishonest.

"What have I risked, Mrs. Bellowes?" she says. "Perhaps not enough. Not yet."

Bellowes looks at her with an expression of pain, almost of sadness.

"I do not understand you, Mrs. Heywoud," she says finally. "Return to your audience. Perhaps their adulation will boost your courage."

Bellowes spins away and Lyons winces apology. Viola watches them leave and tells herself her art is no ignominy. And yet she cannot shed the shame that Bellowes thinks it is.

"Viola!"

From the hubbub she picks out Edward's voice. She sees him at the corridor's mouth arguing with Aitken. And then Aitken points her out and Edward strides towards her.

"You should have shown this to me," he says. She steers him further down the corridor.

"I would have. But we have had other matters to discuss."

"You should have warned me." For an instant he is calm, as if remembering their closeness.

"I did."

"How could I have imagined—"

"Imagined what?"

He shakes his head.

"It's not just that you're naked. It's the way you're posed. The way you look."

She works to hide her pleasure. The photograph has had exactly the effect she seeks. It unsettles him, provokes his anger.

"If I had really understood what you were speaking of," he says, "I'd never have allowed it."

"Perhaps I should have shown it to you. But you would have stopped me. You would have found a way to convince Aitken he needed your permission. Do you not understand, Edward, what this means to me?"

"Bloody hell, Viola. What will Bertie think, and Alice? Are they here?" She pictures Bertie taking in each photograph without a wince or wide eye and Alice by his side doing the same. Edward drops his voice to a whisper. "What would your parents have said?"

Her laugh comes out as a long breath.

"You keep trying to tie me to someone, Ned. To you, to a child, to my parents who have been dead seven years. I am not tied. I don't wish to be tied. To anyone."

She can see he does not know what to make of her change in tone. He frowns a little, looks at her as if listening to the tick and hiss that would signal a snowslide. She scans his face as if it belongs to a stranger, thinks how hard the reading of it is, harder even than Miner's half-face she has learned to understand. She sees a scar, a wrinkle, crow's feet, the dark of his eyes paling to hazel, fine lines of blood inside the whites. She sees the bleached blond of his hair, the pale outline of a beard he has now shaved. She could wait for his response, but she is weary. Weary of opposition and argument, of shock and consternation. She tires of having to defend her work and her decisions.

"There is something I must tell you, Edward," she says. "I am going to leave you."

He looks up sharply.

"What? Are you going to *him*?"

"No," she says, and she is not lying.

"Where, then? You cannot."

"I don't know where. Perhaps to Italy. You know that I was always happy there."

She should never have spoken of past happiness, for now her throat tightens against a sob. She is sad now not for him but for herself and for that few years' younger self who knew nothing, yet, about how happiness could alter.

He has begun to frown. A weight of sadness drops onto her shoulders.

"And the photograph? Not this one. The one from the Pole."

She can see he braces for the bad end of a bargain. She shakes her head. It would be so much easier now to say nothing than to force the words out against this heavy weight.

"We have said much to each other since you returned, Ned, and so much of it has not been kind. But know this. I have no wish to see you hurt." He makes a noise of protest, but she stays him. "I won't say anything about the photograph. I will keep your secret. It can become my secret too."

She sees his eyes redden as a prelude to tears. Kindness has always had this effect on him, and she wonders not for the first time was he shown so little of it as a child that he finds it now rare and surprising.

"What do you want in return?" he says.

"You and I will not divorce," she says. "You will allow me to open a bank account in my own name and you will allow me to deposit into it. A small sum, Edward, just to tide me over while I settle. I don't wish to burden you. It's best for both of us if we go on apart from each other in this way. I will arrange for Isabella to take the photos to the ASL when the exhibit's done. She'll understand. As for me," she says, "you may invent some story about where I am. Perhaps in a few years when people have forgotten the Pole—"

"They won't ever forget the Pole."

"Well, sometime later, Ned, whenever you like, we can have a solicitor draw up some papers."

"Do you not love me?" he says, in a voice so quiet she can barely hear it over the gallery's hum.

"I did, once, Ned. But we have both lied to each other so much, and it's turned to sadness."

They stand together for a moment longer. There is about him something tells her that her offer of silence will fall on him like a weight he cannot lift.

"I must go in," she says, but he is distracted. "Edward?"

"Yes," he says. "I'm going."

She goes towards the gallery space and turns to watch him. He emerges from the corridor with his shoulders back and his head high. He glances once in her direction and then walks out into the street. Viola bites her lip to keep from letting out a sob. She fishes in a pocket for a handkerchief and dabs her eyes as if she merely removes a mote of dust.

"Mrs. Heywoud."

Viola turns with a shuddered laugh to greet the well-wisher who interrupts her. It is Miss French and she hands her a packet of cards and a telegram.

"They have been coming in with the post. Are you all right?"

"Simply moved at the success." Viola gives her a smile.

"It is a success, Mrs. Heywoud. A much bigger crowd than we usually get, if I'm honest."

"Can you do something for me, Miss French?"

"Of course."

"Can you ask Isabella Purvis to come see me? She is a tall woman in a blue-green dress. Her companion wears a scarlet waistcoat."

Miss French goes to find Isabella and Viola shuffles through the envelopes. She must tell Izzy what has happened. She must explain the photographs are hers now, and the ASL's. She can trust Izzy to understand a secret can muster its own morals. Viola flips another envelope aside and sees her name in James' tidy hand. Is he not coming? Does he feel her success so strongly that he cannot come to share it? She goes to the edge of the room where she can read the note in a brief eddy of calm. A single sheet of paper is inside.

> *My Dearest Viola,*
>
> *You said two days ago that you could live in the Broomway. That you could live in a place where nothing is ever clear and where you can never get your bearings. I believe that you are right and that you do have the ability to live with that sort of uncertainty. I cannot. I thought I could, but I cannot. I am like a staid old Zurich banker, it turns out. Quite black and white in my thinking. Not you.*

She skims ahead. Is he saying he will harm himself? What has he done?

> *I am sorry that I have not come to see your public triumph. That, too, is more than I am capable of. We Zurich burghers can succumb to a very unattractive envy. I am sorry if I have hurt you.*
>
> *The Broomway has defeated me, Vi, and I must give in to it. I shall imitate its gray and gloom, its vague horizon, and become vague myself. I cannot stay out in the public world with everything that we have done. Do not come look for me.*

But perhaps I will come to you some day. When you read this,
know I have gone eastward.
   All my love,
   James

He is gone. She takes in a sharp breath and looks up at the room, sure to find it altered by this news. But the room goes on about its business, ignorant of the fact that James has gone. Eastward. Perhaps to Southend and to the very edge of the coast—though there is no edge there, only fading—where the moon's pull on the sea will leave the Broomway large and broad. Perhaps further east, away from England, to France, or Italy, or further still? She rushes out of the gallery to the corridor where she hid before and brushes away tears. In time she reads the letter once more and sees the places that James speaks of lie only on imagination's map.

"Mrs. Heywoud!" A sharp voice, Aitken's, calling for her. "You are needed. A reporter wants Captain Heywoud's artistic wife for an interview."

She must return to the gallery, but James' message pulls her back. He is going somewhere to disappear. Edward will look for him. James' mother and sister will look for him. At some point they will all decide that he cannot be found. They will think him perhaps dead or lost. *Perhaps I will come to you some day.* She sees him on a train platform in Italy, without a case or a camera, in a long coat, come out of a mist to be with her.

She hears more voices coming nearer, senses a commotion in the gallery. As she goes towards the siren buzzing, she thinks again of the blank canvas of Antarctica, of Nilsen's flag insulting the pure expanse of white with its bright shape. What must Edward have thought to see that red, to blink and find that the red persisted, that it was no figment of fatigue. He made a bargain then, without a thought but only pain, to claim what only he could claim at that point on the journey and with Nilsen surely dead. She has made a bargain, too. Across the gallery, Aitken bends and stoops from his great height to chivvy on the visitors. He nudges one man to the left and steers another straight ahead. They do not even notice how he pecks at them to govern what they see. He nudged her, too, and she did not even notice how her heart leapt at the chance for recognition. Surrender up your body and I will make you famous. They are not so different, she and Edward, after all.

She has been walking into the gallery, but now she stops and looks on at the visitors four-deep before her Botticelli. Their summer colors dance against the black and white of her collection. She makes out Isabella's teal. Someone wears lavender and green, the suffrage hues. Now Izzy spies her, starts towards her. Others turn—Bellowes in judgment, Aitken in delight. Izzy sees something in Viola's face and stops. Viola gives her a little smile but there is nothing more to say. Instead, she makes her eye a camera and frames a photograph. Her art upon the walls, the crowd, their looks of pleasure and of shock. She needs no printed photo to remember this. A phantom shutter in her closes and opens again and Viola walks out into midsummer's heavy heat.

Epilogue

At the café Viola takes her coffee white with foaming cream and spices. They call this drink after a monk's robes for its color. *Cappuccino.* She stirs sugar into the cup and looks out at the ring of peaks that rise up from the narrow valley. The light will be good today. It slants down between the jagged summits of the great Cristallo massif, casting an orange glow on the snow-covered chutes. Later, once she has taken the dog for their stroll along the river, she will strap the tripod onto her shoulders along with the camera case and hike the ridge to higher elevations. From there, her long lens will capture spires caught in wisps of snow like wool spun by the late winter wind. She will develop the film—she uses celluloid now—and print the images in the darkroom sectioned from the kitchen of her little house. When she arrived in autumn of last year, the workman muttered darkly about the ground that would soon freeze. She paid him more to dig the chemical drain deep enough.

She sets a few coins by her saucer and tugs on her gloves and shawl and hat. The sun will warm the day, but this March morning holds a chill.

"Buongiorno, Signorina Colfax," the waiter says to her.

Buongiorno, she tells him truthfully in return.

It is a good day in a string of days that brighten as the nights grow short. Six months ago she stepped off the Venice train in Calalzo to wonder was it folly spurred her there from London. She left behind an Edward shattered by his hidden guilt and took with her nothing save her cameras. Was it not enough to walk away from his name and from his money that she must cut herself off from Izzy and London, too? But as the horse carriage took her through the autumn valley and the massif loomed again, known to her but always new, she settled in the scene like a figure in a landscape. Here in Cortina was what she wanted, after all. The stark light of mountain passes.

And yet she cannot leave the light alone but bends and twists it. In her photographs now she seeks out prisms and reflections. She looks for features in the snow and ice that warp the light to tell a story of time backwards, time repeating, time spinning out ahead. In April when the little river runs pale green like a piece of jade, she will go once more to Venice and then on to Milan to bring new work for an exhibition. Photographers and painters there speak of Marinetti's Futurism. Viola sees how these artists push beyond Cubism and its fragments, how they experiment like her with time and shape and speed. This is what she wants. The future, ahead of her, upstream along the jade-colored river running high with melted ice.

She stops to collect that week's post from the Tyrolean building in the center of the town. Letters from Izzy and from Bertie, one from the Milan gallerist who will show her work, and the English newspaper delivered in a package from Bolzano. There is another envelope in handwriting she does not recognize.

Back at home, she praises the dog for no particular reason and calls her to lie down beside the chair. She draws the post to her and begins with the letter in an unknown hand.

Dearest Ma'am, it begins, and then she sees it is from Samuel Miner, dated one week ago and sent from London. He takes little time to state the reason for his letter. Edward has died. Viola breathes in sharply and the dog pops up in excitement great enough to make her collar jingle. Viola closes her eyes against the words, then compels herself to read again.

I regret to be the one to tell you, if the news has not already reached you, that Mr. Edward perished three days since. You may have read about it in the papers. I don't know whether the English news reaches you promptly in Cortina. (Mr. Edward left instructions as to your whereabouts and I am sorry if I was not meant to write.) He had arranged with one of the newspapers to take a reporter on a climb so they could write about it. He took him along on a trip to Snowdon. Mr. Edward was on the Llanberis route. Something went wrong and he fell to his death. There was no hope of reviving him.

Viola sets the letter on her desk.

"Hush," she says to the eager dog and her voice emerges with a choke. "Lie down."

She wipes a hand across her nose and takes up the page again—a cream-colored sheet of thin card. She rereads Miner's words. The Llanberis route. She does not understand. Edward knew every inch of Snowdon, every patch of scree and every knife-edge on the Snowdon Horseshoe. Viola has done the Llanberis route, Snowdon's simplest and ideal for a newsman with no climbing skills. What was he doing? She says it in a whisper.

"What were you doing, Ned?"

Viola looks out at Cristallo and its row of peaks. She remembers Edward and James descending from those ridges with tales of cols and cruxes above the heights that she could climb. She reaches for the newspaper package—she takes the *Observer* in fealty to the paper whose exclusive of the Pole became a different kind of story—and tears it open. There it is on the front page.

POLAR HERO KILLED IN CLIMBING ACCIDENT

Nation Mourns Loss of Edward Heywoud

Below the headline is a photograph that appeared in the same paper over one year ago, when Edward first sent word of success from Madeira. She keeps a copy of this image in a frame in her small room upstairs where light from lamp or window never leaves it free of shadows. The photograph belongs to the far past, before the men's suffering, before the Pole, before their falsehood. In the image Edward stands beside James and both of them are smiling. Their teeth are brilliant white in weathered faces. A dog lies in the snow before them, panting from some recent exertion even in that cold. If only they had remained frozen in that moment, two men beautiful in their hope and happiness, innocent of all that would befall them and all that they would do. She would have spared them their dark future.

Edward is dead. Viola forces herself to think the thought. Edward is dead and James is somewhere unknown, perhaps living by the sea in Essex or in a Highland bothy. She pictures him in remote locations, but perhaps he boards a train in Turin even now to cross the Dolomites and come to her. It does not matter. She does not wait for him and she does not shape her life to anyone except the dog she found cadging scraps by the café when she first arrived. They call her Viola Colfax here—the first name sung, the second guttural like the Austrian words that pepper the Italian—and now only she knows that this week she became the widow of a famous man.

She thinks of the Llanberis route and tries to muster understanding of how Edward could have died. The path runs over soft turf and easy slopes to the broad summit of Wales' highest peak. Along the way, it offers glorious views of the Snowdon massif and virtually no danger. Until it reaches the cliffs at Clogwyn Du'r Arddu. One February they turned back at Cloggy, the three of them, for the ice had hardened into neve along the railway tracks and a simple slip could send a climber over. She searches the article for mention of Cloggy but finds none. But now she is certain this is what Edward has done. Not what has happened to him but what he has *done*: he has gone over Cloggy. And now she understands. This was his choice, his act. She sees him planting an axe for the newsman and then taking the hasty steps that he can turn into a fall. She sees Edward sliding, slow at first then gaining speed and spinning finally so that when he goes over the cliff he sees the rock he leaves behind and not the space he goes to.

He arranged it well, to bring a newsman there as if in message to Viola, to leave the world from a place where he first learned how to search it. How did it feel for Samuel, she wonders, to write the end of Edward's life? He does not say where he will go, what he will do, nor Mary. She trusts that Edward has provided for them.

She looks again at the photograph of James' and Edward's smiling faces, brings the paper close enough that she can see the dust that once was in the lens. She sees the dog. From James' photographs, she knows the dog is Lulu, white with a black head and white tip to the nose. This is the dog who, after this photograph was taken, became thinner and thinner with each image, then was pictured only lying down or carried, and then disappeared altogether from James' final plates. This is the dog Viola saw in Cardiff harbor, three-legged then, at that man Lawrence's side, delighting at new scents of soil and hay, already forgetful of the ice and cold and pain that came before.

Viola reaches down and musses the scruff of her own dog who has dropped a paw onto her lap.

"Come, pup," she says and pushes back her chair. She goes to fetch her coat and hat and gloves, her tripod and her camera, to look for the sharpest light.

Author's Note

My obsession with Antarctica began when I was seven and saw a documentary on public television about Robert Falcon Scott. I'm fairly certain that important aspects of Scott's story eluded me then—his death, his loss in the Polar race to Amundsen in 1912. What struck me was Scott's noble stoicism and the fact of Antarctica itself, this place unlike anything I had ever seen or imagined. I knew about snow and ice because I was already a skier at that age. But this Antarctic stuff was epic, massive, inconceivable in the intensity of its cold and the scale of its vastness. To think that a person could embark on a journey to its center and endure such hardship—I couldn't comprehend it.

Over the decades, I read and reread Scott's journals, and the famous Cherry-Garrard book *The Worst Journey in the World*. I pondered over and over the amazing lines of Scott's last message: "Had we lived I should have had a tale to tell. . . . For God's sake look after our people." I stared at photographs and maps (which usually don't include Antarctica as more than a strip of white across the bottom) and tried to imagine what it must have been like—what it must still be like—to be surrounded by so much white and so much cold. Or, even more awe-inspiring, by the full dark of Antarctic winter. Most of all, I couldn't shake the thought of my hero Robert Scott arriving at the Pole only to find his rival's flag already planted there. What, I kept asking myself, must that have been like?

Scott's journals and letters reveal no bitterness or even envy in defeat. To the very last moments of his life, he remained remarkably calm about what was surely a moment of utter devastation. Though Scott's own story offered no hint of moral compromise, I kept wondering: What if the explorer who saw his rival's victory flag reacted differently? What if that explorer crossed a moral line? What would be the consequences of an act that turned a hero into a coward?

To answer those questions, I began to write the pages that became *Terra Nova*. The title serves as my small homage to Scott's 1910–1913 expedition of that name. For the novel, I invented the fictional explorers James Watts and Edward Heywoud, along with Edward's wife, Viola, an artist like Scott's wife, Kathleen. Through these three imagined figures, I felt I could explore the complexities created by that vast Antarctic continent.

Acknowledgments

began writing this book in the pre-dawn hours of December a few years
ago, each morning pushing my characters a bit further across Antarctic
ice. Every few days, Matthew Juros would ask me how things were going
for "the boys," and he would sit on the couch and listen as I read the new
pages to him aloud. That whole winter, and later on, even when I thought
nobody was getting anywhere with this project—not me, not my poor
explorers—he was always there to offer encouragement and excitement.
For that and for still being there for all our adventures, I am so grateful.
With love to Matt, first listener to this book and dearest partner, I say, as
always, let's go see.

I owe huge thanks to Jessica Case and everyone at Pegasus Books
for bringing *Terra Nova* to the world, including Susan McGrath, Lisa
Gilliam, and Maria Fernandez. I am very proud to be working with a team
and a press I so much admire. Thanks, too, to Megan Beatie who has been
a great champion for the book. Faceout Studio designed a gorgeous cover,
so thank you to everyone there.

I am lucky to have had great writer friends who've offered feedback and
support for this project from the start, chief among them Anjali Mitter
Duva, Jennifer Dupee, Crystal King, Cathy Elcik, Lara McLeod, Cat
Mazur, Kathy Sherbrooke, every wonderful writer in the DLC whose
insights I always learn from, and Gillian English who was there for those
first conversations in London as I tried to figure out what story I would tell.

ACKNOWLEDGMENTS

Jeanne Stanton and Terri Payne Butler were very early readers who helped me see the larger ideas in the story. I am indebted to Veronica Goldstein who worked tirelessly and with such intelligence on earlier drafts of this book. Thank you to Fred Mirliani of the Photographic Preservation Center, to Robert McFarlane whose writing about the Broomway taught me about that geographic feature on the Essex coast, and to the range of other sources I consulted in my research.

Thank you to my children, Eoin Power and Nike Power, to all my friends who heard me talk about this project for years, and to the best sister I never had, Kelley Lessard. Together, you form the very heart of the real world that makes my forays into the imagination possible.

Dogs play a role in this story, not only on the page but in the writing of it. My dog, Finn, my Writing Supervisor, was, like all dogs, the best of dogs. Though his role was limited to watching me in silence while I wrote, his company meant everything to me.

Finally, I must especially thank my daughter, Nike, for her unerring writerly intelligence and her constant support. To have her as a fellow writer—one from whom I learn more every day—is reward enough. To have her as a daughter is gift beyond measure.

A Reading Group Guide for *Terra Nova*

- In Watts' and Heywoud's position as they embark on the "last leg" of their journey, what would you have done about the team and the supplies? Would you have turned back?

- What do you think about Watts' and Heywoud's respective choices about the photograph?

- How do you feel about Viola's actions upon the discovery of the deceit?

- What do you think about Edward's reaction to the revelation of the affair?

- A big theme of the book is ambition. All three of the main characters grapple with it. How does it affect each of them and cloud their decision-making?

- We see art from three characters here: Watts, Viola, and Isabella. What is each character's relationship with their art, and how does it shift throughout the novel?

- What do you think about Viola's project to photograph the hunger strikers?

- Izzy warns Viola about the strikers' determination to starve themselves. What dangers does she think the women hold for Viola?

- Viola is stung by the critique of the suffragettes at her exhibit. Do you think some of it is valid? Or is it unjustified?

- The Artists Suffrage League was an actual organization at that time. What do you think of their approach? What do you think of the tactics of the hunger strikers?

- What do you make of Miner and the mysterious trinket he keeps in his pocket?

- How do you feel about Viola's choice to keep the secret of the photograph? Do you think it was related to the consequences of her own secret affair?

- If you were in Viola's position at the end, what would you choose to do? Would you stay with Edward or leave? If you left, would you make sure James would come with you or go alone?